NO WAY OF TELLING

NO WAY
OF TELLING

—➤◦◉◦◄—

EMMA SMITH

THE BODLEY HEAD
LONDON SYDNEY
TORONTO

For Rosie and Barney with love

Copyright © Emma Smith 1972
ISBN 0 370 01236 4
Printed in Great Britain for
The Bodley Head Ltd
9 Bow Street, London WC2E 7AL
by Fletcher & Son Ltd, Norwich
and bound by
Richard Clay (The Chaucer Press) Ltd
Bungay, Suffolk
Set in Monotype Plantin
First published 1972
Reprinted 1974

CONTENTS

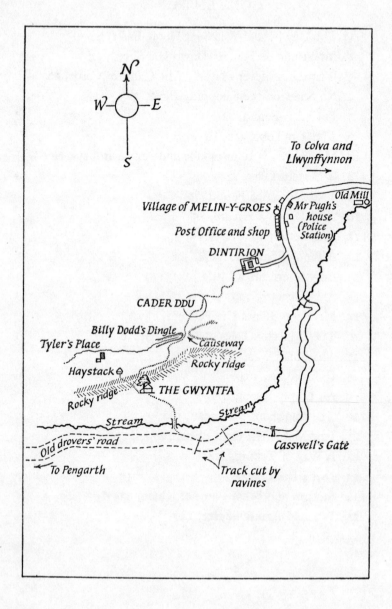

1. The Day School Was Sent Home Early

Amy Bowen, bending and shuffling, climbed out from the back of Mrs Rhys's van into the snowy wind and banged the doors shut, turning the handle on what was now an empty shelter for she was the last to be dropped of the eight children Mrs Rhys brought back from school each day, just as in the mornings she was the first to be picked up. Only tomorrow there would surely be no picking up; no school tomorrow, thought Amy, as she stood by the roadside holding her collar tight together under her chin and watching Mrs Rhys turn the van. The windscreen wipers were beginning to be clogged, she noticed. Busily working to and fro they cleared a smaller space at every wipe.

Mrs Rhys manoeuvred her van until it was pointing round the way it had come, for the road finished here: it was a dead end. The village of Melin-y-Groes was two miles further back, and school itself five miles beyond that in the larger village of Colva.

"You get from here, Amy, just as quick as you can," said Mrs Rhys. She had wound her window down and put out her head. The snow beat into both their faces. "It's coming in thicker every minute and there's quite a step for you to go—will you be all right, do you think?"

"Oh, I'll be all right, Mrs Rhys—I like it," said Amy,

7

stretching up to scoop snow off the windscreen so as to give the wipers a better chance.

"You'll be saying something different time you get home—I know I shall. Never mind about that snow, Amy—let it alone —you'll only get your fingers wet before you start," said Mrs Rhys, putting her gear lever into first but keeping her foot on the clutch as though reluctant to leave her last charge there on her own with not another soul in sight, and the storm increasing. "I don't have to ask if your Granny's well stocked up with food, I suppose—she always is—she's wonderful that way."

"Do you think it's going to last long, then?"

"Well, I shouldn't be surprised, indeed—I always say it's bad when it comes on this time of day. Maybe I should have put you down with young Ivor, Dintirion—the Protheroes would have been glad enough for you to stop with them."

"I wouldn't have wanted to," said Amy. "Supposing we do get snowed in I'd rather be up the Gwyntfa with Granny—she wouldn't enjoy it half so much on her own."

"One's not much company, that's true," said Mrs Rhys. "Well, you make haste then—the sooner you're home the better."

Amy watched the van drive away. It left two black lines on the white road. Then she pulled off a glove and unbuttoned enough of her coat to be able to shove her cotton shoe-bag inside against her jersey where it would keep dry.

There was a box fastened to the post of the five-barred gate. It had a strip of roofing-felt nailed on top and a door in front. Amy opened the door and took out a blue enamel milk-can with a lid. Then she looked hopefully into the little square interior, but there were no letters.

Years ago, according to legend, a certain giant drover called Casswell, being set upon by cattle-thieves, had lifted the gate then hanging here clean off its hinges and brought it smashing down on the heads of his attackers, defeating them. Whether true or not this story was the reason why the present boundary-gate

8

between road and valley was known as Casswell's Gate even though there were now no Casswells living in these parts.

Usually Amy clambered over it but today, so as to avoid getting her skirt wet with the snow already lying thick on the top bar, she unhooked it and went through, dropping the hook behind her. The flakes were big and loose, soft white lumps of snow blowing across sideways on the wind as though they too were in haste to get home. Amy had tied her scarf round her head before she left school and was glad now to have her ears covered. She bent her head, turning it so as to protect her face, and trudged on.

Snow, she thought, was a marvel—it was indeed! Snow was like nothing else: it changed the world, the whole of life, in a matter of moments. Not only the shapes of trees and grasses were changed but daily habits—even laws lost their power and had no meaning when snow fell.

That morning lessons had been uncertain. Mr Williams, the schoolmaster, looked out of the window often and doubtfully, as though the low grey sky held a message of warning. And outside it was very still. No birds were flying about; nothing moved.

"I don't like the look of it," said Mr Williams, twice.

At half past twelve they had their dinner and immediately afterwards he went into the playground, not pausing to put on his overcoat, and stood there for some time staring towards the north where the sky above the hills was dark and seemed to be getting darker. Even as he watched the darkness came down and hid the tops of the hills, and then the whole of them. They were swallowed by the sky. And in place of the stillness that had lasted so ominously all morning, a great draught of air rushed forward: the wind was rising. Crowded together at the window the children could see their schoolmaster's trousers flap and branches begin to sway and bend, and a bevy of small birds burst suddenly out from the cover of a holly-tree opposite and scattered in all directions. Mr Williams came inside in a hurry.

9

"You've got snow on your coat, sir," said Danny Price.

Five minutes later snow was sweeping across the playground and Mr Williams was at the telephone ringing up the various members of School Transport to tell them to come at once.

"It's only going to get worse," they heard him say, "and we'd better have them away from here as soon as we can—if we don't, we'll never be able to get them away at all by the look of it."

There were thirty-nine children in the school and each of them felt it was a special treat to be let off two hours of schooling on a Tuesday, as good as a party almost, even though most of them, living on Radnorshire hill-farms, knew well enough how disastrous a heavy fall of snow coming towards the end of February could be for farmers and sheep. But they crammed on their coats and knotted their scarves and stamped about to get their feet down inside their Wellington boots in a state of great excitement because they were doing it at the wrong time of day; and change is always exciting, reflected Amy as she plodded along, seeing only the ground immediately in front of her; which was why snow was always exciting, she thought—snow changes everything.

Although she kept her head lowered her right cheek was beginning to hurt with the cold. She put up her free hand and covered her cheek with the warmth of a woollen glove, and kept her hand there as she struggled on. Walking was not easy, for at each step her foot slipped a little. After some time her legs ached so much she was bound to rest them. She stopped walking and turning her back on the snow lifted her head.

There was nothing to see; nothing but a white swarming nothingness. The hill that rose up in front of her was invisible and the snow itself had altered. The flakes were smaller now and driving harder. She was uncertain of how far she had come, uncertain of exactly where she was; and as she realized this she felt a curious movement inside her, the sudden squeeze of sudden fright. It was not that she was afraid of losing herself, for the track was clear enough yet and she had only to keep on walking ahead until she reached a path turning off that would lead her down to the stream and across it on a narrow wooden bridge and up the further side to the Gwyntfa, the cottage where she lived with her grandmother, Mrs Bowen. If instead she had had to follow the track, an old drovers' road, on up the valley, up and up and still on for miles over a waste of grass and fern and boggy patches and outcroppings of rock where curlews nested in the spring, that would have been another matter. Anyone might get lost up there.

But Amy's fear was not of losing her way home. What frightened her was being unable to tell where she was on a path she knew so well. An entire hill had disappeared, and the familiar track was not familiar any more, and the snow was increasing, and there was nobody with her. Then she noticed close by her feet a large squarish boulder, its shape already altered by the snow blown against it but still recognizable as a rock on which she often paused when she was coming from school and the weather was sunny and she was not in any hurry. Her panic evaporated. After all everything was where it had always been —not gone, only concealed. She shifted the milk-can to her other hand; the weight of it dangling from its wire handle had numbed her fingers. Head bowed, glove to cheek, once again she set off.

It was a relief at last to reach the turning. Here the path plunged steeply down out of the wind and even, except for a faint sprinkling, out of the snow, so sheltered by oak-trees and overgrown hedges that it was like a tunnel. In summer it was a green tunnel, or like walking underneath a green paper sun-shade. In winter, with the bare twigs interwoven above, it was more like being inside a brown shopping-basket. Half running and half slithering, Amy got to the bottom when she saw with astonishment that her rough-haired mongrel terrier Mick was waiting for her in his usual place on the opposite bank of the stream.

"Why—Mick!" she called out.

Mick resembled no other dog for miles around. He had been abandoned as a puppy by visitors some three years previously, and Mr Pugh the policeman had told Amy she could have him: no one else wanted him—for what use was a dog in this part of the world unless he was a working sheepdog? Mrs Bowen said she thought he might possibly be an Irish terrier, only that his hair was a bit too long for that, maybe. Since he was certainly not Welsh he might as well be Irish, Amy had reasoned, and therefore named him Mick, loving him without in fact caring what he was. Every morning Mick accompanied her so far and watched her cross over the stream, and then turned back; every afternoon he came the same distance to meet her.

He stood up now, wagging his tail.

"However did you know I was going to be early?" called Amy. "What do you think of this weather, boy?—do you like it?"

He barked back at her, eager staccato barks, and then, overcome by excitement, burrowed his nose and tossed up snow, and shook his head and sneezed, and burrowed again, behaving so much like a clown that Amy was bound to laugh. She ran across the plank bridge, balanced the can of milk carefully on one of the steps, and then sprang at Mick, meaning to catch and hug him. But he dodged and she lost her balance and rolled on the ground with Mick beneath her wriggling to get free. When they stood up the snow that clung to them both was speckled with dry leaves.

"Look at us now—covered!" said Amy. "Go on then, boy—tell Granny. Tell her I'm coming."

Mick flew ahead up the slope. Amy retrieved the can of milk and did her best to hurry after him, but as soon as she was clear of trees she felt again the strength of the wind and the sharp bite of the snow it carried with it and she had to go slowly. After all, it was of no consequence how slowly she went now: she was nearly home.

She topped the first rise. From here she was accustomed to seeing in front of her the slated roof and grey stone walls of the Gwyntfa. Low and broad, the cottage was set sideways into the hill, facing east but with the front door placed in the centre of its south wall, the gable end overlooking the slope. To the right of the front door were two windows, one above and one below, and to the left of it, high up, a little peephole that served to light the stairs. The short cropped grass continued to the very step of the porch, and large flat stones sunk into the grass formed a rough sort of path that led away from the porch in either direction. Against the west wall of the cottage was a lean-to shed where they kept the chicken-house and where they chopped sticks and sawed logs. On the other side a patch of ground had been enclosed and dug over to make a garden where Mrs Bowen cultivated vegetables and herbs, and gooseberry- and currant-bushes, and a few flowers. Down in the far corner of this enclosure was the lavatory, a wooden hut like a sentry-box, and the whole scene was crowned by the mountain-ash that grew from a cleft in the rock behind and above the cottage.

None of this was visible to Amy today because of the snow driving between her and every known object, until suddenly there was Mick leaping round her legs again, and there was the porch and her grandmother, wrapped in a shawl, peering out.

"Amy—I'm glad to see you!"

"Isn't Mick clever?" said Amy, stamping her feet in the porch. "However did he know we'd be let off school early? It's lucky we were—I'd never have got home else—it's a blizzard, Granny."

"Come on in, child, and shut the door. There! Well—it's no school for you, not for quite a while by the look of it. Go along and give your coat a shake in the side-kitchen and get your Wellingtons off. I'll make the tea this minute—the kettle's boiling. I'm thankful to see you, Amy, and I don't mind saying it."

2. Mr Protheroe Fetches Down His Sheep

Amy took off her coat in the side-kitchen and shook it, but not too vigorously for fear of the snow flying all over herself. Then she hung it on a peg, gave it another shake, and brushed it down with her gloved hands until most of the snow was lying on the stone flags.

"I've made the tea," her grandmother called.

Amy stepped out of her Wellington boots. She pulled off first her gloves, then the thick tightly-fitting outdoor trousers that she wore over her stockings and under her skirt in wintry weather. Her grandmother knitted these trousers for her in scarlet wool, the same as her scarf, and always referred to them as leggings.

"My stockings are wet, Granny."

"Bring them along in here—I've got dry ones for you, ready. And bring your gloves in too, and your leggings, and your scarf."

Amy unknotted her scarf and gave it a good shake as well. Then she ran across the stone floor and the coconut matting into the other room, shutting the door thankfully on the cold side-kitchen.

"What a lovely big fire—I was hoping there might be. And you've fetched all those logs in. You shouldn't have done that, Granny—that's my job."

14

"Not today, it's not. There's no more jobs for you today, Amy. I've seen to the chickens for you, and they as good as thanked me for shutting them up so early. There's nothing for you to do now but only sit there and drink your tea and warm yourself. And I must say in weather like this I'm more glad than usual to be an old woman and not a sheep—imagine the poor creatures out on those hills—nowhere to go."

Amy imagined them with pity; and yet the very thought of their bleak situation increased her own sense of comfort. She knelt on the rag rug in front of the big black range holding her cup of tea in both hands for the pleasure of feeling the heat from it creep into her chilled fingers. The brass toasting-fork, and the brass handle of the poker, and the brass knobs on the fender, and all the other bits and pieces of ornamental brass gleamed and shone and sparkled in the light of the flames. On the rack above the range stood a plate of welsh-cakes, keeping warm. The grandfather clock ticked away, slow and steady. Mick lay against her knees, flicking his ears with an air of satisfaction for having brought her safely home. Queenie, the cat, was curled asleep, or pretending to be, in Amy's own chair. And overhead on a string that went from side to side of the fireplace hung her stockings and scarf and leggings and gloves, reminders of the storm and her good luck in being safe out of it. Her grandmother leant forward to feel her hands, and then her feet.

"Put your dry stockings on, Amy, and your slippers too. Your toes are like icicles, child."

Except for the lively flames the room was perfectly still, very peaceful. Outside it was quite different. Amy glanced back over her shoulder at the square of window across which snow drove without a pause, and it was like a sample of the wild incessant activity filling the world beyond, choking the sky, the ground, isolating neighbour from neighbour.

"I hope there's nobody out there—nobody lost, I mean. It's bad enough for sheep but worse for people. Do you know on the way home I couldn't tell where I was for a bit—I just couldn't tell, it was so thick. Have you ever been lost in the snow, Granny?"

"No indeed, never! But it's only people like Mr Protheroe are likely to be out on the hills today, and he can take care of himself no matter what the weather."

"Mr Williams said he thought it looked bad. It might keep on for days, he said—and Mrs Rhys, she said the same. Will you mind if it does?"

"Mind?—why ever should I?" said old Mrs Bowen, laughing at Amy. "We'll do very well I think, you and me together. We've got each other for company, and the radio too—that's a blessing —just so long as the batteries don't give out. And there's plenty enough oil for the lamps, and food for no matter how long. So far as *mind* goes it can snow for a fortnight. I shouldn't be surprised if we didn't enjoy it."

At that moment Mick sat up and pricked his ears. Then he ran to the door that led into the side-kitchen and stood there, wagging his tail and listening.

"It's Mr Protheroe, bound to be," said Mrs Bowen, nodding at Amy, and she went across to the dresser for a clean cup and saucer.

Amy, with Mick at her heels, rushed through the side-kitchen to welcome Mr Protheroe and, careless of the storm, flung wide the door that opened directly into their shed.

"Mr Protheroe!" she shouted.

He was climbing stiffly down from his pony, his back towards her. Beyond on the hillside, barely discernible through the swirling flakes, she could see his passive flock of sheep and, further again, crouched in the snow unmoving to hold the sheep where they were, the two dark blobs of Patsy and Nipper, his dogs. Mr Protheroe waved an arm at Amy to make her go in, but she waited while he tied the reins to one of the posts of the lean-to.

"We knew it must be you, Mr Protheroe—you're the only person Mick never barks for."

"Well, who else would it be on such a day as this?"

He followed her into the side-kitchen, stamping his feet and taking off his hat to beat the snow from it.

"At least you're safe back from school, Amy. I wondered a bit."

"We were let off early."

"Ah!—so I understand. And a good job too."

"Come in by the fire and have a cup of tea, Mr Protheroe—do! There's a pot fresh made."

"I can't stop, Amy—I wish I could—but I've got to get back down with this lot. Mrs Bowen, how are you? I was just saying to Amy I'm glad to find her safe at home—that's one worry the less. Molly's been in a fret over Amy ever since it came on to snow. We half expected for Mrs Rhys to drop her off with Ivor. Why, thank you—that's very nice indeed and I don't mind telling you I'm glad of it, though I hadn't intended to stop."

Mrs Bowen had brought him out a cup of tea and a plate of welsh-cakes.

"I knew you'd be in too much of a hurry to come in and sit down, but you can drink that and have a bite while you stand there and it won't hold you up more than a minute. So you're fetching the sheep down—you think it's going to last, then?"

"Seems likely—the forecast was bad. There's five ewes missing and I can't stop to find them now—it's going to be dark directly—dark early today. They'll turn up before night, I daresay. If it's not snowing quite so heavy tomorrow I was thinking could Amy maybe get along up to the stack and see are they there? I'm hoping they will be, for their sakes as much as for mine, and that's the truth. And supposing they are, she could just loose them a feed of hay—could you do that for me, Amy, do you think? I'd be much obliged."

"Of course I will, Mr Protheroe—I'll be glad to," said Amy.

"If this goes on I may not be able to get back up here for a day or two, that's what I'm thinking."

"I can see after the ewes for you—of course I can. But will it go on for long?" asked Amy.

"I can't tell you, girl, not for certain. I'll say this much, though—I've never seen it promise worse—no, never! Well now, it's time I was from here. Molly sent a bit of meat along for you, Mrs Bowen, just in case you happened to find yourself short."

He was fumbling with a satchel he wore slung round his neck and presently managed to tug out a large newspaper-wrapped package which he laid down on the table where the oil-lamps, both brass and hurricane, were ranged.

"Why, mercy me if it isn't a whole leg of mutton!" exclaimed Mrs Bowen. "And only me and Amy here to eat it!"

"You don't know how long you're going to have to make it do for," said Mr Protheroe, clamping his hat back on his head and giving himself a slap or two in preparation for starting. "There's one advantage, it won't go bad this weather."

"Oh, we shan't let it go bad, no fear of that. Give Molly my thanks—I don't know which is the kinder to us, her or you. Now you musn't stop here another minute. It's all very well that short way over the top in fine weather, but on a day like this it's bound to be nasty, especially by Billy Dodd's Dingle, so you mind and take good care."

Billy Dodd's Dingle, which sounded so harmless, was a deep narrow ravine that had claimed the lives of innumerable sheep and even, it was said, in years gone by of a drunken farmer; on which occasion the preacher had delivered a sermon of terrible warning against the evil consequences of drink and spoken of Beelzebub's Back Door. Time had changed and softened the name but not the place, for the cliff edges were as sudden, the slopes as steep towards them, as sheer beyond, as ever they had been.

"Don't you waste your worry on me, Mrs Bowen. I know the short way over the top as well as I know my own back-yard, and so do the dogs. It's not deep yet, though it will be if I stay much longer. What had I better do about the milk? I don't suppose there's a chance of Amy getting down Casswell's Gate for it?"

"Best to wait and see what tomorrow's like. The road may be blocked by then. Or it could blow itself clean out in the night and be over and done with by morning."

"Well, it could," said Mr Protheroe, "but I'd be inclined to doubt it. Now I must be off. You're all right for wood, are you? Oil enough? You don't want to run out of paraffin—"

"We've got everything we need, Tom Protheroe—everything, and a leg of mutton on top," said Amy's grandmother, laughing and giving him a push towards the door. "We intend to have a snug time of it, me and Amy. You don't have to think of us, even. We'll be quite all right, no matter what happens." And seeing him still hesitate at the door, she added: "Why, Tom Protheroe dear, we've been snowed up many a time before and no harm come of it. In all the years I've been here—and they're getting to be quite a few now—I've never come to any harm, now have I?"

"No, that's true enough," said Mr Protheroe. "But we shall be thinking of you just the same, so don't imagine we shan't."

They had occasion to remember these words, his last before going out of the door, later on, deriving from them then what comfort they could.

Amy was struggling into her coat and Wellington boots. "I'm bound to see him off, Granny—I'll maybe not see him again, or anyone else, for days and days."

She ran out into the snow. He was already urging his stout pony up the hillside with the mob of sheep moving slowly ahead and the dogs running to and fro on either side.

"Goodbye, Mr Protheroe," she yelled. "And don't you worry about your ewes—I'll see to them for you."

He turned in his saddle and waved. Before he reached the crest of the hill the sheep were already invisible and he and his pony no more than a faint blur. Then, as she stared, there was nothing to be seen except for the steadily driving snow.

19

3. Why They Never Played Their Game of Cards

The lamp was lit and the curtains drawn. Amy and Mrs Bowen sat one on each side of the fire doing their patchwork. It was to be a bedspread, a present for Amy's father and for his second wife whom they had neither of them ever seen except in photographs. Amy's father had married again out in Australia and there were now three children belonging to him and his second wife. Amy liked to think she had brothers and a sister, even if they did live so far away.

She sat in the rocking-chair, a pillow-case crammed with old pieces of cloth on the floor beside her, and in her lap the cardboard shapes she had cut ready the previous evening. Each bit of cardboard had to have a corresponding scrap of material stretched over it and tacked firmly. Amy did this. Then Mrs Bowen sewed the sections together, her needle piercing only the cloth and her stitches so small it was almost impossible to see them. Later the tacking threads would be cut and the cardboard drop out. Every night they worked away at the bedspread and it grew and grew, overflowing from Mrs Bowen's knees to the floor where Queenie dozed amongst its multi-coloured folds. They spoke seldom, not feeling the need of much conversation, but now and again the stuff they were cutting or sewing would remind them of some incident.

"Here's my old pink skirt, Granny. Fancy me ever being small enough to wear that."

"Fancy indeed! I learnt a lesson off that skirt of yours, Amy. It was so bright I could see you in it a mile away and I had a foolish notion you were bound to be safe just so long as I could *see* you. But you proved me wrong—look at the tear! There was no use in even trying to mend it."

"And I've still got the mark on my leg—it was barbed wire I was caught in, just like an old ewe. And didn't I cry!—but it wasn't so much for hurting myself. It was spoiling my skirt I minded. Still, it makes into lovely patchwork now. It's my favourite colour, pink."

"What a fright you gave me that day," said Mrs Bowen, pausing to look over her spectacles and smiling. "I'll never forget! I hadn't run so fast for years. Run!—I believe I flew!"

They snipped and sewed and talked a little, comfortably, as they did every night. And every night when the clock struck eight they would put away their sewing and have a cup of tea and some welsh-cakes. Then they played cards; sometimes they played Patience, and sometimes it was Beggar-my-Neighbour or Two-handed Whist. When one of them yawned they knew they had played for long enough. Then Mick would be let outside for his last run while they tidied up the room and raked out the fire and lit their candles and Mrs Bowen withdrew from the bottom oven the two bricks that had been lying there all day long absorbing heat. These were their bed-warmers and as soon as each brick had been wrapped in flannel it was time for bed.

Regularly, until tonight, they followed the same routine. But tonight they never played their game of cards, for ten minutes before the clock struck eight Mick growled. First he sat up and looked towards the front door; then he growled. Amy and Mrs Bowen both laid down their sewing.

"Mick—what is it?"

He glanced at Amy and wagged his tail, but immediately afterwards growled again, staring at the red chenille curtain that hung over the front door to keep out draughts. They all stared at the red chenille curtain. Hidden by it were bolts, one at the top of the door, one at the bottom, which they very well knew had not been pushed into place.

"It's just an old ewe, I daresay—there were those five missing—"

"He wouldn't growl for a sheep, Granny."

They looked at each other.

"Oh, Granny—" whispered Amy, and at that moment Mick sprang to his feet and ran across the room, barking. There was a tremendous but muffled thump at the front door, as though something had fallen heavily against it. Mrs Bowen stood up.

"It's all right, Amy," she said. "Who is it?" she called. "Who's there?"

The door burst open and in an instant the storm had rushed inside, filling the room, destroying its peaceful inviolability and bringing instead confusion, a turmoil of Mick barking and barking, the lamp guttering, the tablecloth lifting, and snow blowing across the floor as though it were blowing across a field. In the doorway, half blocking it, was a shape so big and bulky that to Amy it appeared to be not so much a man as a monster leaning there glaring at them with eyes more felt than seen, while Mick snarled and barked, and they by the fire looked on in amazement and fear. Then whoever it was stepped across the threshold into their cottage and slammed the door behind him. The tablecloth sank down; the calendar fell back against the wall.

Neither Amy nor her grandmother had ever in their lives before been confronted by such a person. He was huge, and whether he had a black beard or only bristles on the way to becoming a beard it was hard to be sure. The collar of his short navy-blue coat was turned up. He wore a curious navy-blue wool cap on his head with a peak and ear-flaps. One arm was held across his chest by some kind of tattered rag or scarf knotted round his neck. And there he stood, fantastic but real, in their own front-kitchen: a bad dream, except that Amy and Mrs Bowen knew they were both awake.

Gripping the back of her chair, panting a little, Mrs Bowen said: "It's a terrible night for anyone to be out. Did you lose your way?"

She might as well not have spoken for all the notice he took of her. With legs apart he balanced himself, and while his head remained sunk and unmoving his eyes went searching round the room from corner to corner, lingering on the door into the side-kitchen and the door that closed off the stairs with a dark brooding gleam that terrified Amy. Too stiff with fright almost to stir, she yet managed to reach her grandmother one step off and take hold of her arm. But Mrs Bowen said, quite sharply: "Put on the kettle, Amy. He's frozen, I daresay, poor man. Mick, come here! Mick, lie down! If you'll wait just a minute I'll make you a cup of tea," she said, raising her voice. "Will you come by the fire now and warm yourself?"

This time when she spoke he turned his head and looked at her, but still he said nothing, not a word. Several seconds passed. No one moved, not even Mick, crouched at their feet, as tense as a set trap. Then the head, like the head of a great animal, swung away, and they felt as though some danger had passed by. He crossed the room with a tread that shook the china on the shelves and flung open the door of the side-kitchen and was gone out of sight.

"Who is he, Granny?" whispered Amy, in agonized entreaty. "What does he want? Will he hurt us, Granny? What's he going to do?"

"He's just a man," said Mrs Bowen. She put another log on the fire and gave it a knock with the poker, and moved the kettle over. Amy saw that her hands were trembling. "Now

Amy, it's all right. We shall be quite all right. You mustn't mind about him."

"Oh, Granny—"

"There's no need to be afraid. You just stand by me. You mustn't be afraid, Amy," she said again, firmly, like someone giving an order. "I'll see you come to no harm."

Amy wound her fingers into the thick wool of her grand-mother's old brown cardigan, and so they waited.

They could hear him on the other side of the wall, blundering about. There was the clatter of tins falling, followed by the smash of glass. Then he reappeared, carrying a sack in one hand and in the other a hurricane lamp, lit. He paid no further attention either to Mrs Bowen or to Amy. As though to remind him of their existence, Mick growled.

"Quiet, Mick."

The fire blazed. No one made the tea, in spite of steam beginning to issue like a signal from the spout of the kettle. They watched him dump the lamp and the sack on the chest under the window before wrenching open the staircase door. He was so big and so thickened by his heavy coat they thought he would never be able to squeeze his way upstairs, but he did, and they heard his footsteps cross above their heads. Almost at once he was down again, half-falling into the room and trailing an armful of blankets which he thrust inside the sack. Then clumsily, as all his movements were clumsy, he hoisted the sack to his shoulder, and picked up the lamp. They kept as still as stone. He turned to go. The hand looped in a scarf was already fumbling for the latch when he seemed to recollect that somewhere or other there had been an old woman and a little girl, and very slowly he turned to look for them.

"It's all right, Amy," said Mrs Bowen once more, but softly this time, hearing the catch of breath and feeling the fingers tighten convulsively on her cardigan.

They thought that he was going to speak at last, but he only thrust his face forward as though to see them better—as though they were out of focus, or a long way off; almost as though they puzzled him. In that agonizing pause when all they heard was the slow tick of the grandfather clock and the gentle hiss of the kettle, they had no means of knowing what he might be making up his mind to do. But then, with a sudden inexplicable gesture, he turned away again and jerked the door open. They glimpsed him in the shelter of their porch, a massive black shape with the sack on his shoulder, the snow whirling down beyond him, and then the door banged shut and they were alone. Amy sprang across the room, snatched the curtain clear, and shot the bolts. As she did so the clock struck eight.

"Granny—do you think he'll come back?"

"No—he's gone now. Quiet Mick, quiet!" For Mick had broken into a frenzy of barking.

"Oh, don't hush him, Granny—I know just how he feels," said Amy, bursting into tears.

"There now, he's gone—it's over," said Mrs Bowen, putting her arms round Amy and patting her. "You make the tea, Amy child. A cup of tea is what we both of us need. And I'll just slip the bolts across on the side-kitchen door so as to be sure, though indeed I don't believe he'll trouble us any more. I think we've seen the last of him."

Amy heard her in the next room exclaiming aloud; then the rasp of the bolts.

"The mess in there!" she declared on her return. "Goodness knows how many of our bottling jars he's knocked off the shelf, and there's paraffin all over the floor! I shan't clean it up tonight, though—time enough tomorrow. There now, you've made us the tea—so we'll just stay by the fire a bit, nice and quiet, and get our breath back. You bring the stool over here, Amy, and sit up against my chair. There we are! Now we'll be all right! I'm going to put an extra lump of sugar in your cup of tea—they do say sugar's good for shock," she went rambling on.

"Who was he, Granny?" said Amy, desperately interrupting her.

Mrs Bowen's reassuring chatter died away. It was no use
pretending: they had both been very much frightened. She put
her hand, rather apologetically, on Amy's shoulder.

"I don't know, Amy, any more than you do. Except he was
too big and black to be a snowflake, I'd have said he fell out of
the sky."

"But where was he going? It's not as if we're on the way to
anywhere. We're miles from the road—we're right off the track,
even."

"He must have been lost, Amy."

"Then why didn't he say so when you asked him? Why
didn't he speak?"

"I don't know, indeed," said Mrs Bowen again. "All I
know is, it was me that guided him here, though I never intended
any such thing."

"*You*, Granny?"

Mrs Bowen nodded. "As soon as I saw him with that lamp
in his hand, I knew it. You remember how it was I went out to
the shed, late, after tea, because I couldn't be sure in my mind
if I'd turned the catch of the hen-house door?"

"It's my job usually—that's why you weren't sure."

"And when I came inside again I put the lamp on the window-
ledge while I was getting off my boots—and then you called me
for something. What was it you called me for?"

"To hear the weather forecast."

"That was it! Well—and I never went back after to blow out
the lamp. I forgot. So there it stayed, shining out through our
side-kitchen window for all the world like a beacon calling him
on. How could he ever have found his way here else—or known
there was a house, even? I can't get over the strangeness of it,
Amy—that I should have left a lamp at the window this one
night of all nights. I keep thinking of what it must have been

26

for him, seeing that light and making towards it, and keeping on, and keeping on, through all the storm and darkness."

Amy shuddered. They drank their tea, half-expecting with every sip to hear once again that awful thud against the door. Mick dozed uneasily, raising his head often to listen. Sometimes he growled and sometimes he whimpered.

"There's no one there, Mick," Amy told him, trying to believe it herself. "Granny, what makes you so sure he won't come back?"

"Well, he didn't seem to want to stop—I never saw a man in more of a hurry. He stayed for just so long as it took to help himself to a bit of bedding and Molly Protheroe's leg of mutton."

"He took our leg of mutton?" cried Amy.

"It's gone."

"But it wasn't cooked—he can't eat it raw!"

"I daresay if a person's hungry enough he wouldn't trouble himself too much was it cooked or raw."

"Do you think he was hungry—as hungry as *that*?" asked Amy, dubiously. "I don't think so—I think he was *wild*! Like one of those animals they bring round with the circus, only he'd got out of his cage. Oh, Granny—can I sleep in your bed tonight?"

"You may have to," replied Mrs Bowen, "if you want to keep warm. Those were your blankets he took."

"And he never asked us, even. He never spoke—he never said one word to us, not one word. Oh Granny, he was *horrible*!"

Mrs Bowen raked the fire and put the guard in front. She looked round the room absently, as though she were seeing it fresh in the way a stranger might see it. Then she sighed and shook her head and gave her eyes a rub, like someone very tired.

"Well, yes—he gave us a big fright. But Amy—he never harmed us. He could have done. There was none to stop him."

She took a taper to light the two candles standing ready on

the mantelpiece. Then she hesitated and laid the taper down. Picking up the lamp instead she crossed to the front door.

"You surely don't mean to open that door, Granny?"

"I've got to let Mick out for his run, Amy, same as we always do."

"Not tonight—it wouldn't matter for just this once. He'd manage all right, wouldn't you, Mick?—he'd understand."

"I must, Amy. If I don't open this door tonight we won't either of us sleep for thinking what may be outside it."

They looked at each other solemnly: it was true, Amy realized.

"Do you mean to go right properly outside yourself, Granny? —not just let Mick out?"

"I was thinking I'd maybe have a breath of fresh air while I was about it."

"Then I'll come with you. Yes, I will—I want to."

Amy held away the red chenille curtain while Mrs Bowen drew back the heavy bolts. Then with a thundering heart she opened the door just sufficiently wide for both of them and Mick to squeeze through, closing it instantly behind them; and there they were, outside, partly protected by the porch from weather, but not at all from anything else. They could hear the wind roaring away in the bare trees at the bottom, but round their own cottage there was for a moment a comparative lull. Mrs Bowen lifted the lamp high for them to see into the night as far as they could. All they could see was snow, steadily falling. The nearer flakes, dropping casually down across the beams of the lamp, looked wonderfully white and slow. But a little further off these drifting fragments seemed to alter, to draw closer together and quicken and darken until the spread of lamplight was confined by moving walls, hurrying down and down in endless descent.

A staggered line of footprints, deep shapeless holes, led up to the porch, but already they were beginning to be blurred and softened by new snow and Amy, seeing this, was glad, for she felt that in blotting out his marks the snow was blotting out their visitor as well. Then they heard the wind roar up the hill towards them. In a fine cloud the fallen snow lifted and whirled. The lamp went out.

"Quick, Amy—inside!"

They snatched the door open and were through in a flash.

"Granny—where's Mick?"

He was missing. But it was easier now to open the door a crack and shout:

"Mick! Mick!"

He came in a flurry of snow and excitement, and leapt round the room wagging his tail and sneezing. The bolts were triumphantly shot into place. They stamped their feet and laughed, exhilarated by their own daring.

"I'm glad we went out, Granny—you were right. Now we *know* he's not there."

But later on, in bed, it was hard to be quite so certain.

"Granny?"

"Yes?"

"What was that noise? Didn't you hear it?"

"I heard a bit of snow fall off."

Amy lay still, considering this explanation.

"There's all sorts of noises go on every night," said her grandmother's voice, reasonably. "We don't hear them mostly on account of we're not mostly listening."

Amy shut her eyes, hoping to be able to shut her ears as well, and so to shut out all anxiety, but at once clear in her mind she saw that single line of footsteps filling up with snow. Her eyes flew open.

"Granny!"

"What now?"

"There should have been more footsteps—going-away ones too."

Her grandmother said, after a pause:

"But those may very well have been the going-away ones, Amy—how can we tell?"

"Then where were the coming-here ones?"

This silence seemed to last for much longer. Amy tried to sense in the dark whether her grandmother was thinking it over, or had simply dropped asleep.

"Why, Amy," said Mrs Bowen at last, "they could have been anywhere—we didn't look for them, specially."

But Amy turned towards the old woman, clutching at her for comfort, whispering loud and fast:

"I know why we didn't see his going-away footsteps—they were so close up to the house, that's why. And that noise *was* him, Granny, and I think he's in our shed this very moment. He's there—*now*. He never went away at all."

Mrs Bowen sat up. There was the scrape of a match and then Amy saw her, bending sideways to light one of the candles. She wore a white cotton nightgown made by herself, as all her nightgowns were, with a high neck and long sleeves, and her hair fell forward over her shoulders in two thinnish grey pigtails.

When she was sure the candle was properly alight, she reached for a shawl and wrapped herself in it, and then she arranged the bolster and pillow behind her for greater support. These preparations calmed Amy. It was a relief to know that her grandmother was fully awake. It was even more a relief to see her, and to see the room appear round her, conjured out of the black void by one small wavering flame. Amy lay, covered to the tip of her nose by bedclothes, and allowed her eyes to rest gratefully on the chest-of-drawers which, although invisible, had been there all the time, exactly the same as usual.

"Well, Amy," said Mrs Bowen, finally, "this is what I think—if he's there, then that's where he is, and there's nothing we can do about it. There's no one can hear us if we shout, and the two of us put together aren't so strong as that man's little finger. We might as well know it—we're on our own. And if this snow keeps on it'll be a good few days before we see another face. It's no *use* for us to be frightened—that won't help us one little bit—and besides, it's a feeling I don't enjoy. So now— I don't mean to bother any more tonight about where he is."

Amy kept her eyes on the chest-of-drawers and counted the knobs. A slight sensation of sleepiness crept over her. There were eight knobs. Her grandmother's words went round and round in her head: they were sensible words.

"Granny? How long are you going to stay awake?"

"Longer than you."

"What about the candle?"

"I'll blow it out, later."

"I don't understand—" said Amy, struggling to disentangle a thought, a picture, some remembrance, from the yellow knobs of the chest-of-drawers going round and round in her head.

4. No Snow on the Chopping-Block

Amy overslept. She opened her eyes with a feeling of vague disquiet. Something was wrong. Why was she in her grandmother's bed and where was her grandmother? Then she heard the clock downstairs begin to strike, and it struck nine times instead of seven, twice too often. Horrified, she sprang out of bed. She had overslept and Mrs Rhys would have gone long ago. But when she pulled the curtains apart there was no view at all: the panes of glass were blocked in, a solid white. Snow! And then she remembered yesterday, and all that had happened—everything.

Her grandmother was calling to her from below.

"Amy! Come along down. Don't stop to put your clothes on —I've made the tea. You can have my shawl to keep warm in."

Bare-footed, half-awake, half-asleep, Amy pattered downstairs. Mrs Bowen was just stooping to put the pot of tea on the hob in front of the fire which burnt with the loud crackle and fuss of a fire only recently lit. Mick came to meet her, wagging his tail. Queenie had already settled herself for the morning in Mrs Bowen's well-padded basket-chair. Except for the time on the clock everything had the appearance of being the same as usual. Yawning, Amy sat back submissively in the cushioned rocker and allowed her grandmother to tuck the shawl round her and even, as though she were once again a very little girl, to pull on the stockings that had been hanging since she came home yesterday on the string over the fire.

"I didn't see the sense in rousing you any earlier, Amy—it's not as though we've got a very busy day ahead of us. Mind, there's any amount of mending if it's work we're after, and the brasses can always do with an extra polish."

Amy listened without replying. She was letting herself get used to the idea that today was really, in spite of appearances, different from most days: up late, no school. There was another difference too; but this she averted her mind from, feeling not yet quite ready to think about it.

"I heard the news at eight o'clock," said Mrs Bowen, "and it was all the same—tales of snow, far and wide. It seems it's the heaviest fall we've had for years, and there's more on the way, so that's a fine prospect. Here's your tea now, Amy—drink it up and then you can get yourself dressed and see to the chickens, and time you've done them I'll have the breakfast ready."

The more her grandmother continued to talk and behave as though nothing strange had taken place the night before, the more Amy found that she could not exclude the happening from her own thoughts. She drank her tea in silence, frowning, and with every sip the possibility of there being something else besides chickens outside in the shed intensified. She tried to persuade herself that her fears were nonsense. It was morning now. The sun was shining. And yet, just *supposing* when she opened the side-kitchen door and stepped out—she put her cup down hurriedly.

"I'm going to get dressed, Granny, and—and then I'll see to the chickens. I believe it's stopped snowing—it looks quite bright outside."

Had her grandmother really forgotten what horrid surprise the shed might hold in store? Amy longed to remind her and yet it was impossible for her to mention the subject while her grandmother remained so unconcerned.

"I don't suppose it'll last," said Mrs Bowen, measuring porridge. "Take that kettle, Amy—it's your water for washing. And make haste—it's too cold for you to be loitering about with no clothes on."

Amy took the kettle and went slowly up the narrow twisting boxed-in stairs. There was no passage in their cottage, or even landing. A partition divided the top floor in two halves, with the stairs emerging directly into Mrs Bowen's bedroom, which Amy had to cross in order to reach her own room beyond it.

In each bedroom there was a marble-topped washstand and on each washstand a matching set of china jug, basin and soap-dish. Amy's jug and basin were small, made on purpose for a child. They were white, decorated with wide rings of pink and gold, and they had been bought for her by her father before he had emigrated to Australia, long before she could remember. Amy thought them very pretty.

She mixed the hot water from the kettle with cold water from the jug and rapidly soaped her face and neck, with a dab or two at the ears. Having washed the soap off with a flannel she scrubbed herself dry on a rough towel. Resolved now to do what there was to do quickly, and yet still dreading to do it, she scrambled into her clothes at top speed and ran down the stairs and into the side-kitchen.

As she pulled on her Wellingtons and overcoat she eyed the door that she was going to have to open. And then, suddenly, she realized that her grandmother must have been out already: the bolts had been drawn back. Amy flushed warm all over with relief. So that was all right! She lifted the lid of the corn-bin and filled a scoop with grain; but after a moment or so of consideration she put the scoop down and went into the front-kitchen.

Mrs Bowen was stirring the porridge. She glanced up.

"Why, Amy," she said, "whatever makes you so solemn, child? You can't surely be imagining that man's out there in the shed, can you?"

"Did you go outside when I was asleep and have a look?"

Mrs Bowen moved the pan off the fire. She took Amy's scarf from the string where it was dangling ready and tied the two ends of it firmly underneath her chin.

"Of course we did, me and Mick, first thing. You don't suppose I'd have left that for you to find out? There's only the chickens waiting for you in the shed, Amy, nothing else, and it's late so you'd better make haste—they'll be wanting their breakfast as much as you want yours."

"Weren't you afraid, Granny? Supposing you'd opened the door and he'd been there?"

Her grandmother laughed.

"Well, to tell you the truth I didn't stop to think too much. There's times when it's better to do a thing straight off, when it's got to be done, and think about it after."

Amy was silent, pondering the matter while she watched her grandmother stirring. Finally she said:

"You're braver than me, Granny. You're older, of course, but I don't know if that's why. Is it?"

Mrs Bowen too was silent a moment or so before she answered.

"I'd say brave isn't mostly what people are, Amy, it's what they decide to be—and if there's no choice, then they can't very well decide any other, can they? You don't have to fret about it—you'll find you're brave enough whenever the time comes that you've got to be."

"Shall I?" said Amy, with an anxious sigh. "I hope you're right, Granny. Come on then, Mick."

She opened the side-kitchen door. Snow had blown up against it and frozen, making a low barricade which she stepped over.

The morning was flawless. There was no wind. Amy's breath steamed on air that was clear and cold and still. Nothing broke the silence, nothing moved. She stood in the shed with the scoop of corn in one hand, marvelling at how a world so white and so smooth could have been created by anything as rough and dark as the storm of the previous night.

Their shed was formed by a roof sloping out from the west wall of the cottage, supported on oak posts. It was wide open to the hillside except for its north end, which had been closed in by sheets of corrugated tin. Against this closed end, at right angles to it, was the chicken-house, raised above ground-level on blocks of stone so as to preserve it from dampness and rats. A narrow space existed between the chicken-house and cottage wall, screened on its third side by the corrugated tin, and in this convenient nook they kept their few garden tools, empty flower-pots and similar odds and ends. The rest of the shed was used mainly for chopping sticks and sawing up logs. In summertime swallows built their nests under the sloping roof, and Amy used to sit on the chopping-block during late warm afternoons, her feet on a carpet of accumulated wood-chips, watching the birds dart in and out. Now it was not summer and there were no swallows; snow had covered the chippings and the chopping-block, she suddenly noticed, had gone.

It had gone!

But that was impossible! How could a great chunk of wood, immensely heavy, all at once have gone? The chickens were rustling inside their prison, impatient to be let out, but Amy could only stare at the place where the chopping-block always was, and where it now was not. Then her eye fell on Mick, snuffling away busily in the corner, and then she saw the chopping-block: there it was, removed as though by magic, and brown and dry although everything else in the shed had at least a speckling of white. It was brown and dry because he must have been sitting on it, squeezed between the chicken-house and the wall of the cottage, while the storm battered the thin shield of corrugated tin at his back and eddies of snow whirled under the roof to settle in every cranny, every crack, covering the blankets he was wrapped in, and the sack at his feet, and the sieve and the hank of twine hanging above his head. The picture was so vivid to Amy that she stood petrified in front of the chopping-block, as though the ghost of his awful presence still crouched upon it.

"He was here, Mick, in our shed, like I said he was."

Mick came out from underneath the chicken-house and wagged his tail at her.

"And then, when it stopped snowing, he went away."

She dumped the scoop on the ground and floundered out from the shelter of the shed to scan the white slope beyond. Plain as print, there they were, the missing footsteps, the ones that had worried her last night, leading uphill behind the cottage in the same direction as Mr Protheroe had taken—so long ago, it seemed—when she waved him goodbye yesterday afternoon. She stared at those footsteps as though by staring she could force them to tell her something more, something finally reassuring, but all they told her was the way that he had gone.

In a sort of a dream Amy took hold of the shovel and scraped a patch of ground clear of snow. She tipped the grain on to the bare patch and then undid the door of the chicken-house, and the chickens came crowding out, a wild commotion of squawks and ruffled feathers. Amy watched them pecking for a few moments. Then she cleared away the snow piled in front of the side-kitchen door. When that was done she leaned her shovel against the wall and went inside.

"Granny," she said, "he was in our shed all night, just like I thought he was."

Mrs Bowen was pouring porridge into their two bowls. She stopped pouring.

"He was ?"

37

"Tight up in the corner he must have been—that's where I found the chopping-block. It's what he sat on. You didn't happen to notice it was gone when you went out with Mick, did you?—I didn't either, at first. He moved it."

"You're a lot sharper than me, then, and that's a fact, for I never saw a mite of difference. Though to be honest with you, Amy, I didn't give much more than just a glance to the shed, enough to see he wasn't there, and for this reason—which I don't mind telling you now it's all over and done with. What I had fixed in my head was that he might have passed the night in our toilet. Don't laugh at me—he could have done. It would have been shelter for him. So that's why I wasn't too particular about the shed."

"Did you look in the toilet?"

Mrs Bowen gave a brief nod.

"I didn't stop to clear a way to it, neither—there was snow so high it all but came over the top of my Wellingtons. And I can't tell you the relief to my heart it was, Amy, to find that toilet empty. I was afraid he'd be there for sure—I was afraid he'd be dead, died of the cold."

She said much the same words when she had been out with Amy into the shed and studied the chopping-block and the footsteps.

"Oh, Amy—all night out here! He must have been about starved," she exclaimed; by which she meant that he must have been near freezing. "Only to think of it! We were warm in bed at least."

But to Amy, even as the chopping-block had seemed to have been moved by magic, so did the footprints going up the hill have a supernatural quality about them.

"How is it he managed to keep on the path, Granny? There's not a sign of it this morning. With all this snow on top there's no way of telling what's underneath. How did he know there *was* a path, even?"

"Well, I suppose he must have seen Tom Protheroe's tracks, and the tracks of that old mob of sheep, when he first got here—though mind, it was snowing so hard there couldn't have been much left of all their trampling and mess; but I daresay there was just enough to tell him there'd been a flock driven that way not long before, and he reckoned wherever it was they were going, he could go too. I believe he set out directly he went from here last night, Amy," said Mrs Bowen, "hoping to come on a road or a farm while there were still tracks enough to follow—you remember what a hurry he was in? But it must have struck him so rough when he got to the top of the hill, he was obliged to give up and come back down here to our shed, and wait for morning."

"It's lucky for him he did wait—he'd have gone straight over the edge of Billy Dodd's Dingle in the dark," said Amy.

Gradually during breakfast their disturbed feelings settled down, rather as the spluttering fire had settled down into a comfortable glowing furnace. With every spoonful of porridge the man who had caused them such terror came to seem more and more remote, like the storm itself, a memory, something extraordinary to discuss and to wonder at, but past. He had appeared out of the night as though he had been a part of its blackness, and when the night was gone so was he. Now it was morning and the sun shone and presently all that remained of him, his footsteps, would melt and be gone as well.

Mrs Bowen fetched out a pot of her cherry jam, a rare treat. They sat on, drinking cup after cup of weakening tea. There was nothing to hurry for today.

"Where do you think he's got to now, Granny?"

"Well, I don't know how far he's got, but it seems likely he'll finish up in the Protheroes' back-yard—providing he gets by Billy Dodd's Dingle. A real nasty old track it is over the top in bad weather, and bound to be a lot worse today than it was for Tom Protheroe yesterday afternoon—*he* wasn't anxious to linger and he was on a pony. Still, I daresay it might be passable yet, though I shouldn't care to try it myself."

"I wonder what Mrs Protheroe will think if she sees him."

"Think?—she won't pause to think. If I know Molly Protheroe she'll have him inside the house and those dirty old clothes off him and be scrubbing him down in the bath before he's got the chance to turn himself around and make a run for it—and I wouldn't be surprised she didn't shave that beard off him too," said Mrs Bowen, beginning to laugh and then finding herself unable to stop.

"She'd do it, too!" declared Amy enthusiastically. "I believe she'd do anything, once she'd set her mind to it. She doesn't care a bit what she does, or what she says. And she never gets cross either—not properly cross. Of course she scolds the boys now and then, but that's nothing. I like Mrs Protheroe a lot," said Amy, her eyes wide and sparkling with admiration.

"Why, naturally you do—how can anyone help but like her? There's not a kinder soul in the world than Molly—and she's clever as well—and full of fun. I'd have told Tom Protheroe a hundred times how lucky he is, only he knows it well enough without being told," said Mrs Bowen, wiping away her tears of laughter and speaking warmly of the woman who lived in what had once been her own home long ago during the short time that she was married, and later the home of her son and his wife, Amy's parents, during the time—even shorter—when they were married; for Mrs Bowen's husband had died after only six years, and her daughter-in-law while Amy was still a baby. Other children and grandchildren, not hers, had grown up at Dintirion.

"A better mother than Molly Protheroe I can't imagine—nor a nicer lot of boys than those three of hers and Tom's," said Mrs Bowen, her thoughts beginning to wander a little.

But Amy was more in the mood for jokes than reminiscences. "Fancy if that leg of mutton Mrs Protheroe sent us should happen to turn up on her doorstep again—what a surprise she'll get!"

"She'll most likely think it's the postman coming with a parcel," said Mrs Bowen, pretending to be serious.

"What a funny sort of parcel—what a funny postman!" exploded Amy.

They let themselves laugh and laugh. After so much anxiety it was like a tonic to be able to. But all at once Amy sprang to her feet.

"Oh, Granny—the ewes! Those five that were missing—I said I'd watch out for them."

"So you did, and I don't know how it can have slipped my own mind either. Leave these few crocks where they are—there'll be plenty of time for them later. We'd best get up to the haystack now before it comes on to snow again—it said on the news it was going to."

"Are you coming with me? You don't have to, Granny. It was me that promised Mr Protheroe."

"A breath of air will do me good," declared Mrs Bowen.

In spite of the serene and smiling aspect of the morning, in spite of the way they had just been making fun, Amy was secretly glad to be having her grandmother's company; and Mrs Bowen knew in her heart that she would not have been altogether easy if Amy had gone on her own.

5. Four Are Found

Amy carried the shovel in case they should come on one or more of the sheep stuck in a drift, and Mrs Bowen took a stick for her own benefit, and so they set out to climb the hill behind the Gwyntfa.

But whereas Mr Protheroe, and later on their visitor, had both veered to the right, Mrs Bowen and Amy bore away to the left, for their cottage stood at the junction of two pathways. The one that went off to the right was the oldest, a branch, some people held, of the old drovers' road; but it had been so little used for so long, except as a mutual convenience by Protheroes and Bowens, that its existence was officially forgotten and it was no longer marked with a dotted line on the ordnance survey maps. Yet for those who knew, it was a way that could be followed over the crest of the hill and down the further side, where it then skirted Billy Dodd's Dingle, climbed the flank of Cader Ddu—that bleak forbidding mountain—and finally fetched up at Dintirion, the Protheroes' farm, which stood on the outskirts of Melin-y-Groes, and a little above it, connected to the village by its own short steep stretch of macadamized road.

Dintirion was said to have been a court-house long ago; but Mrs Bowen herself believed it had once, even earlier, been some kind of a fortress, and warnings of invading hosts been carried back to it along that very path centuries before by breathless runners from a look-out post situated on the hill above the

Gwyntfa. For this was the Welsh Marches, wild border-country; and why else should a path, otherwise of little importance, have a core of stone, invisible to the eye but apparent to the feet, unyielding, firm, defying time and the seasons? Amy and the Protheroe boys had always supported this theory, largely because it had provided them with good dramatic material for a game that could easily be worked in with the less interesting business of herding sheep. Besides, Mrs Bowen had been a teacher and so they respected her historical opinions.

The other path was not ancient and had no mysterious foundation of stone; it was simply a track of beaten earth, also leading over the ridge behind the Gwyntfa, but in a north-westerly direction, and nowadays it stopped at Mr Protheroe's haystack. Once it had gone on, down to the small farm-house concealed in a clump of trees at the bottom. This part of the path had long since merged with the rest of the rough slope and disappeared, while the farm-house itself had fallen into ruins.

But when Mrs Bowen first came to the Gwyntfa, a widow with her little boy Dilwyn, there had been a gnarled and taciturn old man living there all alone, like a hermit, and Mrs Bowen had done her best to be neighbourly: every morning she climbed the same track she and Amy were climbing now, so as to look down from the top of the hill and see if old Tyler had spread a rag of white cloth over a thorn-bush, his sign that he was in need of something. That was more than thirty years ago and the walls and roof of the old man's house had been collapsing then, she said. When he was gone the house stayed empty, no one else caring to live in such an out-of-the-way habitation. People spoke of it still as Tyler's Place although its proper name, marked on the ordnance survey maps, was Cilnant, and although it now belonged for the sake of the land that went with it to Mr Protheroe, who allowed it year by year to become more derelict, considering that any money spent on it would be money wasted.

This morning, however, it was the present, not the past, that claimed their attention. Each time Amy breathed in she could feel the air go down cold inside her, and each time she breathed out she felt a faint tickle round her nostrils as her warm breath froze. It was hard going. At every step she watched the black Wellington boot she planted ahead of her sink, and heard the crunch it made, and then, as she pushed her weight off it, felt it slip back. She grew damp inside her clothes with effort.

They reached the top at last, puffing, and turned to survey the wintry landscape, an undulating whiteness that stretched away, silent, without a living creature in sight, broken by nothing but the grey stone walls of the cottage and lower again by the mottled brown of trees marking the course of the stream. Nor was there any movement except for the twist of smoke coming from their own chimney. But the sky had clouded stealthily over; it was a dull grey now, matching the cottage walls, and getting darker every minute.

"We'd better make haste, Amy," said Mrs Bowen. "That sunshine was too good to be true—I thought it might be. Early and bright at this time of year is never to be trusted. Mick, come here—you stay with us, boy. There's no rabbit with a grain of sense would be out on such a day, so don't you go looking for one."

And taking the shovel from Amy, Mrs Bowen set off at a resolute pace towards the haystack which stood beyond the brow of the hill, a short distance down the further slope.

Every harvest Mr Protheroe built the stack here, hauling the bales from Dintirion by tractor to provide for his hill sheep in winter. By the middle of February there was not much of it left. Underneath a rusty tin roof the remaining bales were sheeted over with black plastic, firmly pegged to the ground. Whenever Mrs Bowen saw the stack she said the same thing as she did today, and in the same tone of exasperation:

"Tom Protheroe ought to build a proper barn. What's the

use of this—a bit of old roof, and on the weather side too! I've told him and told him—he just can't be bothered. Why, Amy," she exclaimed, her voice changing, "those ewes of his are here after all! So they did find their way—they're not so silly as they look. Keep back, Mick! Wait there, boy—sit!"

For the sheep were showing signs of uneasiness at the presence of a dog. They had bunched together against the plastic sheeting, while the boldest stood out in front and stamped her foot. Mick sat down.

"There's only four of them," said Amy. "There ought to be five—he told us five, didn't he? I'd better take a look round the other side."

Lifting and lowering each leg as straight as she could, Amy made her way round to the far side of the stack. Snow had piled up against it so deeply that in spite of her care some got over the top of her Wellingtons and slithered icily down inside.

"She's not here, Granny—and I've got snow in my boots."

Whenever she opened her mouth her teeth ached. Her sweat had dried and felt clammy with the cold. Closing her lips together tightly, Amy ploughed her way back.

"Do you think she's got herself stuck in a drift somewhere, Granny?"

"She most likely has," said Mrs Bowen, pityingly.

"Oh, Granny, we must find her—she'll die if we don't."

"Well indeed, if she does die then die she does, Amy, and that's all about it. We can't go searching the hills for her. Only to step off the path might easy enough bring us up to our own necks in snow—you know that, Amy, as well as I do."

They looked at each other uncertainly, and then at the sky, and then again at each other.

"Hadn't we better fetch these ones home with us, Granny? Suppose we can't get back up here tomorrow?"

"I was just thinking the very same. If we can manage to carry a bale between us, they'll follow."

45

Together they tugged out a bale from beneath the plastic sheeting.

"We can catch the shovel in under the string, Granny, and then you can take hold of the handle and pull it—see? And I can pull another one, if I only make a line first to pull it with."

Amy, as she spoke, was picking up discarded lengths of binder-twine, of which there were plenty lying about on the ground under the plastic sheeting; these she knotted together until she had a line long enough to go over her shoulder. As soon as she had tied it to a second bale they set off, and the sheep, magnetized by the hay, followed in short jerky runs, stopping every few feet and turning their heads apprehensively to make sure of the whereabouts of their enemy, the dog. As well as she was able to for panting, Amy called out instructions to Mick:

"Wait, boy—wait! Come on, then—just a little—that's enough! Wait, boy—sit!"

Against the stark whiteness of snow the sheep looked a dirty yellow. Tempted on by the hay ahead, and driven by fear of the dog behind, they proceeded in hopeful, fearful rushes to the top of the hill. Mrs Bowen and Amy were breathless.

"Oh Mick, you are a clever dog—you know just what to do! No, no—you just stay there. Don't you frighten them off the path. It won't be so hard for us going down, Granny. Why don't we sit on the bales and toboggan?"

"You can try it if you like," said Mrs Bowen. "I prefer to stay on my own two legs."

Amy did try, but the bale of hay sank into the snow like a rock and stuck, so she had to give up the idea of riding and pull again instead. It slithered along quite easily downhill, and again the sheep followed, trotting hurriedly down the broad furrows scooped out by the bales. Last of all came Mick, advancing and stopping as Amy told him. Before they reached home the air clouded and she saw snowflakes beginning to

46

settle on her grandmother's head and shoulders. They dragged the bales into the shed and Amy waited for just long enough to break open one of them and loosen the hay so that the ewes could have their reward, before hastening inside after Mrs Bowen and Mick.

"My feet are like icicles—and sopping wet. It's that old snow in my boots. Oh look, Granny—it's coming down thick—we were just in time!"

They were thankful as well as triumphant.

"What we need," said Mrs Bowen, "is a good warm right through. The kettle's on and we'll have a cup of tea in half a minute. Take those stockings off, Amy—there's a dry pair on the line for you. I don't know why it should be so, but wet stockings put a chill in the marrow of a person's bones quicker than anything else."

It was a relief to be home, and home was so snug. They were pleased with themselves for bringing four of Mr Protheroe's sheep down from the hill. Success made them almost forget about the stranger who had so much frightened them the night before.

6. The Tin Toboggan

Snow fell steadily. It fell without wind, without commotion, dropping quietly down as though it meant to go on for a long time and had no need to hurry.

The morning passed by in peaceful activity, accompanied by music from the radio, turned low enough not to interfere with conversation; as soon as a serial story began they switched it off. Amy had spread newspaper at one end of the scrubbed table and was polishing the brasses. At the other end Mrs Bowen kneaded dough. Presently she set it to rise. Then she wiped her hands on her apron.

"I think I'll run my eye over the stores now, Amy, so as to satisfy my mind. Not that we're short—I don't mean that—but considering we may have to keep going on what we've got for we don't quite know how long, it might be as well to make sure just what it is we *have* got."

And opening the doors of the big cupboard that stood against the far wall of the front-kitchen, Mrs Bowen proceeded to count aloud the jars of bottled fruit and the tins of this and that ranged neatly inside. There were various canisters with names painted on them: LENTILS, RICE, CURRANTS, SAGO. Mrs Bowen gave each one a shake in passing to judge how full it was.

"Plenty of lentils. Plenty of rice. Not much sago—well, that's no hardship considering we neither of us care for it."

"Don't get any more sago, Granny—I hate it," said Amy. "Why don't you get something we both specially like instead, and then I'll paint the name on the tin for you—crystallized ginger!"

"H'm—you'll be lucky!" said her grandmother.

There were pots of jam and pots of marmalade. There was tea and sugar and dried milk. Other sorts of food supplies were kept in the cold side-kitchen but they both knew well enough what these were without the inconvenience of having to go and look: a ham, and the remains of a flitch of bacon done up in muslin against the flies, and one of Mrs Protheroe's huge home-made cheeses, and several squares of Protheroe butter were all piled on to a wooden rack hung from hooks in the ceiling. There were strings of onions out in the side-kitchen, and bunches of herbs, and an earthenware crock partly full of salted runner-beans, and jars and jars of pickles. And in spite of it being now nearly the end of February they had still a few apples left—cookers on one shelf, eaters on another. Mrs Bowen knew all about providing food for long isolated winters: she had had years of practice.

"We shan't go hungry, that's a comfort," she said as she closed the cupboard doors. "It's only fresh milk we have to go without. I know we ought to keep a goat, Amy—it's folly for us not to—only somehow I can't bring myself to fancy the taste of goat's milk."

Amy went on polishing.

"I wonder who he was, Granny—that man."

"Oh—him!"

Mrs Bowen came and sat down at the table facing Amy.

"I don't suppose we shall ever know," she said.

"Shan't we? What if he stops for a day or two in the village? What if it turns out he's old Mrs Hamer's long-lost son?"

"Now Amy, that's nothing but nonsense you're talking—Mrs Hamer's got no long-lost son that ever I've heard of."

Amy rubbed the knob of the poker with extreme vigour, held it up, looked at it, twisted it this way and that to make it sparkle, and laid it down.

"You don't suppose he's a murderer, do you, Granny?"

"He didn't murder us," said Mrs Bowen, rather shortly.

"I just can't help wondering who he was, that's all. He was so different. And he was hurt. I think he'd broken his arm."

"It couldn't have been broken, Amy. When an arm gets broken the fingers don't have any power in them. I distinctly remember he put that hand on the latch of the door and opened it—so it wasn't a broken arm."

There was a pause while the scene recurred to both of them, detailed and yet somehow remote.

"He stole our blankets and meat and our lantern, so he was a thief anyway," said Amy, summing up.

"Well yes, there's no denying he took what wasn't his, and he took it without asking," said Mrs Bowen." And yet it struck me he didn't know what he was doing half the time. He acted like he was in a daze. Those were funny sort of provisions he took, Amy—a jar of pickles and raw meat. He may have helped himself to a few apples, but they wouldn't do much for him. There's plenty more in our side-kitchen would have made better eating than that. What about all the bacon up there on the cratch—he'd have found it a lot easier to cook a bit of bacon than a leg of mutton. And there's that pile of butter and a whole cheese not started—he missed to see them and all he had to do was raise his head."

"Maybe he was in too big a hurry."

"He was in a hurry right enough," said Mrs Bowen. "And yet—there was a moment when I had the feeling—" She stopped and lifted her hands and let them drop with a helpless gesture.

"Go on, Granny—what kind of a feeling?"

"That's what I can't say. I don't exactly know. Now Amy,

quick—turn on the radio. Let's hear what they have to tell us about the weather."

The forecast gave warning of more snow expected, and the news that followed was chiefly about the widespread chaos already caused: roads blocked, trains at a standstill, buses overturned, people stranded in cars and lorries, expectant mothers rescued by helicopter.

"There's many by the sound of it worse off than we are," said Mrs Bowen.

That afternoon Amy found it hard to settle down. At first she thought it might be a good opportunity for writing a letter to her father, and she got her pen and ink and paper out of the table drawer, but after a line or two Australia seemed so very far away and the letter so dull that she left it lying on the table and wandered restlessly through the side-kitchen and into the shed, not allowing Mick to come with her for fear he should agitate the sheep. As soon as she appeared they raised their heads with nervous expectancy and took a few steps towards her.

"What is it you want?" she said, speaking aloud so as to accustom them to the sound of her voice. "You've got hay to eat, and shelter. I can't give you water. It would freeze straight off. You'll have to lick snow—that's what sheep do in this sort of weather."

It worried her whenever she thought of the fifth ewe—alone somewhere, struggling perhaps, hoping for help that never came. Snow was still falling, but thinly, and the air was brighter. After the heat of the front-kitchen the contrasting sharp cold was almost a relief. Amy looked in the hen-house. There were six eggs. An old speckled hen sitting fluffed up on a nesting-box cackled at her disagreeably, not liking to be disturbed. Two of the eggs were warm, just laid. She put all six safely in a bucket and looked round for the hacker meaning to chop some kindling, more as a way of occupying herself than to be useful for there were plenty of sticks chopped already. The cold was beginning to bite through her jersey. After a minute or so, failing to find the hacker, she went inside.

"Six eggs, Granny, and another one soon—unless that old speckledy hen's just having a rest. Do you know where the hacker is ?"

"Why, hanging up I suppose, where you put it last time you did some chopping," said Mrs Bowen with a touch of severity. To forget to hang the hacker on its proper hook and to leave it instead lying carelessly on the ground was a well-known failing of Amy's. "You'd better find it, Amy—it's not going to do that hacker any good to have snow piled on top of it."

Amy pulled on her leggings. Then she went into the side-kitchen and put on her coat and her boots, and then she stamped back into the front-kitchen and put on her scarf and her gloves. She felt cross with her boots because they were wet and clammy. Her mind refused to concentrate. So many worries kept flitting in and out and not one of them would stop for long enough to let her solve it: there was the ewe that was lost, and there was the hacker which she felt sure she had neither hung up nor left lying on the ground, and there was the difficulty of writing to her father, and the difficulty of giving Mick a run when there was nowhere for him to run except in the shed which was full of sheep. Amy sighed. Mrs Bowen, who was mending a pillow-case, looked up.

"Whatever is the matter with you, Amy ? You're so jumpety."

"I know I am. I feel I want to do something, only I don't know what it is, and everything I get started on turns out to be wrong and just a nuisance. Perhaps I'll take Mick out the front away from the ewes and clear a path for him there."

But no sooner had Amy begun laboriously shovelling than she realized that snowflakes were no longer falling round her; the air was suddenly empty. All at once she knew exactly what it was she wanted to do. She flew into the cottage.

"It's stopped snowing, Granny—and I'm going to make a toboggan, the way Ivor showed me. That's what we need this weather, I've just thought—a toboggan!"

"Why Amy, what a good idea!" said Mrs Bowen, thankful that she should have hit on a cure for her fidgets.

"And when I've done it we're going up to the haystack, me and Mick, to see if that old ewe's there yet. Do you think she might be?"

"It's worth a look," said Mrs Bowen.

Amy put Mick to wait in the corner beyond the chopping-block while she was working.

"You sit still, Mick, until I'm ready—if you so much as wag your tail those ewes are bound to think you're after them."

From down behind the hen-house she dragged clear a sheet of corrugated tin left over from the time they had closed in the north end of the shed. Two winters ago she had stood by and watched Ivor Protheroe make his toboggan, and helped him whenever he let her, so she knew how it was done. Ivor had told her that corrugated tin made the best and fastest toboggans of all. He said it was a fact. He said he had proved it.

Amy stood on the tin in order to keep it firmly anchored while she banged away with a hammer, her object being first to fold in the two jagged corners and then to double over the last four inches at one end. It reminded her of hemming in needlework classes, only this was done not for neatness but for safety: Ivor had impressed upon her what awful consequences there would be if any raw edges or spiky points of tin were left sticking up in front.

By further banging and pulling she then managed to bend up another ten or twelve inches at right angles to form a kind of a prow. As an additional measure of prudence she muffled this upstanding front in a sack, which she tied on tightly with binder twine. Finally, for pulling she borrowed the side-kitchen clothes-line. It was finished! Amy stood back and contemplated her handiwork. Ivor would have done better, no doubt, but for her particular purpose this was good enough, Amy decided. Mindful of the sheep, she carried Mick several yards up the hill and told him to wait for her there while she went back to the shed and fetched her new toboggan.

Once again she toiled up the steep slippery slope, treading squarely in the furrows they had made that morning and which the recent fall of snow had blurred but by no means obliterated. By the time she reached the top the sun shone in a clear sky and the whole world was divided equally into a brilliant golden blue above and glittering golden white below: blue and gold and white, nothing more. She might have thought herself the sole form of life for miles except that a hare must have dashed erratically along the ridge only a few minutes earlier and vanished, leaving behind its message of scuffed-up prints. And the lonely mewing cry of a buzzard reached her faintly; she saw it half a mile further up the valley, turning loosely like a dry leaf in an eddy of air. The day was so bright with sun and snow she had to narrow her eyes.

"Oh Mick," she cried, using one of her grandmother's favourite expressions of delight, "isn't it a sight for sinners!"

She rushed at Mick to chase him ahead of her down to the stack, and he bounded sideways and fell over, and sprang up and bounded on again. Amy followed running, but the toboggan came gliding behind her so swiftly and lightly over the top of the snow that it was hard to keep her ankles out of its way. So she stopped and straddling it rather awkwardly, sat down. She sat down—and in a flash, before she could even catch her breath, was away. The success took her by surprise. She almost hit the stack head-on, and then, swerving, nearly missed it altogether to go shooting on down the hill. Frantically she dug in both feet. The toboggan slewed round and came to a halt in a flurry of snow, facing back the way it had come. Mick danced round her, barking.

"It goes as fast as Ivor's did," she told him. "I'm not sure it doesn't go a bit faster."

But there was no ewe waiting for them in the lee of the stack and if it had not found its way there by now it probably never would. It must be stuck fast in a drift somewhere, and the thought of a plight so terrible damped Amy's enjoyment. Soberly she hauled out two bales from under the plastic sheeting and, puffing and grunting, got them aboard her toboggan. There were about fourteen bales left, she reckoned, or perhaps a few more. Bent double she dragged her load to the brow of the hill.

Certainly bales were more comfortable to sit on than bare tin, but Amy felt herself less able to control the toboggan when she was perched up on top of them, and so she brought it down the hill to the cottage very slowly and cautiously.

Mrs Bowen was clearing frozen snow off the front-kitchen windows. She heard the noise of shouting and barking and came round into the shed to watch their arrival.

"Why Amy," she said, "that was a brainwave you had! What a help it's going to be to us."

Amy was pleased by her grandmother's praise. "I mean to fetch all the bales on it—not all today, I don't suppose. There's about a dozen or so of them left. Maybe fourteen—fifteen."

"And you can manage on your own, do you think—or shall I come with you?"

It was when Mrs Bowen said something like this that Amy was made aware, with a pang, of the great difference in their ages and also of what the difference meant: Ivor would have been longing to try out the new invention. But her grandmother had done the journey once today and once, for choice, was enough. She was old, and old people were obliged to portion out their strength, having only a limited daily supply of it. Amy felt she could go up and down, up and down, again and again, and still not be tired.

55

"I can manage all right," she said.

Mrs Bowen inspected the toboggan thoroughly, and admired it.

"I'm glad you thought to put that sack on the front, Amy— it could be dangerous when you come to have a spill if there'd been tin sticking up."

"Ivor showed me what to do. I ought by rights to bang the sides up as well, so as to stop the snow coming in over— that's what Ivor did—but I shan't bother for now. His was a real beauty, though. He'd got some old bicycle tyres and we cut them open—I helped him—and we made holes in the tyres and holes in the corrugated and bound them over the edges with string, all round. It took us a lot of time, but it was worth it. Mine's not as good as that, not nearly."

"I think you've done it very well," said Mrs Bowen. "You can always add a few improvements later, if you feel inclined. Do you mean to stay out much longer? I believe it's getting colder again, if that's possible."

"I'll bring a few more bales down yet. You see, Granny, what I'm planning to do is to make a wall with them—here— between these posts, and that'll give the ewes some shelter. Oh, Granny—she wasn't by the stack, that other one. I don't like to think of where she's got to."

"No more do I," said Mrs Bowen.

It occurred to Amy while she was collecting the next load that possibly instead of being stuck in a drift the missing ewe had taken refuge in Tyler's Place, and with this thought in her head she stood by the haystack gazing down towards the group of trees that concealed the ruined farmhouse. It was a good way off—half a mile at least. More than that. A mile?

Amy transported two more bales to the cottage, trudged up to the top again and tobogganned down to the stack. Again she stood calculating the distance between her and that group of trees. Her legs were beginning to ache; so were her arms.

56

Getting there would be easy enough—she could whizz down on her tin toboggan in next to no time at all; but coming back would be harder: a long walk, uphill and out of the sun, the path uncertain, afternoon nearly over. At that moment, for no apparent reason, there flashed into Amy's mind a remembrance of the hacker as she had last seen it. Of course! She had driven it into the top of the chopping-block, and there it had stayed, upright, its blade firmly embedded.

Amy turned away from viewing Tyler's Place and lugged another two bales to the top of the hill.

He must have wrenched it out when he decided to use the chopping-block for a seat. Did that mean it was now lying under the snow on the floor of the shed where he—not she—had flung it?

One of the bales had slipped backwards off the toboggan. She struggled to get it on board again. Every time she had to shove or drag a bale it was bigger and heavier, she could have sworn, than the time before. Her face flushed, her thoughts troubled, Amy raised her head and immediately was overcome by astonishment.

She was so accustomed to vast acres of emptiness that at first the two black dots were almost unbelievable. They appeared to come speeding directly out of the sinking sun, down from the uplands, swooping across the snow as birds swoop through the air, coming from the west by the same way the drovers had used long ago but at a pace no drover had ever dreamed of. Their approach was so rapid that it was like some kind of conjuring trick. Nearer and nearer they came, racing along the other side of the valley. Thrilled, amazed, motionless, everything else forgotten, Amy watched them. They were people! They were real!—alive!—two men! They were on skis!

Exactly opposite to her, at the place where the turning she took every day from school dropped down from the high track to cross the stream, they stopped. She thought that to them she

57

must seem like a flag on the skyline in her scarlet trousers and scarlet scarf, and she waved. They were certainly looking towards her. Neither waved back. One of them pointed, but that was at the cottage. Perhaps they were going to come across? She waited hopefully. But instead, after a few more moments of what might have been consultation or argument, they shuffled their skis round, thrust their sticks into the ground, glided on, and were gone.

Amy was curiously disappointed that neither of them had answered her wave. They must have seen her. She had waved and they had not—as though they had disapproved of her waving. Probably they were just too busy talking, that was all. But her pleasure at an apparition, otherwise so marvellous and strange, was a little damaged.

She decided that this was going to be her last load of hay for today. It was hard work and she was tired. By the time she had ridden down to the cottage, though, her tiredness had lessened and her spirits revived. After all, what news it was! Conscious that she did have something quite out of the ordinary to tell, Amy burst into the front-kitchen.

"Granny—did you see those people? They were on skis—that's what they do in Switzerland. Imagine—in our valley!"

Mrs Bowen had seen nothing, and so Amy described the spectacle for her.

"They must have come from right over the other side, from Pengarth. How far would that be—five miles?"

"More like eight," said Mrs Bowen, marvelling with her. "So it's visitors in winter now, is it?—we've only had picnickers before, summer folk. That's what the millionaires do, Amy—winter sports they call it, don't they? Fancy though—*here!*"

"I wish they'd come across the stream for a cup of tea," said Amy. "I waved at them and they were in two minds about it—I could tell, the way they stood there."

"I daresay they were wanting to know how much further

58

they had to go before they came on a road. That's a longish way to have travelled with no sign of human habitation. Still, it won't take them many minutes to get down to Melin-y-Groes on those contraptions, I don't suppose. Most likely they're there by now. Maybe we ought to learn to use those things, Amy. They'd be handy for us in winter time."

Mrs Bowen was cheerful but Amy felt an unexpected twinge of envy that strangers should be able to reach the village so easily when they themselves were cut off from its lights and faces and voices.

"Oh, I do wish they'd called in," she said, with a deep sigh. "We could have told them about last night, Granny, and asked them to keep a look-out for that man. We could have sent a message to Mr Pugh and then he'd have caught him, and then I'd have got my blankets back."

"Why Amy," said Mrs Bowen, "it was only chance you glimpsed them at all. We're no worse off than we were before. I think you'd better stop in now, and I'll make the tea. You've been out on that hill for long enough. The sun's gone—and there's not a speck of snow melted for all the shining it's done today. That just shows how cold it is. I've fed the chickens, Amy, but I left it for you to shut them in, by and by."

"I'll do it now, while I've still got my coat on," said Amy. "That's six bales I fetched down this afternoon, and tomorrow I mean to fetch down the rest of them. Mick—you stay in with Granny. I shan't be long gone."

The chickens were already inside their hut; Amy had merely to push the slide across and turn the catch. Then she began to build a wall with the bales of hay between two of the shed-posts. There were not enough bales yet to make a proper wall, but if the storm were to get up again in the night it would give the ewes at least a certain amount of shelter, Amy felt.

She only wished she could have done as much for the ewe that was missing. All day at the back of her head she had been worrying about it, unable to forget that it must be *somewhere*, and on its own, possibly hurt, certainly hungry, needing her help. People and sheep were not the same; they had different thoughts and different feelings, she knew. And yet she kept imagining it might have been her that was missing; and if it had been and nobody bothered to come to her aid—what then?

She had promised Mr Protheroe to care for his five ewes—five, not four—and the promise made her responsible, bound her to do her best. Amy was ashamed because she felt that her best was what she had avoided doing. Suppose the missing ewe was down at Tyler's Place? It could be. She had considered exploring the ruins and had turned away: it was far, and it was late, and she was tired—but chiefly she had not gone because she had been afraid to go. She would go, she *would*! Tomorrow, early, before breakfast, she would toboggan down to Tyler's Place.

The resolve lightened her heart. Some sort of wild I-dare-you-to urge drove her to run out of the shed and flounder uphill along the north-easterly track, treading in the very footsteps that had lain there since morning untouched except by snow-flakes. She defied the footsteps, destroyed them, kicked them to bits, as she went. Long before she reached the top she lost her breath and threw herself spreadeagled flat on the frozen snow. She heard Mick barking, barking.

"I'm *here*, Mick," she whispered, waiting for him to find her.

But he must have gone in again; there was silence. Night was approaching. The snow glimmered almost blue—blue-white, coldest of all cold colours. Amy felt the icy touch of it against her flushed cheek, and sat up.

Two men, their skis balanced in long dark lines across their shoulders, were just about to reach the front door of the cottage.

7. Mrs Bowen is Inhospitable and Amy Disobeys

Amy came down the side of the hill in a series of flying leaps and arrived breathless at the very moment Mrs Bowen, her shawl round her shoulders, stepped out into the porch and closed the door deliberately behind her. One of the men stood a yard or two off, supporting the skis and the ski-sticks. The other was in the porch entrance. He turned as Amy came up and looked at her and she halted by the step and put her hand against the nearest post to steady herself and looked back at him. His eyes, even in the failing light, were brilliant and piercing. Her heart thumped, but that was from hurrying: she was not frightened, she was excited. After a few moments he turned again to Mrs Bowen who had been standing waiting without a word.

"Good evening. Is your husband about, I wonder?"

"No, he's not," said Mrs Bowen, explaining nothing more.

"Ah!" said he, knocking his boots gently against a post of the porch, so as to make the snow fall off them. "Then we'll wait until he comes."

"You'd have a long wait," said Mrs Bowen shortly. "He's been dead for thirty-five years."

Amy was puzzled by her grandmother's dry manner and surprised that she, who was usually so hospitable, had failed to invite her callers inside. It was not as though they were anything like that wild creature who had broken in on them the night before. The tall man talking to Mrs Bowen was polite and smiling. Everything about him seemed to Amy wonderful— his voice, his clothes, his eyes, her first sight of him swerving down the valley out of the setting sun as though he had been some sort of angel or hero, too good to be true. Yet he had been true after all. She had longed for them to cross the stream and her wish, like a wish in a fairy-story, had been granted: they were here. They were actually *here*, and Amy had an over- whelming desire to be allowed to keep them, to make friends with them—with this one anyway, the one with the soft pleasant voice and the dazzling eyes who was saying to Mrs Bowen:

"Is there somebody else we can speak to—your son, perhaps?"

"Well, no—so far as speaking goes I'm the one for that," said Mrs Bowen, not troubling to add that her son was in Australia.

Amy heard her with dismay. Why was she being so rude, so unlike herself? He would be bound to take offence and go. She watched his face anxiously. But no!—he was still smiling, his voice remained agreeable. Indeed, he almost sounded as though he were amused by what Mrs Bowen had said.

"You mean to tell me you live here alone?"

"There's the two of us," said Mrs Bowen.

Again Amy felt those extraordinary eyes turned on her like lamps, and said eagerly, wanting to speak to him herself:

"She's my granny."

"I see! Do you hear that?" he called out, laughing. "Nobody here but an old woman and a child. We thought it must be a shepherd's cottage," he said to Mrs Bowen, "right up here in the hills like this, on its own."

Amy could tell from the way her grandmother pulled the

shawl tighter round her arms that she was angered by his words. But it was true, after all—she *was* an old woman. He had not meant to annoy her.

"You must find it very isolated—no neighbours. Don't you get lonely?" he went on.

Mrs Bowen made no reply.

"You won't mind, I suppose, if we take a look round?" he said, and to Amy it seemed that his voice had become a degree colder: it was hardly surprising.

"Oh?—and what for?" said Mrs Bowen.

A look round! Amy knew what for at once, and knew that her grandmother knew—had known it all the time. So they were not just holiday-makers, out on their skis for the fun of it. They were the police, and they were looking for that man. How dull she had been not to have realized it straight away when she first saw them. But it was their clothes that had misled her. In Amy's experience policemen could be seen to be policemen by the uniform they wore, as in the case of Mr Pugh down in Melin-y-Groes.

The tall man, instead of answering Mrs Bowen, had walked across to the one supporting the skis and ski-sticks. Whatever he said was spoken too low for Amy to hear but the other man, who was short and dark and wore a green knitted cap with a bobble on top, immediately propped his burden against the porch and tramped off round the side of the cottage in the direction of the shed. Amy could see that he was holding something and for one confused moment she imagined it was a black torch, unlit, before understanding that it must be a revolver. She had seen plenty of guns in her life but they had always been shot-guns with long barrels, the kind that farmers used for shooting rabbits. It was no rabbit this man was after. Amy felt a curious gap in her breathing.

His tall companion strolled back to the porch where he rested one foot nonchalantly on the step Mrs Bowen had cleared of snow that afternoon. Mrs Bowen stood, adamant, in front of the door. Why? Amy wondered.

"Are there any other houses near here?" he asked conversationally. "Or any buildings, for that matter—outhouses, barns—that sort of thing?"

"No, there's not," she answered curtly, "no buildings at all. The nearest farmhouse to us would be Dintirion, Mr Protheroe's place, and that's some miles off."

"I see. So there's nothing over the brow of this hill, then? When we were further up the valley we rather thought we could see another roof, but we must have been mistaken."

Amy could bear her grandmother's inexplicable taciturnity no longer.

"It's Mr Protheroe's haystack they'd have seen, Granny," she broke in. "That's what it was—sure to have been. They could have seen it easy enough when they were up higher, couldn't they?"

"Don't talk so silly, Amy—a haystack's not a building," said Mrs Bowen with a sharpness that was altogether different from her usual tone of voice.

The man in the knitted cap reappeared. Once again there was a consultation out of earshot.

"Granny, where's Mick?"

"In the side-kitchen where no harm can come to him," said Mrs Bowen enigmatically.

"Why don't you tell them?" whispered Amy, going close to her grandmother. "About *him*—why ever don't you?"

"Hush, Amy!"

The tall man had turned towards them.

"Where do those tracks in the snow lead to—the ones going up behind your cottage—to that haystack?"

"It's no haystack," said Mrs Bowen. "Not any more, it's not—just a few bales left over, that's all, with a rusty old roof on top."

64

"The size of your haystack is of no importance to me," he said, quite gently. "I'm simply wanting to know if it's where the tracks lead to. Do they?"

"Well, of course they do—where else?" she answered irritably. "We've been fetching down hay for those few sheep that's back in the shed there—we're minding them for our neighbour, Mr Protheroe. They're his sheep and it's his haystack, not ours. So now I've told you all there is to tell and if you'll excuse me I'm going back inside—it's cold work standing about out here. Come along, Amy—it's time you were inside too."

But Amy was offended by the undeserved sharpness with which her grandmother had spoken to her, and she stayed where she was. Except for Mrs Bowen putting her hand on the latch, nobody moved.

"We shall have to have a look at this haystack," said the tall man imperturbably. "Perhaps you'll be kind enough to lend us your little granddaughter and then she can show us the way."

"You don't need any showing," said Mrs Bowen. "A blind man could follow those tracks—they're clear enough."

"I'll go with them, Granny—I'd like to go," burst out Amy.

"No, Amy—I'd sooner you came on in."

"Oh, but she wants to show us the way—don't you, Amy? You needn't worry—we shan't keep her out for long."

He had called her Amy as casually as an old friend would have done. She was startled; and pleased, because it showed that somehow he knew *she* welcomed him even though her grandmother was so hostile. Grateful for such tolerance, Amy took a step towards him and as an old friend might have done, he caught hold of her hand. Again she was startled. His manner was careless but his grip was unexpectedly tight. It told her, like a secret between them, that no matter what her grandmother said he fully intended Amy to go with him.

"I don't mean to sound rude," declared Mrs Bowen fiercely,

"but I don't care for Amy to be out on the hill with strangers—and it nearly dark too."

"Oh, come now!" he said, refusing to treat this scruple seriously. "She'll be perfectly safe with us. I give you my word."

Amy stood passive, her hand in his. She was glad he had asked her to guide him to the haystack and she meant to do it. Never before had she defied her grandmother; but then, never before had she felt for her grandmother what she felt now: resentment. Why should she be deprived of this treat, this moment of glamour? Why should she not go with him? Why not? He was on their side. He was what they had needed so badly last night and might even be in need of again—someone to help them, a protector. So why not?

"Amy!—you heard me!"

It was her grandmother who was behaving badly, Amy argued with herself—she was behaving unfairly, unreasonably! And mixed in amongst all Amy's other emotions was a small wicked desire to punish her.

"I'll be all right, Granny—really I will."

"Amy!" cried Mrs Bowen.

But Amy took no notice.

They skirted the shed. He paused to flash a torch up and down the length of it. The sheep shifted uneasily. Again, climbing the slope, he reached for Amy's hand. He had brought a ski-stick with him and went so fast she was glad enough to let herself be towed behind, though whether he did it playfully, or really so as to help her, or even because he thought she might otherwise change her mind, Amy was not sure. Half-way up he stopped. The man in the knitted cap who had been following, stopped as well.

Her companion leant on his stick.

"I'm afraid your old grandmother isn't very fond of strangers," he said.

"There's not many come this way," she replied, meaning it

66

as an apology, and added shyly: "I waved to you this afternoon."
At once she regretted her words: they seemed to reproach him.

"Yes, I saw you. It was most kind of you. Thank you for waving."

He was not annoyed with her; he was smiling. She caught a gleam of his teeth in the dusk and felt relieved. He was very good-natured.

"Has there been anyone else to wave to today?" he asked.

"Oh, no!" she said, thankful the question was easy to answer truthfully.

For Amy's conscience perplexed her. She longed to pour out to him the whole story of what had happened last night, but because her grandmother had kept silent about it she felt under an obligation to keep silent too. It distressed her to do so. She knew they ought to tell him; it was wrong not to tell him. Why should they show mercy to someone who had behaved like an enemy, breaking into their home, terrifying them, stealing things?

And yet when, in her mind, she called their intruder an enemy she seemed to hear her grandmother's voice: "He never harmed us, Amy." And when she tried to conjure up his dreadful face all she could see was that arm slung, wounded, across his chest. "He acted like he was in a daze . . . he didn't know what he was doing." A confusion of echoes and pictures filled her head on the snowy darkening hillside.

"Amy!" She was recalled by an actual voice, a soft, slow, insistent voice. "I want you to tell me if you've seen anyone about—anyone at all—since it started to snow?"

Suddenly she knew, forlornly, that he had brought her out here alone, had taken her hand and called her Amy, simply so as to ask her this question and be answered without interference. It had meant no more than that. Well, she could astonish him with her answer if she wanted to! She did want to, and yet she heard herself saying, evasively:

"There was Mr Protheroe—that was yesterday, though, just

67

after I got back from school. We got sent home early. He was fetching his sheep down. It was coming on hard then, a real blizzard. He missed to get five of them—there's one out somewhere now."

The remembrance of the lost ewe pained her as sharply as a forgotten thorn in the finger.

"And you've seen no sign of anyone else?"

"What sort of a sign?" she asked him, stupidly.

"I mean, have you noticed anything unusual? Anything to make you think there might have been someone about—during the night, for instance?"

"No!" said Amy quickly, loudly, and her heart sank like a piece of lead for she had committed herself to a lie and now he could never be her friend. Never! She had deceived him without even knowing why she had done it. They went on up the hill again in single file.

At the top the two men halted and stared in all directions.

"The haystack's on a bit, down there," said Amy, timidly.

They looked briefly where she pointed and then resumed their intent scrutiny. It was dark now, and yet because of the snow not very dark. Mysteriously pale, the land stretched away. The sky was starry. And still there was no wind, no sound, no movement, not even a sense of time passing, only a sense of waiting and of a curious empty vastness.

"Nothing!" said the man in the knitted cap at last, uttering what was the first clear word Amy had heard from him.

"You'd better run along home," the other one said to her. He spoke neither kindly nor unkindly, merely as though she had ceased to be of interest. He dismissed her. So that was over.

Amy watched them descend the slope towards the dim outline of the tin roof and the pitch-black pile that lay beneath it. Presently all the shapes merged together. Then she heard the rattle of the stiff plastic sheeting being flung back, or dragged off. Having played innumerable games of hide-and-seek she reflected, almost scornfully, that anyone with any sense wanting to hide would avoid the haystack simply because it was so likely. Her gaze wandered. Somewhere down there, right at the bottom was Tyler's Place. By now it was too dark for her to be able to see even a smudge of the surrounding trees. But just suppose, she thought, those footprints this morning had been misleading? Hunted animals doubled back on their tracks. Or suppose he had fallen over the cliff of Billy Dodd's Dingle and then followed the stream down? It would have brought him to the ruins of Tyler's Place. Suppose he was there now—just suppose?

She glanced again towards the haystack. There were faint fitful gleams of light in its vicinity, as though they were switching torches on and off. All at once Amy felt the great loneliness of someone left out of a game: unwanted. She was about to turn and make for home when a breath of wind touched her cheek. She looked up and the stars overhead were fewer. Towards the north there were none; there the sky was blank, and the blankness was moving, spreading fast. Soon there would be no stars left. The wind was rising and bringing the snow-clouds with it.

At this moment Amy's attention was attracted and held by a scarcely visible spark of light. It was too low to be a star, and it was not one of their torches either. It was nowhere near the haystack—not near at all but far off, made feeble by distance.

She heard the voices of the two men talking, and then the stamp of their feet and the scrunch of snow. They had given up their search among the bales of hay and begun to climb the slope. A feeling of panic came over Amy. Hide-and-seek was a frightening game; it was too frightening. Always when Ivor leapt out at her, caught her, she screamed. Suddenly, passionately, she wanted them not to see the light, for if they did the game would be ended and the end would be more frightening than the game.

Amy was shivering. Every moment the wind increased. It blew cold on the bare skin of her face and whipped at her scarf. She tilted her head to watch clouds rush at a terrifying speed across the sky, putting out the stars, and as she watched the two men loomed into view. A few paces more and they would reach her and stop and turn round and see what she was able to see; and then that small give-away light down there, still foolishly shining, would be extinguished like the final star.

"Didn't I tell you to go home?"

The voice that a short while ago had sounded to Amy so pleasant, now, in her guiltiness, seemed harsher. She had got to prevent them from turning round. Any pretext would do. She began to gabble:

"Down there—down there, look! Down by our shed, see! By the cottage—look!"

"Look at what?"

"I saw something—down by our shed."

He took hold of her shoulder. "What did you see? What was it?"

"A light," she said, faintly.

"I can't hear you."

"A light—I saw a light," she shouted. "Down by our shed, I saw it."

"Are you certain?"

Amy was silent. Her frenzy subsided. She felt cold and tired, muddled in the head, depressed. She was certain of nothing.

"It was her old granny of course," said the man in the knitted cap, impatiently. "She's probably wondering where the girl's got to."

But the steely fingers dug into Amy's shoulder. "What made you think that it wasn't your grandmother? Who else might it have been?"

"I don't know," cried Amy. "Whoever it is you're looking for, I suppose—whoever it is you've been asking all those questions about and hunting down there in the haystack for. You're the police, aren't you?"

"Yes," he said after a moment, short and sharp, and let go of her shoulder.

Amy kept very quiet. They seemed to forget she was there and talk spoken above her reached her in fragments, torn by the wind.

" . . . passed him further back . . . "

" . . . impossible . . . "

"Well, I told you . . . dead . . . couldn't have got as far as this."

" . . . tomorrow . . . tonight . . . "

Beating their arms, stamping their feet, they turned at last for a final surveillance, but even as they turned the first blast of the storm struck them in a splatter of icy pellets, and if a light still shone down at Tyler's Place it was invisible now, hidden from the watchers on the hill by countless million snowflakes whirling between.

8. A Certain Look

Mrs Bowen and Amy regarded each other.

"Well?" said Mrs Bowen.

"They've gone."

Mrs Bowen poked the fire.

"They were the police, Granny."

Mrs Bowen straightened up indignantly.

"I knew that. You don't think I'd have let you go off with just anyone, not knowing who? I wasn't afraid they'd do you any harm."

"You didn't want me to go, though."

"You went just the same."

"I'm sorry, Granny," said Amy, deeply contrite. "I don't know what it was came over me."

"Oh, well—I daresay you were right. Never mind about it now—come by the fire, Amy, you must be just about starved. What did they say, then?"

"They asked me, had I seen anyone?"

"I knew they were bound to. Oh, well—it's all for the best, I daresay. Drink up that tea now—it'll warm you—and I'll put a piece of bacon to fry in just a minute."

"I said I hadn't."

"You said you hadn't what?"

"I said I hadn't seen anyone. It was a lie, Granny. I told him a lie."

Mrs Bowen had picked up the kettle. She set it slowly back on the stove and stared at Amy in amazement.

"Whatever made you say that?"

"You didn't tell them either. Why didn't you?"

"You mean they've gone off and still not knowing anything about that man? I made sure you'd tell them." Mrs Bowen sat down suddenly. "Oh, Amy—I only hope we've done right."

"I know where he is, too. I saw a light. He's down at Tyler's Place."

"Never!"

"He is. There was a light—I saw it. They didn't see it."

In the long silence that followed they could hear the fluttering of the fire and Mick on the hearthrug sighing in his sleep as he settled himself more comfortably, and outside in the darkness the loud commotion of the wind.

"Why didn't you tell them, Granny?" said Amy at last, again.

"Indeed, Amy, you may well ask, and it's hard to say now, exactly," replied Mrs Bowen. "Two things I suppose it was that must have made my mind up for me. First, there was Mick. He was in such a fret—backwards and forwards—and I naturally took it to be you he was wanting to go after. So I let him out by the front, thinking he'd make less disturbance for the sheep that way, but then when I looked out of the window I saw he was running straight on down the hill. Then he stopped, and there were these two men coming. Up jumps Mick and on he goes again to meet them—barking, of course—"

"I heard him," said Amy.

"But he wasn't interfering with them, just bringing them in, like any good dog ought to do."

Mick, hearing his name, had woken up.

"And then," said Mrs Bowen, "I saw that one in front, the tall one, put out his boot and give old Mick such a kick as lifted him right clean off the ground—he came running back to me. I thought at first he must have had some ribs broken, he was whining so pitifully, but it was fright as much as pain—he's never had such a kick as that in his life before, poor old fellow, and no reason at all for giving it. He wasn't acting nasty or going to bite—nothing! It was no way to treat a dog and I took against that man when I saw it—he didn't know I'd seen, mind. And there was more to it than just a kick—it was his manner of doing it—so cool!—he could have been kicking a tin can out of his way, same as boys do, for the fun of it. Well, after that I wasn't going to help him to find anyone—not anyone!—that's how I felt."

Amy was down on her knees, her arms round Mick hugging him gently for fear of bruises.

"Oh, poor Mick! But he couldn't have done it on purpose, Granny. Maybe he was meaning to kick up a bit of snow at Mick to stop him coming on, and his foot slipped—it could have done."

Mrs Bowen pursed her lips and shook her head disbelievingly. Amy said, laying her face down on Mick's rough fur:

"What was the other reason then?—two reasons you said you didn't tell them for."

"It wasn't a *reason*, the other—there's not enough sense in it for that. I can't pretend it was more than just a feeling I had. Do you remember last night when that man was at the door—there—how he turned around before he went and looked at us?"

Amy nodded. She remembered.

"Well, it was that look of his. There was something about the way he looked at us then—something it's hard to find words for—that kept coming back at me. Wild was what you called him, and so he was wild, like an animal. But you know how it is, Amy, with animals—wild ones especially—if they're in some kind of trouble and you happen to come by, you can tell the way they look at you they're wondering can they trust you this once? They doubt they can—it goes against their natural instinct. And

74

yet they're bound to hope there's maybe a chance you'll help them—you can read it in their eyes. And I read it in his—or I thought I did. And then these men today, they seemed to me to be like hunters. There!—I can't explain it any more than that and I know it sounds like a pack of nonsense."

"No, it doesn't," said Amy. "I felt the same."

"You did?"

"I felt sorry for him—all of a sudden, when I saw that light of his down there."

"Well, indeed! And me thinking you were so gone on those two at the door."

"So I was," said Amy, nodding her head while she stroked Mick very gently. "So I should be again, I suppose. The tall one—he was lovely, I thought. I never saw anyone like him before," she said, rather sorrowfully, thinking of him already as something beautiful just missed out of her life, glimpsed and gone for ever.

"Lovely!—he wasn't my idea of lovely," said Mrs Bowen.

"Oh, Granny, he was!—he had that way of talking. And his clothes—you could tell they must have cost a lot of money, they were so soft. His jersey was all fluffy—didn't you notice? He reminded me of cream-toffee," said Amy, dreamily. "That was exactly the colour of him, his clothes, and his face, and even his hair when he got his cap off—cream-toffee!"

"Get along with you, Amy! I thought I was bad enough with my fancies, but I declare you're worse. Toffee indeed! How could you possibly see? It was all but dark out there."

"No, it wasn't, not so dark as that," said Amy, determined to keep hold at least of that first vision. "But Granny, what sort of policemen were they, do you think? Why didn't they have uniform on? Were they English?"

"They were English all right by their voices. They didn't come from round here, that's certain. London, they may have come from. As for the uniform, police don't always wear uniform,

75

specially when they're out to catch someone. It shows up who they are too much."

"London!" said Amy, awed. "He must have done something downright bad if they've had to come all the way from London to fetch him."

"Oh, Amy, how can we tell what he did—or why he did it? We don't know anything about him."

"Yes, we do—we know where he is. We know he's down at Tyler's Place."

"Well, yes," said Mrs Bowen. "It seems as though we do know that."

They ate their tea in almost total silence. After tea they got out the patchwork quilt and snipped and sewed, and still there was very little said. They listened to the news and the weather forecast on the radio: snow was sweeping the country and more expected. Mrs Bowen switched the radio off without a word and they went on sewing.

"Granny," said Amy presently, "I was thinking of something."

"We're both thinking of something, I daresay," answered Mrs Bowen, "and I wouldn't be surprised if it didn't turn out to be the same thing."

"I was thinking about last night when we went out with Mick—you said if we didn't go we'd never be able to sleep for fear of what there might be outside."

"So I did. Well, and what of it?"

"We went, didn't we? And then we came back in, only we'd left Mick out—remember?—by mistake. And so then we opened the door again—and we called—and he came—"

Mrs Bowen put down her sewing and looked at Amy and waited.

"Well?" she said again, to help her on.

"I was thinking," said Amy. "He didn't bark then, did he? What I mean is, we didn't know it but that man must have been there in our shed, *then*. And Mick must have found him—he went off round the side, didn't he?—that's why we came back in without him. So I can't help wondering—it was funny for Mick not to bark. Do you think that means he liked him?"

"You'd better ask Mick," said Mrs Bowen.

"The only person he never barks for generally is Mr Protheroe," said Amy.

Mrs Bowen continued to sit with her sewing left forgotten in her lap. After a while she sighed.

"I'm very much afraid we've acted foolishly, Amy, and worse than that—done wrong, maybe. It was my fault I know, and I blame myself entirely. But if only I'd spoken out that man would be in handcuffs by now, and he must deserve it or they wouldn't be after him. Though mind you, when I kept my mouth shut I'd no idea he was still so close—I thought he'd be miles from here."

"Why didn't you tell about Tyler's Place then, when that tall one asked were there any other buildings and that round here? You must have thought he might have been down there or you'd have said."

Mrs Bowen pondered this with a look of surprise on her face.

"You're right, Amy—I must have had it at the back of my mind. And yet—would you believe it?—I never knew there was such an idea in my head, not till you mention it now. There!—that just shows how sneaky your own mind can be."

Amy glanced over her shoulder at the door. The bolts were firmly across, top and bottom. She knew the side-kitchen door was barred in the same way.

"He won't come back tonight, will he?"

"No—I don't think he will. He took all he wanted then. I'd say he was meaning to get on to Melin-y-Groes and missed to find his way—he must have come round in a circle and fetched up at Tyler's Place. Supposing it is him that's there," she added as an afterthought.

"It must be him. I saw that light—I told you," said Amy.

"A light's no proof it's him. There could be others out on the hills. It could be Tom Protheroe even, going after his ewes."

"You know it wasn't Mr Protheroe, Granny—he wouldn't even *try* to come over the top, this weather. He'd come round by the road, if he came at all—you know he would—and up the valley and up by our place, and call in. It wasn't Mr Protheroe."

"Well, no—I daresay it wasn't," said Mrs Bowen.

They tidied their sewing away earlier than usual that evening and dealt out the cards for Two-handed Whist, but their attention was not on the game. When Mrs Bowen wasted a King as though it were a card of no consequence Amy said nothing, not having noticed. And when Amy after trumping her grandmother's Queen of Diamonds immediately led the ten of that suit, Mrs Bowen remained silent for the same reason. Neither remembered to count their tricks. Amy shuffled the cards together and dealt again.

"Suppose they do come back tomorrow, those policemen—shall you tell them then?"

"Suppose!—suppose! Oh, Amy—I don't want to bring harm to anyone—not to anyone at all. But how can a person be sure of what's for the best? I wish I knew," said Mrs Bowen, brushing the cards away from her with a gesture of despair.

9. Two More Are Found

That night Amy slept in her own bed underneath an odd assortment of coverings: the old ironing blanket, various coats and shawls, and on top of everything else the partly-finished patchwork quilt. She had fallen asleep at once, too exhausted to stay awake listening for strange noises; too exhausted, she almost believed, to care if there had been any.

She awoke early and lay on her back, her mind calm and clear, contemplating her resolution as she might have tried a knot to see if it held. It felt quite firm. Two or three times before in her life she had awoken with the sensation of sleep having settled some course of action for her, banishing fear. There had been the morning she had known as soon as she opened her eyes that this was the day she would climb to the top of the great oak at Dintirion—a dare of Ivor's that had burdened her for weeks; and again there was the morning when she knew at once she was going to cross Mr Pratt's field with the bull in it that very afternoon, walking, not running, from corner to corner: a dreadful dare invented by herself. And in each case she had done what she knew on awakening she would do.

Amy slid her feet out of bed and groped for the chair where she hung her clothes at night. It was still too dark to see properly. With the clothes clutched in a bundle against her chest she crept through her grandmother's room.

"Amy?"

"It's all right, Granny—it's only me."

"Whatever are you doing, child?"

"I felt a bit hungry—I thought I'd get something to eat." This, she realized immediately, was not going to provide her with enough excuse. "I can't sleep, Granny, so I might as well dress myself. I can get a few things done early, before breakfast. I was thinking I might—might do a bit of work on my toboggan," she added ambiguously.

"But it's not half past six yet."

"I know."

She waited, fearful of being forbidden, peering through the faint greyish obscurity towards the bed and the shape that was her grandmother.

"I'll get you a cup of tea, later," she offered quickly.

"Never you mind about that," said Mrs Bowen, but sounding reassured. "I'll be down myself before too long. If you do go out to the shed, Amy, you mind and see you wrap up well," she called after her.

Mick emerged, yawning and stretching, from underneath the front-kitchen table where he slept at night in an orange-box padded with an old coat, and wagged his tail sleepily.

"We're going out, Mick," Amy told him. "You'll wake up soon enough then."

There was no comforting fire to dress in front of, only ashes. Amy scrambled into her clothes as quickly as she could. Then she went into the side-kitchen and drew back the bolts and opened the door. It was not snowing. The pale morning light was thick and still, like cold grey soup. Amy shut the door, frowning. She put on her coat and leggings and her Wellington boots and tied her scarf tightly over her head and under her chin. She had one glove already on when she recollected telling her grandmother that she was going downstairs to get something to eat. Partly so as to make this true, and partly because she had learnt that it was as well when setting out on any expedition to take food, Amy ran back and helped herself hastily to four mince-pies from a tin in the store-cupboard. One she crammed into her mouth and the rest in a pocket.

"Come on, Mick."

Their sudden appearance alarmed the ewes who huddled away in a panic, but for once Amy spared them no attention. Her mind was fixed now on a single objective. She took her tin toboggan and set off uphill through the deep newly-fallen snow. Even at the top she did not pause. She never looked back or round about her, but sat down immediately on the toboggan, pulled Mick on to her lap, scuffled with her heels to get started, and in a moment was off.

They swerved past the old haystack and flew on down the hill, down and down, on and on. With eyes stretched wide she stared ahead, desperately trying to steer a course on a track that was overgrown at the best of times and now lost under snow, with even the snow itself scarcely visible in semi-darkness. They seemed to be going much too fast. Surely she ought to be aiming further to the left? She dug in her left heel: that was too far—she dug in her right. They missed a thorn-bush by inches, leapt over a bump. The ground flattened and then dropped again, and still they flew down and on—on and down—as though there were no end to the hill and Tyler's Place had vanished like a dream.

Again the ground levelled. The toboggan went more and more slowly, almost stopped, crept over a rise and once again gathered speed. Ahead, strung across their path, was a ragged hedge, and beyond it a low cluster of trees. Amy saw what she thought was a gap in the hedge and steered for that. When she was close upon it she realized that it was not after all going to be wide enough to let them through and she tried to stop, but they were too near and going too fast. She jammed her heels down, skidded sharply, lost control, and was flung off against a barrier of hazels.

For several moments she lay where she was in the snow with

Mick held tight in her arms. She had expected to be hurt and it was a surprise to find that she was not. Then Mick began to wriggle and she stood up and looked back the way they had come, and her heart failed her: how were they ever going to get to the top again? She felt as though they had come to rest at the bottom of a huge dim white pit, and the thought of it choked her with dread. Her resolve disintegrated. She wanted only to get free, to escape. Escape from what? From whom? Amy bent and peeped between the bare sticks of hazel at Tyler's Place.

Not much of what had been a house remained. The north wall had long since fallen, spilling its great stones in heaps on the ground, and alders and sallies had seeded and sprung up amongst them. Jagged roof timbers stuck out over space. The main kitchen had lasted the longest, being supported on one side by the massive chimney-breast. It was even slated, although the gaps in the slates enlarged with every passing year.

Once Tyler's Place had been a familiar playground for Amy. Here, during the weeks of summer when school was closed, she used often to meet the three Protheroe boys, Colin and Ray and Ivor, who would ride over on their ponies with a satchel of bread and cheese and cake and apples for dinner whenever there was not too much work to be done on the farm. This remote and private spot had seemed then to be utterly theirs: Tyler's Place was their place, and many long hot afternoons had been spent by the four of them in total and satisfying possession of it before Mrs Bowen had come herself and seen the sliding hanging slates and the tottering chimney stack and said it was unsafe, and they were not allowed to play there any more. It was two and a half years since Amy had been down to Tyler's Place. In that time it had changed—not so much decayed further as simply become strange to her, as though the welcome had faded out of it: almost as though it had died.

"Mick—shall we have a look? Shall we?"

Mick licked her cheek.

But still she stared through the hedge, wondering. There was not a sound. It was the absolute silence that frightened her most, the sense of emptiness, of Mick and herself being quite alone. And yet if this were so, why should she feel frightened ?

"There's no one there, Mick," she whispered.

She was sure there was no one there. The silence said so, over and over, like a heart-beat: no one—no one—no one. If she dodged through the gap it would be quite safe. She could go right up to the house and look in and nothing would happen to her; nothing—nothing.

But then, what about the light she thought she had seen down here last night ? Could she have been mistaken ? Well—perhaps. In that huge dark landscape, with torches flickering on and off, and stars appearing and disappearing, and her own feelings unsettled, it was possible that she might have imagined she saw the faint spark of a hurricane lamp shining far below. Yes, Amy admitted to herself, it was possible.

Even so she meant to approach with extreme caution, to avoid the gaping doorway and gaping windows in front of the house, and instead to creep up on one side of it and climb the flight of stone steps that ended abruptly in air. Once there had been a barn standing back at right angles to the house and the steps had then led up to a loft, but now they led nowhere for the loft had long ago fallen in, and most of the barn as well. Only a fragment of its wall survived, and these ghostly steps with which Amy had an old and intimate association. Summer after summer she and the Protheroe boys had swarmed up and down them, had conquered and held them, been defeated, leapt from the top of them, pushed each other off them. The steps had been used as a platform for speeches, as a tier of seats during endless discussions, as a starting-point and finishing-point in nearly all of their games. Amy had never before seen them in winter, and now they were thick in snow, and she was going to climb them alone.

She squeezed between the stems of hazel, bringing down a

light patter of snow. One hand she held over Mick's muzzle just in case after all the silence was a lie. It would have been a comfort to her to feel that she could get across the intervening open ground in a single dash, but the snow lay too deep for running and she was forced to plod slowly forward in full view of the blank window spaces. It seemed a long way to the tangle of sloe-bushes and brambles at the foot of the steps. When she reached them, she paused. The hammering inside her quietened; the silence continued. No one had shouted. No one had given the least sign of having seen or heard her. The only watcher had been the house itself; emptiness filled it, surrounded her, hung from the trees. Even if there had been someone here last night, he was gone now. She was sure of it.

Suddenly Amy ceased to be afraid. This was Tyler's Place and she had known it all her life, and it knew her. Except that the Protheroe boys were somewhere else, and instead of being August it was February, and very early in the morning, everything was really the same as everything always had been.

She climbed the steps to the top, where she set Mick down. A mountain-ash had rooted and grown up in the right angle formed by the building and the house. Amy took hold of one of its branches and leaned over, steadying herself with her other hand on a rafter. The slates at this corner of the roof had slipped off, leaving a yawning hole. By craning as far as she could she was able to look directly down into the dim interior of the old farm kitchen.

It was so indistinct that at first she could make out nothing. She thought there was nothing to make out: that she had been right and the kitchen was empty. Then she found herself staring at a pale splodge, a blur, not understanding what it was. As she stared, it moved. Had it really moved or had she blinked? Amy kept her eyes steadily on the pale blur, straining to see more clearly. And then all at once she realized that she was looking straight at a sheep. Relief overcame her—more than relief: joy! Her fearful enterprise had been worth while, had been justified after all. It was the missing ewe!

She almost fell down the steps in her haste to get to it, and floundered round to the doorway that was always open, its door having disappeared years before.

"Wait!" she said to Mick. "Wait there, now!"

She ran in and dropped on her knees on the cold and grimy flagstones, embracing the ewe as though it were indeed her dearest friend. But even as she did so, even as the ewe, twisting in her grasp, bleated nervously, Amy heard another sound. It came from behind her, the small careful sound of something or someone shifting position. Her heart gave a jump and stopped and her breath stopped with it and her blood dried up and she dared not move. She shut her eyes tightly and waited and time passed and nothing happened. She listened with bursting ears and before her own breath came out in a rush she heard, like an echo the wrong way round, a breath not hers, a long soft sigh.

Inch by inch, Amy stood up. She thought she could never turn her head and yet in spite of herself she turned it: and there he was, a huge mountain of a man lying sprawled on the floor with her blankets heaped on top and beside him, within his reach, their hacker.

He lay there, watching her. He neither moved nor spoke but stayed as he was, pushed up on one elbow, watching her. Mick in the doorway whined and then gave a short sharp bark. From the corner of her eye she could see the doorway. She knew how close it was. All she had to do was to run for it, and through it, and away. But would he not leap after her as she ran and catch her with one mighty bound from behind? Her legs were too weak. She was shaking. And as she stood there, trembling, unable to save herself, he lifted an arm and held it out towards her, the hand doubled back into his chest. He was showing her something: what was it? The sleeve of his coat and the sleeve of the jersey underneath it and the shirt under that, all hung

85

down in tatters, sliced open from shoulder to wrist so that even in the murky half-light she could see the great crooked wound, clotted with blood, disfiguring his bare arm. She stared in horror. He made no sound; he was speechless, showing her his wound, as though it was all he had to show or say. Then he groaned and lay back flat on the ground and turned his head away. Amy walked very quietly to the door.

He might be dying.

She reached her toboggan and peered again through the hedge as she had done when she first arrived. Tyler's Place looked as it had looked then: deserted. Not a sound came from it, not a wisp of smoke, no movement, nothing.

Amy was cold. Her grandmother would have lit the fire by now. It would be snug at home with the kettle on the boil and porridge and hot buttered toast for breakfast and cups and cups of hot tea. And still she remained crouched, irresolute, staring across the snowy gap at Tyler's Place, and through the stone walls at what lay inside.

"He won't hurt us, Mick," she said. "It's him that's hurt."

Slowly, fearfully, she retraced her steps until once again she stood in the doorway. Here she stopped, uncertain of what to do next. He lay so still she was awed. His face was covered. There might not have been a man there at all, but only an untidy mound of blankets on the floor.

"Would you like a mince-pie?" she said at last.

There was a violent disturbance amongst the blankets, so that Amy stepped back and half turned, ready to flee. Head and shoulders heaved up. In the filthy bristling face she saw astonishment, and a gleam, surely, of something more. Again he reminded her of a wild animal, only now it was not of a wild animal roaming dangerously loose, but caught in a trap, and she seemed to hear her grandmother's words: "They're bound to hope there's maybe a chance you'll help them. You can read it in their eyes."

Very warily, with a mince-pie balanced on the palm of her outstretched hand, Amy advanced. He let her draw near without moving, without a word. When she was close enough for him to have been able to grab hold of her if he had wanted, he picked the mince-pie off her hand with huge dirty fingers and put it in his mouth. Amy's breathing grew easier. She felt about in her pocket and dug out the crumbled remains of the other two mince-pies.

"That's all I've got."

Now at last he was talking. Words poured from him. She noticed that when he spoke his face altered, lit up, so that instead of looking like a wild animal he looked like what, after all, he really was—simply, a desperate man. He was touching his chest, motioning towards the doorway with wide sweeping gestures. She shook her head.

"I'm sorry—I don't know what you're saying."

He stopped talking. Amy sat down like a visitor, politely, on an old iron kettle-stand, and glanced about her. The ewe shuffled and stamped: Mick had come inside, sniffing along a trail that led him to their sack in a corner. She called him away.

"Mick—here, boy! Keep still, now."

The rusty fireplace was stuffed full of twigs and bits of chopped wood and on the floor was a pile of hacked-off branches and broken rafters. Obviously he had intended to make a fire to warm himself by and no doubt to cook the leg of mutton on. Why had he never lit it, then? Had he run out of matches, or had he feared the smoke would give him away and preferred to stay hungry and cold to being caught? Her eye fell on their hurricane lamp. He had given himself away, though—to her, at any rate.

"The police are after you, mister," she said. "They came to our place, searching. He's foreign, Mick. He can't understand a word I'm saying, no more than I can him. I don't know what

87

we ought to do. Is your arm very bad?" she asked him, getting up for a closer look.

The sight of it made her feel sick.

"You ought to have that seen to," she said. "I think it's gone poisonous, that's what I think it's done. They do, if you don't disinfect them. I think we'd better fetch him back up to Granny with us, Mick—if we leave him here I do believe he'll die."

10. Amy Draws a Picture

Amy burst into the front-kitchen, boots and all, her eyes alight, her cheeks as bright as her scarf.

"Granny, Granny, I've got him, he's here—he's in our shed!"

Mrs Bowen stood transfixed, the toasting-fork raised in one hand.

"Amy! *Him?*"

"It's all right, he won't hurt us. He's got a great horrible gash on his arm. I think it's gone bad."

"*Amy!*" said Mrs Bowen again, absolutely unable to get out another word.

"He's foreign, Granny. It's no use talking to him—he can't understand. And we've fetched the ewe back up as well—she was down at Tyler's Place with him. And Mrs Protheroe's leg of mutton. He didn't have a fire to cook it on—they'd have seen the smoke, wouldn't they? I think that's why he didn't have a fire. Or it could have been he didn't have any matches."

"You've been down to Tyler's Place?—and that man was there?—and he did you no harm?"

Amy triumphantly nodded her head to the first two questions and shook it with equal vigour for the last.

"Oh, Amy—only to think what might have happened! Such madness!—whatever made you do it?"

Amy was silent, glancing round the room, which was exactly

as she had imagined it when she was at the bottom of the hill: the fire blazing, brass winking, a smell of toast in the air.

"And he came back up here with you, just like that?" said her grandmother, incredulous.

"His arm's bad—he showed it to me. So what could I do? We wouldn't have let an old ewe with a bad leg stay on down there, would we? And it's a lot worse, what he's got, than a bad leg on a ewe, Granny. It's worse than anything I've ever seen before."

Mrs Bowen had one hand pressed to her heart. "You must just allow me a minute, Amy—I can't get myself used to the notion, that's all."

"What do you mean to do then?"

"Why, we'd better have him in, I suppose," said Mrs Bowen.

The man who had so terrified them two nights earlier was sitting on the chopping-block, his head tilted back against the hen-house. His eyes were closed. Mrs Bowen studied him.

"You wait till you see his arm," whispered Amy. "It's *horrible*."

"He doesn't any of him look too good to me," said Mrs Bowen. She raised her voice. "Hey, mister!" she called. "You'd better come in—come on inside."

He opened his eyes and seeing Mrs Bowen started up clumsily, knocking against the hen-house. His scarf had been knotted again to make a sling for his wounded arm. Mrs Bowen was beckoning to him.

"Come on in."

They put him in front of the fire in Mrs Bowen's basket-chair and gave him a bowl of porridge which he emptied in a few ravenous gulps.

"Give him some more, Amy," said Mrs Bowen, bending over the frying-pan. "It's food he wants first—we'll see to that arm of his after. And fetch me out the blue carving-dish—we can't expect him to balance an ordinary-sized plate on knees as big as he's got."

He finished all the porridge and devoured two considerable helpings of bacon and eggs and fried bread. Amy lost count of how many slices of toast she buttered for him or how many times her grandmother refilled his cup with tea. They waited on him vigilantly, like a pair of robins feeding a great cuckoo hatched unexpectedly in their nest, until at last he lay back in Mrs Bowen's chair and lifted both hands to tell them he had had enough.

"What's he saying, Amy?"

"Why, he's thanking us, of course," said Amy, proud of him for showing good manners. "He's smiling, Granny! See what a nice face he's got when he smiles!"

"Well, if you can make out what he looks like back of all that bristle and stuff you're a whole lot cleverer than I am. Smile or not, he's a sight to scare the crows. And I only wish to goodness he could speak a bit of English like anyone else—it seems unnatural to hear him talk and not to understand a word he says. Now Amy, you drink up that cup of tea and have a slice of bread and butter yourself—there's no need for you to go hungry as well."

"I can understand him all right. It was him pulled that old ewe out of a snowdrift. That's what he was doing when I saw the light—he wouldn't have shown a light if it hadn't been he was getting the ewe out."

"He *told* you that?"

"Well, he kind of explained it with a bit of acting. I acted for him how I'd seen the light and then he acted for me how he'd heard the ewe bleating and gone out and found her in a snow-drift, stuck fast, with her wool all tangled up in barbed wire."

The grandfather clock struck once, a soft reminder. Mrs Bowen glanced up: it was half past eight.

"Amy—fetch me the bowl from the side-kitchen and make haste."

Amy flew to obey her.

Mrs Bowen bathed the wound in warm water and disinfectant, having first spread a towel to catch the drips. She sucked in her breath gently as she did it, commiserating.

"I never have seen a nastier gash than this—no, never! I wonder how he came by it—if he could only tell us that we'd know better what it's all about. I don't like to let it go without proper attention—it ought to be stitched by rights, but no use thinking of that, I don't suppose—and anyway I daresay it's been left too long already—stitching ought to be done straight after. Why look, Amy—he's got a tattoo and I thought it was dirt—I was trying to clean it off."

Amy stood by holding the bowl of water. She was growing accustomed to the sight of the torn flesh and could look at it now without flinching. But when she glanced at the man's face she was startled: it was indeed a sight to scare the crows, with the black brows drawn together into an agonized frown, eyes glaring from underneath, nostrils distended. He uttered no sound but Amy could see his other hand clenched tight on his knee.

"You're hurting him, Granny."

"Well of course I'm hurting him, bound to be, aren't I? How he stands to let me touch it I don't know, let alone picking and poking the way I'm doing, but I've got to get it clean, Amy, else there won't be a chance of it mending. He's brave enough, I'll say that for him—I'd have been screaming long since."

"Do you think those policemen are going to come back here, Granny? Was that why you said for me to hurry?"

Mrs Bowen laid a folded length of flannelette sheeting over the wound and fastened it on with strips of plaster. Then she began to bandage the whole arm from shoulder to elbow.

"All I'm thinking is—if they were to walk through that door now, Amy, it wouldn't be much good for us to say there'd been nobody by. There, I've done what I can, but I don't like the look of it. Rightly speaking he ought to have a doctor."

Amy was at the window.

"They've been once and he wasn't here. What makes you think they'll come back, Granny?"

"Because when the police are after something they'll search for it over and over, same as I would if I dropped a needle on this floor—I'd know it was somewhere about and I'd keep on and on until I found it. The sooner he's from here the better for all of us."

"But where's he to go to?"

"That's not our business, Amy."

"Why, Granny! You can't want them to catch him—not now?"

"I never said I did. If that's what I wanted I'd be more inclined to keep him here. But as soon as ever I've put some food together for him he must go—and I mean it for his own sake, Amy, not just for ours."

"He'll think we don't want to help him any more."

"You must make him understand then—you said you could. And Amy—leave Mick out by the porch. He'll give us a bit of warning, suppose anyone comes."

Amy went outside with Mick. It was snowing again, a veil of small flakes dropping lightly without wind from directly overhead where the sky was low and grey. There was not a glimmer of sun. There was nothing to be seen but the snow falling.

"Stay there, Mick—good boy!"

She shut the door and leaned against it, full of misgivings. For if Mick were to bark, suddenly, what could they do? It would be too late already. Her grandmother was right: he must go at once—now—before the Gwyntfa changed for him from a haven into a snare. But how was she to explain? Acting was all very well but it might be unreliable. She wanted to be sure he understood exactly what she was telling him.

Amy sat down at the table where Mrs Bowen was hurriedly making bread-and-cheese sandwiches, and got her block of writing paper and a pencil out of the drawer.

93

"Dear Dad," she read, "I hope you are well. Me and Granny are well. There is nothing much to say. It is snowing here."

She tore off the sheet of paper and crumpled it up. On the next page she drew two matchstick men. She drew them sideways so as to be able to show the skis on their feet, and in the hand of one of them she put a gun. At the top of the page she drew the cottage, with a row of dots and arrows from the figures to the door.

"How can I make him know it was yesterday they came, Granny?"

"Show him the calendar."

"He won't know what date it is, will he?"

"Never mind about that—he's not so dull. Show him today—it's the 22nd—and point him the day before. It shouldn't be hard for him to puzzle that out if he's as sharp as you say he is."

He sat so still that Amy thought he must have dropped asleep, lulled by the comfort of food and warmth. It was disconcerting to find instead that he was wide awake, staring intently into the fire, absorbed by unknown calculations. She touched his shoulder. He looked up and said something, but she shook her head, not recognizing the sounds. He said them again, two syllables, over and over.

"I think he's saying London, Granny."

"Well, if that's where he wants to go to he might as well be saying the moon, this weather."

Amy handed him her sheet of paper. Would he realize what it meant? She watched him closely and saw his expression change as he looked at it. Then he was on his feet. His actual words were incomprehensible to her but he was plainly asking: was this true? Had these men really come?—here?—to this house?

"Yes!" she cried aloud, as though by some miracle he could all at once understand what she said. "They're after you—two of them. They're the police and they came for you yesterday and you can't stop here in case they come again."

94

And in pantomime she repeated what she had said and had tried to draw for him.

It was clear that he did understand her: he was transformed. He might have been a different man from the one Amy had found lying on the floor at Tyler's Place like a huge piece of wreckage washed up and abandoned, past caring what happened to him, hungry, cold, in pain, defeated, despairing. He looked now as he had looked when they first saw him—dangerous and wild. He crushed Amy's sheet of paper and tossed it away, buttoning his coat. Mrs Bowen thrust a package of food into each pocket. He caught her arm, stooping over her, and again they heard him utter those two savage-sounding syllables.

"You'll never get to London, boy," said Mrs Bowen, pityingly. "It's hundreds of miles from here, and snow every inch of the way."

He turned towards Amy, who stretched her hands wide apart to indicate immense distance.

"Ha!" he said.

He was fumbling for something inside his shirt, lifting whatever it was with difficulty clear over his head and then forcing it roughly into Mrs Bowen's hand. When he patted Amy's shoulder she almost lost her balance. Then he was gone. By the time Amy had darted through the side-kitchen and into the shed he was already several yards up the hill, ploughing steadily forward through the thickening snow. She forgot all caution and shouted after him, pointing away to the right in the direction that led to Dintirion.

"London—that way!"

He half turned and raised his hand, but kept going straight on without altering his course.

Mick had come rushing round from the front porch to join her, and was causing consternation amongst the sheep. But still Amy stood in a state of anguish, watching that huge bowed figure vanishing little by little into the white oblivion of snow. She went slowly into the side-kitchen and shut the door, and slowly into the front-kitchen.

"He hasn't gone the Dintirion way, and there's no other way on past Tyler's Place—he'll get lost if he tries. Unless he means to stop on down at Tyler's Place for a while. Do you think he does? But then why was he asking for London? Or was he thinking to try along the bottom of Billy Dodd's Dingle?"

"Amy," said Mrs Bowen, "we've done what we can for him and now it's best if we put him right out of our minds."

"Yes, I suppose." Amy wandered round the room. "Maybe it's just as well he didn't take the top way—he'd as likely as not have gone over the cliff—it's snowing again. Do you think we ought to have sent him down the valley, Granny? It would have been a big risk for him, though—now, in daylight. Night-time he could have gone—"

"Haven't I just said, Amy, there's no sense for you to keep on thinking about it. What's done is done."

"I know it's done," said Amy, wretchedly, "but how can I stop myself *thinking*? How can I stop myself wondering if what's done mightn't have been done better? What was it he gave you, anyway?"

"Oh, that! I declare, I'd forgotten it."

Together they examined the small enamelled medallion hanging on a thin silver chain.

"Why look, Granny—there's a little picture on it. Is it a lucky charm?"

"I think it's what they call a holy medal. I've heard of travellers wearing them, and sailors. That's meant to be a saint, I'd say. It could be St Christopher. I believe he's a sailor, Amy—those clothes he was wearing, and that tattoo on his arm—and now this medal, or whatever it is. He reminds me of fellows I used to see long years back when I was a child in Cardiff. Sailors, they were, and I believe he's the same."

96

"He was trying to thank you, Granny—that was why he gave it."

They looked at each other, much troubled.

"Poor man," said Mrs Bowen. "He won't get far. They'll catch him, sure to. And what's he done?—that's what I keep asking myself. And as for our share in stirring the pudding, Amy, I don't feel easy about it, not a bit. He must be a criminal."

"We don't know he is."

"He *must* be, Amy. And we've been helping him. That means we're going against the law."

"It can't be wrong for us to give food to someone who's hungry—or to look after a person who's hurt."

"Well, no—maybe not, if that was all. But we ought to be helping those policemen to catch him, not helping him to get away."

"They don't need us to help them. You've just said they're bound to catch him anyway."

Mrs Bowen stooped down and raked the fire.

"If they come back here, Granny, do you mean to tell them about him?"

Mrs Bowen went on raking the fire as though hoping she might be able to rake an answer out of it. Then she put away the poker and straightened herself and sighed, as she always did when doubtful.

"I'm sure I don't know, Amy. I don't know what I ought to do. Who would ever have thought it could be so hard to tell right from wrong?"

"You keep on wondering what he did, that's why. But we don't know anything about that—it's only guessing and that's not fair. It's how he's acted to us, that's what we ought to go on. That's what counts for us because that's all we know for certain. He took those blankets and food and stuff, but I don't blame him any more—he didn't hardly know what he was doing that night. He never hurt us, though—you said it yourself. And Mick doesn't bark at him, not now, and he was stroking Queenie, and he gave you that medal. He thinks we're friends of his, Granny—you can't give him away when he thinks we're his friends."

"I don't want to give him away," said Mrs Bowen, weakly, overwhelmed by Amy's passionate defence.

"They could have made a mistake about him, couldn't they? Whoever it was did that to his arm he's the criminal—that's what I think—to have done that. I liked him, Granny," said Amy, pleading with her grandmother to say she had liked him too.

Mrs Bowen dropped the medallion into the drawer of the table and began to pick up the dirty cups and saucers.

"Maybe we shan't ever hear any more about him—that would be the best that could happen."

But Amy went into the side-kitchen and put on her coat and Wellingtons with a fiercely resolute air.

"I'm just going to fetch down a few more of those bales," she told her grandmother.

"Amy!"

"I shan't go a step past the haystack—I promise I shan't."

They eyed each other with perfect understanding of what the bales of hay would do: wipe out his footsteps sooner than the snow could cover them.

"All right, then," said Mrs Bowen.

11. The Letter

It was dark outside and very cold. Snow had been falling off and on all day, increasing towards evening when the wind began to rise. Amy, shutting the hens in, had observed a difference in the way the flakes came down; all day their lazy haphazard descent had been strangely companionable to her. For hours she had toiled to and fro between haystack and cottage, fetching the rest of the bales from the other side of the hill and then struggling with the great heavy awkward scratchy bundles to complete the wall she had already started to build between two of the shed-posts. And whenever she paused from her labours and looked up, there was that delicate movement all about her; somehow, without knowing why, Amy had found it reassuring. But towards evening the pace had altered, and the flakes drew together, massing like an army, and instead of slipping down in idle irresponsible spirals they began to drive sideways as though they had a purpose to accomplish and there was no more time to be lost. Then Amy was glad to close the door on approaching night and the hurrying snow.

But the sense of foreboding stayed with her long after the door was closed. Usually when they pulled the curtains across they shut out the weather and forgot about it. Tonight Amy found she was not able to shut out the snow. In her mind's eye she saw it still, and the fire was not warm enough, nor the lamp bright enough, nor yet the walls thick enough, to prevent her vision of the miles and miles of empty hills surrounding their cottage, with the wind like a marauder sweeping across them.

"I don't feel inclined for any sewing tonight," she said.

"I'm not all that set on it myself," agreed Mrs Bowen. "Why it should be I don't know but sewing seems to call for a steady mind. I'll get on with some darning—that'll come easier."

"And I'll write to Dad," decided Amy.

She had no recollection of her father. He had emigrated to Australia when she was only nine months old, unable to bear the catastrophe of his wife's death in surroundings where they had been happy together. Consequently, for Amy he existed as a more or less mythical figure, the hero of a collection of stories told and re-told by her grandmother, the face she had looked at too often in half a dozen photographs. Yet sometimes she missed him very much, aware, painfully, of a gap where there might have been a living person, a silence when there should have been a voice.

She dipped her pen. "Dear Dad" she wrote again, and again the difficulty of communicating with someone so far away and so unknown held her with pen poised staring at the blank sheet of paper. The man who had sat in her grandmother's chair that morning was more real to her than her own father.

"What shall I say, Granny?"

"Tell him we've all but finished the patchwork quilt."

"He won't think that's very interesting."

"Tell him how far you've got in school, then."

Amy considered the possibility of turning fractions and Francis Drake into items of news. She sighed and dipped her pen again.

"That's no good."

"Well then, tell him what's been happening here the last day or two."

Amy bent over the table. "It has been snowing for three days nearly," she wrote. "There is a lot of snow. A funny thing happened. Me and Granny—"

She stopped writing. Mick had jumped up from the rag mat and cocked his ears. He was whining. Mrs Bowen and Amy looked at each other. There was a knock at the side-kitchen door.

"Granny?"

"I'll go," said Mrs Bowen.

They knew who it was even before they had opened the door: Mick told them—he kept his tail low and just moved the tip of it in the faintest wag.

"But in heaven's name," said Mrs Bowen to Amy, her hand on the bolts, "why ever should that man have come back here? Such folly!"

She spoke as one dismayed, and according to common sense they had every reason to be dismayed by his reappearance. And yet somehow when they saw him actually standing on their threshold Mrs Bowen and Amy were pleased. The kettle was over the fire in a flash. Mrs Bowen, with a gesture of triumph, whipped open the oven door to show him the leg of mutton spitting inside; she had decided to cook it that night to prevent any possibility of its going bad, and now he could join in the feast. But he shook his head when she invited him, pointing at the clock and then at himself and then towards the side-kitchen: whatever the purpose of his visit he had no time to stop for a meal. He was in a hurry and when he saw Amy's writing things on the table he gave a grunt of satisfaction. This, clearly, was what he had come for. Without delaying another moment he sat down at the table, took up Amy's pen, folded back the top sheet of paper, and with big awkward strokes began to write.

"And us believing you were half-way to London by now," scolded Mrs Bowen.

"Maybe he thinks it might be best after all to stop on down at Tyler's Place till the snow's gone, or till he's mended a bit."

"Thinks!" exclaimed Mrs Bowen. "How can we tell what he thinks, Amy? Whatever it is goes on inside that man's head is about as plain to you and me as a crow on a dark night!"

He took no notice of their chatter. Writing was hard work for him. He laboured at it, breathing heavily. Mrs Bowen placed a cup of tea on the table near him and looked over his shoulder.

"Oh, Amy," she said, "if I could only just read what he's setting down there on that piece of paper we'd be wiser a lot. It always has seemed to me such foolishness for human beings to talk in different languages. 'Tisn't as though our ways are so different—when it comes to food and drink and a warm fire to sit by and a bed to sleep in we're all much the same, as far as I can see. Birds and beasts have got more sense."

Two sheets of paper had by now been covered on both sides with the blotched untidy writing. He was sitting back, reading over to himself what he had written, his lips silently moving. Then he picked up the pen again and asked Amy a question. She came and leant on the table beside him and he showed her his signature scrawled at the bottom of the letter, at the same time tapping his chest. Then he pointed to her, again asking his question.

"I'm Amy," she told him. "Amy! Look—I'll show you."

In capital letters she wrote on the cover of her writing block: AMY BOWEN.

"Amy!" she said. "I'm Amy! Can you say it? Amy!"

"A-mee!" he repeated.

"Why, that's good! Oh, Granny, doesn't it sound funny, him saying it! She's my Granny, mister—can you say Granny? Granny! Go on—see if you can say it—*Granny!*"

In a deep growl he tried to copy her: "Grrra-nee!"

"Amy—don't laugh so! You'll offend him."

But he was too busy to be offended. At the foot of the last page he was adding some final message that included, Amy noticed, her own name. When he had quite finished he folded the pages clumsily and stuffed them into the envelope and gave it to Amy. She eyed him anxiously. What did he mean her to do with it? He rubbed his head, perplexed by her perplexity. Amy waited.

"London!" he said at last, pointing to himself and then raising his shoulders in a shrug that indicated extreme doubt of ever reaching London. He took the letter away from Amy and held it up in front of her, speaking with passionate conviction, his eyes alight. Then he gave it back to her, pressing her hands over it and still earnestly explaining. What he said, word for word, she had no idea, but his meaning was clear enough. Amy understood that it was a solemn trust he left with her, and she told him:

"I'll take care of it. I'll post it for you, as soon as I can—as soon as the snow goes. I promise I will."

He was satisfied. He tossed off the cup of tea and stood up.

The front-kitchen was filled with the smell of roasting mutton. Mrs Bowen had just stooped and lifted the big meat tin out from the top oven.

"Amy—you cut him some bread and butter while I slice a few bits off this joint for him."

"I don't think he wants to stop, Granny."

"He'll surely have a bite to eat before he goes—it won't take many minutes."

But Amy was right: he was determined to be off—only first there was something he wanted to show them. From an inner pocket he had tugged out a battered old wallet and from this a card with a photograph pasted on to it. Amy stood on her toes to peer across his arm.

"Why look, Granny—that's him in the photo!"

"I believe it must be, though it's hard to credit."

"Now we can tell what he's like without a beard. I told you he'd got a nice face underneath. Is it his passport?"

"I don't know if it's a passport, exactly, but I do believe he's a sailor like I said, Amy, and this card is what tells all about him. That'll be the name of his ship there, see—and that's the place he comes from, or the other way round."

"And there's what he wrote at the end of his letter—that's his own name—Bar-tol-o-meo something," she said, pronouncing it syllable by syllable. "Bar-tol-o-meo?" she asked him.

He had been holding the card between them, looking at each in turn to see how much of it they were making out. Now he put the card back inside his coat and patted himself.

"Bartolomeo! Bartolomeo!" he said, nodding at Amy.

"He's got a name that's big enough to fit him, anyway," said Mrs Bowen. "Well, Bartolomeo, if you're in such a hurry to be off you'd better take this leg of mutton with you. You've had it before so you may as well have it again—at least it's cooked this time. Just you wait while I wrap it in a newspaper—I don't suppose you'll be too fussy about a drop of grease working through. There now—you button it up inside your coat and it'll serve to keep you warm."

At the side-kitchen door he surprised them. With his good right arm he encircled Mrs Bowen and lifted her clean off her feet. Amy caught a fleeting glimpse of the startled expression on her grandmother's face, a mixture of concern for the safety of the lamp she was holding and horror at finding her soft wrinkled cheek pressed into a tangle of black whiskers. Then she was herself swept up and for one dizzy moment lost in a jumble of duffle-coat and bristly hair and the smell of hot mutton. A moment more and they were alone again in the side-kitchen.

"Well!" said Mrs Bowen.

"He *kissed* us!" cried Amy, ecstatic.

"Kissed indeed!" said Mrs Bowen. "I feel more like I was grabbed hold of by a grizzly bear."

Absolutely confounded they returned to the front-kitchen, where Mrs Bowen put the lamp carefully back on the table before beginning to laugh.

"And him with that meat stuffed inside his coat like a hot brick—and me with the lamp—I was frightened out of my wits I'd let go of it. Suppose I'd set his beard on fire!"

They were both laughing so hard it seemed only natural for

Mick to be barking too. He barked and barked and they, not heeding him, laughed and laughed. The sudden loud peremptory rapping on the front-kitchen door came as an interruption for which they were quite unprepared.

12. A Blob of Ink

Like flames extinguished by a douche of water their laughter stopped. But Mick went on barking. He was snarling as well and making short rushes across the floor.

"It's them, Amy. It's those policemen again," said Mrs Bowen in a low voice, glancing rapidly round the room. Quickly she put another cup on the table so as to make two, and filled them both with milk and tea, spilling a little. The rapping sounded again.

"Now there's no need to worry, Amy. It's lucky for us they didn't come five minutes back," she said in a whisper. "Who is it?" she called out, going to the door.

For answer there was another burst of knocking and the latch rattled impatiently. But still they were made to wait. Mrs Bowen was signing across the room at Amy, and Amy was utterly bewildered. What did the signals mean? All at once she realized: the letter Bartolomeo had given her was clutched in her hand, in full view. Hurriedly, she pushed it up inside her jersey, out of sight.

Mrs Bowen nodded at her encouragingly.

"Catch hold of Mick," she said, and then at last she pulled back the bolts and opened the door.

"Oh—so it's you again, is it!" Amy heard her saying.

Without a word they thrust their way past Mrs Bowen, like men desperate for admittance.

"You could have shaken some of that old snow off in the

porch first," said Mrs Bowen, severely. To be so unceremoni-
ously pushed aside was not her idea of good manners. "I don't
want all that wet stuff brought into my house," she said, showing her displeasure.

They were covered in it. Even their eyelashes were clotted
with snow. It fell off them in heaps. While Mrs Bowen stood by
clicking her tongue disapprovingly, Amy felt her eyes drawn
to various puddles on the floor where previous deposits of snow
had melted, and surreptitiously she moved the lamp on the
table further back.

The tall man was already taking off his coat and his cap and
his gloves. He threw them down on the oak chest with a gesture
of relief and stamped his feet.

"I was beginning to think you weren't going to let us in at
all," he said to Mrs Bowen, and added, casually reprimanding
her: "It isn't the sort of night one cares to be kept hanging
about on the wrong side of a bolted door."

"Maybe not," she replied with spirit, "but then, it was quite
a turn you gave us, knocking. We don't expect to have callers,
not in such an out-of-the-way place as this is, especially after
dark—and with the snow, too. 'Whoever can that be?' I said to
Amy—"

"Did you?" he cut in, rather dryly. "The usual method of
finding out is to open the door and see. However," he went on,
sniffing, "since I believe you're about to offer us hot roast lamb
as compensation for our inconvenience, I'll say no more. I
accept the compensation! How very good it smells!" And he
sniffed again.

"If you mean you're hoping for a slice of mutton, then I'm
afraid you're going to be disappointed," said Mrs Bowen,
promptly. "Amy and me have had our supper and we finished it
up, every bit, and Mick's had the scraps. So you see I can't
offer you what's not there, can I?"

"Surely it can't *all* be gone?"

107

"Oh, yes, it can! There's not a morsel of mutton left in this house, not unless you count the smell of it—you're welcome to that," she said, with a hint of malice. But then she relented: "I'd be willing to cook you an egg each, and a piece of bacon, if it's food you're in need of—would that do?"

"It doesn't sound as though we've got much choice," said he. "Very well, then—let it be eggs and bacon. Only you'll certainly have to give us more than one egg each—three at least. We're hungry!"

"Oh! Hungry is it? Then you've come to the wrong door. You should have kept on through Melin-y-Groes another few miles till you got to Llwynffynnon—that's the place where people can order any meals they happen to fancy any time they happen to fancy them," said Mrs Bowen, once again thoroughly vexed by him. Who did he think he was, knocking on her door and demanding food as though she ran a café in town?

Amy hovered unhappily in the background. She no longer felt what she had first felt for the tall fair smiling policeman; later events had modified that initial infatuation. She still viewed him with admiration, but her allegiance had shifted, so that the admiration was coloured now by extreme anxiety as to what he had it in his power to do, and also by the guilt of knowing that in going against his purpose they were going, as her grandmother had said, against the law. There was one thing, though, of which she felt absolutely sure: it was important to please him. To get annoyed and show that annoyance as clearly as her grandmother was doing, was bound to be a mistake. Amy bit her lip and pressed her fist against her jersey. Instead of the beating of her heart she was aware of the stiff shape of the letter concealed there.

"Give us whatever you've got," said the man that she had once hoped would be her friend, and there was a change in his voice. The light bantering note had gone, and instead it sounded curt and cold. Mrs Bowen had gone too far, as Amy had feared might happen, and he was not amused by her any more; he was displeased. "That dog of yours seems to be a pretty vicious animal," he said.

Mick, tucked underneath Amy's arm, had all this time been snarling quietly but continuously.

"Vicious he is not," declared Mrs Bowen, quite unabashed by an altered tone. "There's no dog in the world with a sweeter temper than our Mick. He'll bark, of course, as any dog will, but it's not often I hear him snarl. No doubt he has his own reasons for it. Amy, you'd better put Mick in the side-kitchen, and bring in a cloth to wipe up all this mess. No, no—don't take the lamp, child. Where are your manners? We can't leave visitors standing in the dark. Here's one of the candles for you."

Amy was glad to escape into the side-kitchen. Now was her opportunity for hiding the letter, only she must be quick and where was she to put it? On the floor perhaps, under the coconut matting. Or up on the cratch with the butter and cheese? But it might get greasy there. She swivelled on her heels, the candle guttering. Where?—oh, *where*? Finally she slipped it beneath the strip of newspaper lining a shelf and stood a jar of pickles on top. That would surely be safe enough; and after all, she reflected, it was only for a short time.

"I'm sorry, Mick," she said, kneeling to hug him and explain why he was being banished. "You mustn't snarl at a policeman, though, not even if he did give you a bit of a kick by mistake. It's cold out here, I know, but 'tisn't for long, boy—they'll soon be gone."

She took a cloth and a basin and going back into the other room set about mopping the puddles off the floor. Mrs Bowen was over at the dresser, talking, her back turned as she reached down plates from the shelves, and got out knives and forks from the drawer.

"If I don't seem to be all that hospitable," she was saying, "you'll have to excuse me. The fact of it is, with me and Amy

109

being here on our own, and the snow coming on so sudden, there's not much more in the way of provisions than just enough for the two of us. You're the police, Amy tells me," she added abruptly.

At least her grandmother sounded more friendly, thought Amy, crouched low on the floor, mopping away. She peeped up at the tall man who was warming his hands in front of the fire. He too gave the impression of having recovered his good humour.

"Yes," he said.

"From London, are you?" asked Mrs Bowen, deftly laying the places.

"Yes," he said again.

He gave no indication of resenting either of her questions. Amy was thankful. Perhaps everything was going to turn out peaceably after all.

"That's a long way to have come," said Mrs Bowen. She took the candle and disappeared into the side-kitchen.

Left alone with the two men, Amy studied them covertly. How different they were; and not in appearance only. Ever since their arrival the little dark one had been restlessly prowling round the room, picking up objects, tapping the barometer, lifting the lid of their old oak chest, actually looking inside the grandfather clock as though hoping to find more there than just weights and a pendulum. But the other, tall and fair, had propped his shoulders comfortably against the mantelpiece and so remained, unmoving, his legs crossed, apparently occupied by his own thoughts.

It was him that Amy was watching now. From the first moment he had fascinated her; puzzled her too. She felt there was something about him, something important, that he kept out of sight, and his elegant lounging attitude, his soft laughing voice, even his clothes, even his blonde hair shining smooth as silk in the lamplight, were all like a disguise for this secret quality that she could sense hidden, like rock hidden under a grassy track, but could not identify. He looked up suddenly and Amy was caught staring, speared on the shaft of his brilliantly pale blue eyes.

"Let me see now—you're Amy, aren't you?" he said.

She nodded, standing back by the table, shyly.

"And your grandmother—what's her name?"

Before Amy could answer Mrs Bowen reappeared carrying a bowl of eggs and some rashers of bacon. She blew out the candle with a breath violent enough to have blown out a bonfire. Amy realized that the truce had been brief and was over.

"Since you ask, I'm Mrs Bowen. And now that it seems we're telling names I suppose I might as well know yours."

"You might as well, Mrs Bowen. Let us by all means introduce ourselves, and then we shall feel more confidence in each other, shan't we? I'm Chief Inspector Catcher of Scotland Yard in London. How do you do? You can call me simply Inspector, Mrs Bowen, if you like—it's shorter, isn't it?—easier to remember. And this is my assistant, Mr Nabb."

He was smiling at her but Mrs Bowen faced him without a flicker of response. Then she turned on the other man.

"And what do you think you're doing?"

He had opened the door at the foot of the stairs and as he did so Queenie, who had crept softly up behind him, streaked past and out of sight.

"Just looking."

"Well, this is my house you're in and you'll ask my permission before you start opening doors and *just looking*. Lifting lids and handling private property—I saw you!"

Amy had never known her grandmother to be so indignant before. It made her horribly nervous. But the Inspector was still smiling. He bent towards Mrs Bowen and spoke gently.

"The police", he said, "have a right to look wherever they want to look. It's their duty. And your duty, Mrs Bowen, is not to hinder them in any way."

Mrs Bowen went very red.

"I don't need to be told my duty, Inspector. That's my affair, and no concern of anyone else, I'll thank you to remember. But if you've a right to go poking about in my house then I've got a right to know what for."

"Why yes, of course you have," he answered her soothingly. "We're on the trail of a very dangerous criminal, Mrs Bowen. He's seven foot tall and six foot wide—a regular Goliath, I'm told. You can count yourselves lucky to be enjoying the benefit of police protection in return for food and shelter—it's really not safe for you, and a child, to be up here in this cottage on your own with someone like that about."

"What's he done?" said Mrs Bowen.

Amy took a step forward and gripped the back of a chair. Now at last they were going to know. The two men exchanged glances.

"He murdered a fellow," said Mr Nabb, laconically.

There was a pause. Amy felt her mouth go dry. So he was a murderer after all.

"Well, you won't find any murderer in my house," declared Mrs Bowen, banging at the fire with the poker and slamming the pan on top.

"But we have to look, Mrs Bowen," said he. "The police have to look, and they have to keep on looking, in every house and in every barn and building until he's been found. We know he's in this district. We've traced him as far as Pengarth. He came up from Cardiff on the back of a lorry—apparently the lorry-driver didn't realize he was carrying a passenger as well as a load of crates underneath his tarpaulin—and he was seen leaving Pengarth on foot, making for the hills. That was three days ago, and nobody's seen him since. Now, we've completely circled this stretch of uplands—forest, you call it, don't you?— though I can't think why when there's not a tree for miles; we've been all round the boundaries of it. We've asked in your village down there, and we've got our own people posted ready in all the other outlying villages—there's not been a sign of him. Therefore, if he's gone in and he hasn't come out, he's still here, somewhere. It's just a question of finding him—digging him out, like a fox—and this is where you can help us, Mrs Bowen, by pointing out any places where you think he might have taken cover—"

Amy had already recognized the map Mr Nabb was unfolding. There was one exactly like it on the wall of her classroom at school. It was an ordnance survey map and she knew that every single building, large or small, occupied or not, was marked upon it. Afterwards she had no recollection of deciding what to do; she only remembered doing it.

"I'll show you the Gwyntfa," she said, snatching the map from Mr Nabb's hand and spreading it open on the table. The bottle of ink still stood as Bartolomeo had left it, the top unscrewed, her pen sticking out. Amy picked up the pen and, bending low, poised it accurately. Then she uttered a little cry of dismay.

"Oh, there now—look what I've done!"

"Where's the blotting-paper?" said Mr Nabb. He spoke through clenched teeth, evidently infuriated by Amy's act of clumsiness. "Get some blotting-paper—blot it up!"

"I can't," said Amy, trembling but thankful. "There isn't any."

"Then why couldn't you have left that ink alone, instead of messing about with it? All you were asked to do was point, that was all—just point with your finger."

"I'm sorry," said Amy humbly. "I was going to put a little cross by our place—it's there, see?"

She was afraid to raise her head in case she found Inspector Catcher watching her from the fireplace; in case those pale blue piercing eyes looked directly into her mind and discovered that she had just on purpose obliterated Tyler's Place with a splodge of black ink.

"Oh, Amy," said Mrs Bowen, coming and resting a hand on her shoulder, "what a pity for you to have done that to Mr Nabb's nice map. Ah, well! Never mind! We can maybe scrape it off when it's dry. Now then, let me see—it was buildings you were asking about, wasn't it?—or any likely place a person might hide in. There's a bit of a quarry somewhere further back, over the other side of the stream—that's it, I think. It'll be brimful of snow just now, I'd say, but it might be worth your while to take a look at it. And there was a house once—an inn, it was—higher up the valley. Is it marked still, Amy? I can't tell for sure—my eyes aren't as sharp as they used to be. I don't suppose it's more than just a heap of stones by now. And then down here, alongside the road—that's where Mr Price's place is. He's got a big farm."

Mr Nabb listened silently as she pointed out other farms and buildings to him; and silently, when the ink-blot had dried, he folded the map together. Amy's block of writing-paper, which had been underneath the map, was revealed lying on the table, her name printed in bold capital letters on its cover. He had glanced at this block of paper before when he was nosing round the room, but left it alone. Now, with the persistence of a terrier searching for the scent of a rat, he picked it up, and turned back the cover, and there was the page that Bartolomeo had taken such care, out of politeness, not to tear off; the page on which Amy had begun for the second time to write to her father. Mr Nabb studied it with interest.

"That's my letter," said Amy, flushing.

She meant that he had no business to read what was private, but Mr Nabb, it seemed, was not impressed by privacy, for he read it just the same. First he read it to himself, and then he read it aloud:

" 'A funny thing happened.' Oh? And what *was* the funny thing that happened?" he asked her.

"Why, you of course," she blurted out. "It's the first time I ever saw people on skis. Isn't that what you call them—skis?"

Mrs Bowen was over by the fire again. She had started to fry the bacon.

"I'm going to have to trouble you to sit down," she said to Inspector Catcher. During the whole of the previous exchange he had continued to support himself negligently against the mantelpiece. "You're in my way there—I can't get on with the cooking." He obliged her by moving a step to one side, but no more. "Amy," she called, "you make haste now and cut the bread and butter. It's getting late and they'll want to be off directly they've eaten their supper."

"And where do you suppose we shall be off *to*, Mrs Bowen?" asked Inspector Catcher.

"Why, how should I know?" she answered him, astonished. "It's no affair of mine where you're going after."

"Oh, but it is your affair, Mrs Bowen, because we're not going anywhere."

"Not going anywhere?" she cried, aghast. "You surely don't mean to tell me you're thinking of stopping the night here?"

"Well, of course we're going to stay here for the night," said he, with a touch of impatience. "You don't seriously imagine we shall be setting out at this hour, in the middle of this wilderness, in the teeth of a blizzard, to look for some other accommodation? Come, come, Mrs Bowen—be reasonable! How good that bacon does smell, after all. It's not burning, is it?"

"But I can't have you," said Mrs Bowen bluntly. "I'm sorry— I can't, and that's final. I haven't the facilities. There's only the two beds for a start—I'm not going to turn Amy out of hers, and I've no intention of turning out of mine, not for you or for anyone else."

"Mrs Bowen—please! There's no need for you to work yourself up into such a state of excitement. We can manage perfectly well without beds, and really I don't believe that even you can grudge us a seat in front of your fire. Didn't I tell you a few minutes ago you'd be getting police protection in return for food and lodging? Considering the circumstances I should have thought you'd be only too glad to have us under your roof for the night."

"We've done well enough up to now without protection, police or otherwise. We're not used to company, me and Amy—to be quite plain with you, we don't enjoy it. And I can't understand why ever in the world you didn't stop on in Melin-y-Groes, seeing you were down there making enquiries. There's Mrs Rhys—she does Bed and Breakfast. Or come to that, why couldn't Victor Pugh have put you up? He's got a spare bedroom, that I do know."

"And what makes it more likely for Victor Pugh to have put us up than for anyone else to do it? Is he the only person in your village with a spare bedroom?"

"No, he's not," said Mrs Bowen sharply, "but he's the only policeman."

"Oh, so that's what his name was—Pugh! Perhaps I ought to explain to you now, Mrs Bowen, that we've come to an arrangement with Constable Pugh. He's going to keep an eye on the village down below while we have our headquarters up here in the hills with you. That's because in a manhunt the best strategy is always to spread out as much as possible. You never can tell at which point the man you're hunting may try to escape from the net, you see."

"Amy! Hold these plates for me."

Mrs Bowen scooped up the bacon and broke four eggs into the frying-pan.

"Headquarters, did I hear you say just now? How long were you thinking of staying for, then?"

"For as long as it takes us to find our man—that might be tomorrow, or it might be the day after. Of course, if it goes on snowing as hard as this it may take us even longer—who knows?"

"But I can't feed four mouths, day after day, till goodness knows when—there's not enough food," said Mrs Bowen.

"Oh, nonsense!" he replied, easily. "I can tell you're a very provident housekeeper simply by looking at you, Mrs Bowen. I'm sure you've got plenty of stores tucked away. You'll manage to feed us all right."

Mrs Bowen made no reply. She was stooping over the frying-pan and so it was Amy who saw Mr Nabb pull open the drawer of the table.

"What's this?" he asked.

The medallion was dangling from his fingers.

"Granny!" said Amy, urgently attracting Mrs Bowen's attention. Mrs Bowen turned round.

"That?" she said. "It's what they call a holy medal, I believe. Amy—come on over here. These eggs are about done and I need you to hold the plates for me again. Did you butter the bread like I told you to? That holy medal," she said, raising her voice, "was given to my son before he went off to Australia, the purpose of it being, as I remember, to keep him safe on the journey. I don't recall now who gave it—that's going back a good few years, that is. But as he wasn't one for medals and such things himself he passed it on to me, and it's been in the drawer there ever since. Amy—you've forgotten the cheese—whatever next? Don't just stand there staring—fetch it out of the cupboard this instant. Didn't you hear the Inspector say he was hungry?"

Amy had listened to her grandmother in growing stupefaction. All her life she had known her for someone incapable of telling a lie, yet now she related this piece of fiction with such composure and such fluency that Amy could visualize the scene as clearly as though she had actually witnessed it herself. In Amy's imagination her father wore a navy-blue duffle-coat with the collar turned up.

"Put that back where you found it and pull in your chairs,"

said Mrs Bowen commandingly. There was a certain sparkle about her, as though she had just enjoyed an invigorating experience. "You might as well eat your food now, while it's hot, as I've been to all the trouble of cooking it for you."

They did as she told them. But because Mr Nabb's eyes were never still he had no sooner picked up his knife and fork than he laid them down again and bending sideways groped along the floor. When he straightened himself there was a small piece of crumpled paper in his hand. Amy's heart gave a horrible thump of warning. She shrank back, away from Mr Nabb. Without saying a word he smoothed the paper out flat on the table, and there were Amy's two little matchstick men with skis on their feet and a row of dots and a row of arrows pointing towards the cottage door.

To Amy it seemed that now everything was revealed, that this drawing of hers was a piece of evidence so incriminating that only to look at it was enough for the whole guilty truth to be known immediately. But Mrs Bowen remarked in a perfectly matter-of-fact voice:

"That wasn't such a bad drawing of yours after all, Amy. It was a pity for you to have thrown it away—your father would have liked to have seen it. But never mind, you can make another picture for him easily enough—and now the Inspector's here, and Mr Nabb, you can study better how to do it right."

13. Amy Overhears a Little Joke

Amy took Mick upstairs with her when she went to bed and arranged his old coat on the floor and told him to lie down and stay there. But he was restless. She kept her candle alight and watched him. He turned round and round on the coat and pushed it with his nose and scraped it with his paw.

"Mick—lie down!"

He flopped at once in obedience, but his ears were still pricked. He tilted his head, first to one side, then to the other. A murmur of voices reached them through the floor-boards and various bumps and scrapes that could have been the sound of chairs pulled up to the fire. Amy found herself listening as well, trying to match every noise to a possible movement. Mick growled. Then he sprang up and wandered round the room, sniffing and hanging his head close against the cracks, trembling as though he could hear rats on the move.

"It's no good, Mick—they're going to be there all night, and I'll never get any sleep if you don't settle down."

But in the end she was obliged to climb out of her bed and tie Mick to one leg of it with an improvised rope made by knotting a pair of stockings together. She crouched on the floor, stroking him, and the murmur of voices below went on.

"I wonder what they're saying—I wish I could hear."

It was cold. She took the old ironing-blanket off her bed and wrapped it round her shoulders. Then she picked up her candle and tiptoed through the doorway into her grandmother's room. Queenie was curled up at the foot of Mrs Bowen's feather quilt.

"Amy?"

"I can't sleep, Granny. I wish they'd stop talking—it keeps me awake."

"There's nothing in this world could keep me awake tonight, I don't believe—I'm tired to the bones of me. It must be telling that pack of lies has worn me out."

"You were a wonder, Granny. I'd no idea you could make things up like that," whispered Amy admiringly.

"Nor I didn't myself, and I don't know that I feel so very comfortable about it, neither. Fancy, to find out at my age I'm a liar born—an old woman like me, and never suspected it all these years. It came so easy, Amy—a natural gift, you might say. I ought to be ashamed. Well, so I am, in a way."

"I do wish that little one, that Mr Nabb—I wish he wasn't so nosey," said Amy.

"Nosey!—that's the very word for him," agreed Mrs Bowen. "And even supposing it is his job to be, I don't like him any the more for it. He's disrespectful. But it's the tall one I can't abide—I can't abide him, Amy. Whatever he says it seems like he's laughing at me. Why should he laugh at me all of the time? He may think he's a whole lot cleverer—and I'm not denying he is—but that's no reason. A person doesn't show his cleverness by laughing at people—he just shows he's got no manners at all—none!"

"How long do you think they're going to stop here?"

"Till they find him—that's what they said, didn't they?"

"Yes, that's what they said. Oh, Granny, I just can't bear for them to catch him. Are they sure to?"

"Now Amy, have sense. Right or wrong, we've done all we can for that poor man, and very likely we did more than we should have done. They say that he killed someone—maybe he never meant to—we can't judge, we don't know. But he must take the consequences now, and for you to stand there in your nightdress with your teeth chattering won't help him one little bit. So you be a good girl, Amy, and get into your bed and go to sleep. That's what I mean to do."

And Mrs Bowen turned her back and pulled the bedclothes round her ears, leaving Amy to feel as much alone as if her grandmother had suddenly vanished out of the room. She stood forlorn by the high pillow, shivering, and the candlestick in her hand shivered with her. She was not sleepy. The voices in the front-kitchen mumbled on. Whatever were they saying? Talk, talk; and then a pause; and then talk, talk, talk again.

Very quietly Amy crossed to the head of the staircase and leaned into the short matchboarded tunnel, listening. But the door at the bottom was shut and not a single word came clearly through it. She knew that the deeper, harsher voice was Mr Nabb's and the other, softer and slower, belonged to Inspector Catcher. Amy put her candlestick on the floor so that its gentle flicker illuminated the stairway, and then with infinite caution lowered herself two steps. They had stopped talking. She waited. As soon as Mr Nabb began to speak she lowered herself again, but when she reached the third step from the bottom she dared not press the latch for fear that even the faintest rattle would give her away.

So there she huddled, the ironing-blanket clutched around her shoulders, her feet as cold as ice. The conversation had lapsed again. Perhaps they had heard her creeping down the stairs; perhaps at this very moment they were staring across the room in her direction. Then there was a thud, a clink, a clatter; someone swore, someone laughed, and under cover of the noise Amy pressed the latch and pushed: the door stood open a crack, not more than an inch, but enough. Their voices reached her as distinctly as though she were sitting beside them.

"For heaven's sake, Harris—leave that fire alone, can't you!

121

You'll wake the old woman up with all the racket you're making."

"Serve her right—give her a taste of her own medicine. She hasn't shown very friendly to us, I must say. What's the matter with her? Don't they trust the police round here?"

The Inspector laughed again. Something about his laugh struck Amy as peculiar. She felt as though the laugh were a clue, if she could only understand it, to some bigger puzzle, something that had been worrying her all the time at the back of her mind. Her heart began to beat faster, louder, with a sense of painful anticipation. Why had the Inspector just called Mr Nabb by another name?

There was the chink of a glass, the sound of someone shifting in his chair—*her* chair. It was strange to be able to hear but not to see them; not to see the expression on their faces, whether they frowned or smiled, or how they sat, leaning back or bending forward.

"What makes you so sure he's alive, anyway?" said Mr Nabb. "You're always so sure you're right, Vigers. I think we're wasting our time here."

There was a pause and then the smooth, soft voice replied:

"He's alive all right—I know it. You're in too much of a hurry to get back to civilization, Harris. That's why you think he's dead in a snowdrift—you want him to be, so as to have it all over and done with. It's a pity you're not enjoying yourself. I am."

"Enjoy! I don't see how anyone—except for a nut-case—could enjoy himself spending the night in a barn with the temperature below freezing-point."

"But that was last night, Harris. Tonight you've no reason to complain—I've provided you with a warm fire and a comfortable chair."

"A chair! Why can't we get lodgings in the village and sleep decently in beds? It's safe enough—they won't have got wind of us—not likely! They're cut off by the snow down there, same as here."

"What you're saying is sheer nonsense, Harris. That village isn't cut off, the same as here. It's got a policeman and it's got a telephone line—it's in direct communication with the world. And if we're one jump ahead of the Embassy people now—which we are—it's only because they don't know we're ahead of them; they don't know we're here. Can't you understand that once we attract attention to ourselves we lose our whole advantage, quite apart from any other consequences. I don't count the woman in the Post Office. She's not a risk. She swallowed your story, obviously, and your appearance, Harris, if you'll forgive my saying so, is sufficiently nondescript not to excite interest. But I am not nondescript, and if I'd gone into the village with you attention would undoubtedly have been attracted, and we should have been remembered, and in due course we could have been described. We don't want that to happen, do we? So let's have no more of this absurd talk about lodgings in the village."

"Well, I still think he's dead," said the voice of Mr Nabb, sulkily. "How can he be alive? Didn't Oscar say he'd all but cut his arm clean off him? That was three days ago. Three days without a bite to eat, and an arm half gone, and then this snow on top to finish him off—of course he's dead! Or as near as makes no difference."

"But it does make a difference, Harris, you blockhead—all the difference in the world. If he's *not quite* dead he may still be able to speak. Don't you realize that we can't afford to let there be any possibility, however slight, of that man speaking?"

"There's no one round here could understand a word he said if he did open his mouth. And besides, we don't know for sure if old Alvarez told him anything, do we? It's only guesswork."

"Are you trying to exasperate me, Harris, or can you really be so stupid? He was boxed up at sea with the old man for more than a week. He was the only one on board who spoke the same

123

language as Alvarez. He took him his meals. He looked after him when he was ill—nursed him, the captain told Oscar, as a mother nurses her child. Don't you think it likely that in such a situation old Luis Alvarez would have passed on his secrets, would have shared his information? Why, of course he did! There's nothing more certain! And that sailor knows very well indeed the value of what he's been told. He's seen a man killed so as to stop it going any further—he only saved his own life by the skin of his teeth. He knows, all right! And because he knows he has to be dead, Harris; he has to be quite dead, with no doubt about it, either. It's not good enough for you to hope he is and think he might be. We're here to make sure of it. I say he's still alive and I'm right, Harris, because I was born with an extra sense which you haven't got. It's the jungle instinct. It warns the stalking tiger when his victim's close. Tigers can tell, Harris—and so can I. And I know that he's somewhere close now—I can feel it."

Amy shuddered. Supposing his instinct told him more, that she was there, even closer than the man they hunted, listening to them from behind this very door? Panic welled up in her, stopped her ears. She shut her eyes and pressed against the side of the staircase, afraid. But nothing happened. The door was not snatched violently open. No one had heard her sigh of terror, the loud clamour of her heartbeats. Gradually, as her panic receded, her ears became aware again of Mr Nabb's aggrieved voice, grumbling on:

"... and then this other game of yours—this Catcher and Nabb stunt, eh? What's the idea of it? Supposing they'd spotted what you were up to, poking fun—they might have started to wonder a bit more. It's the sort of a carry-on that leads to trouble—and where's the sense of it, anyway?"

"It was a little joke of mine, Harris—a very small joke to amuse myself, that's all. Why not? One has to amuse oneself. And even if they did have enough intelligence to understand, it wouldn't matter in the very least. What can they do to us? Absolutely nothing! They're entirely at our mercy, Harris; and mercy they shall have, in exact proportion to the hospitality they show us. That seems perfectly fair—don't you agree?"

"One day you're going to make a little joke that won't turn out so funny, Vigers, you mark my words. You say you're always right—but that's where you're going to be wrong, one day. People aren't always as stupid as you think they are. Take that old woman upstairs—so far as you're concerned, what is she? Nothing but an old fool—and that girl of hers the same. But I know better—I've watched them. They're sharp, the two of them. And I'll tell you something else, Vigers—I don't trust them. You've got your instinct, you say—well, I've got mine. And if I find out that they know more than they've let on to know, they're going to be sorry for it, I promise—they're going to be very sorry indeed—"

"Put that bottle away, Harris, and hold your tongue. You're like an old woman yourself, the way you chatter on. You bore me. You're talking absolute rubbish. These people are stupid, and if you waste your time watching them it merely means you're as stupid as they are. Now make up the fire. I'm going to sleep."

"Oh! So it's me now, is it? I bore you, do I? My company's not good enough for you, I suppose. Bores and fools, that's what you think—that's your opinion of everyone—of everyone except for yourself, Mr Brilliant—"

"Be quiet!" said the voice of the man who had told them his name was Catcher, and it was not soft any more; it cut like a knife, so that even Amy, listening, shrank away. "The only reason you're sitting in the same room as I am tonight, Harris, is because you happen to be able to ski. Do you think that gives you the right to speak in such a way—to *me*? You've made a mistake, as you'll discover when once this job's done. I shan't forget it. I never do."

Then there was silence from the front-kitchen. But Amy sat on in the dark and the cold, unmoving, minute after minute, while the voices repeated over and over in her head odd fragments of sentences muddled together, incomprehensible and terrifying:

". . . Catcher and Nabb . . . poking fun . . . a little joke of mine, Harris . . . people aren't always as stupid as you think they are . . . a little joke . . . I've watched them, they're sharp, the two of them . . . it's the jungle instinct, tigers can tell . . . didn't Oscar say he'd as good as cut his arm clean off him . . . seen a man killed to stop it going any further . . . tigers can tell . . . Catcher and Nabb . . . entirely at our mercy, Harris . . . it was a little joke of mine . . ."

Amy went up the stairs at last on hands and knees, too stiff to be careful; but if a board or two did creak no one appeared to notice. She crawled into her grandmother's bed. At her frozen touch the old woman awoke.

"Why, child! You're like a stone! Where have you been?"

"Listening. And oh, Granny—they're not policemen at all—they're not the police! They can't be!"

"Not the police! Whatever do you mean, they're not the police?"

"Shush, Granny—shush! Don't say it!"

"It's you've just said it, not me."

"But not so loud—"

Mrs Bowen heaved herself round in bed and lit the candle. Then, propped on one elbow, she looked at Amy, and Amy looked at her; and as they looked the fearful possibility became for both of them a certainty.

"Do you know, Amy, I feel as though somewhere deep inside of me I always knew it," said Mrs Bowen. "From the very beginning I was uneasy about those two. And yet again, there was no way of telling for sure they weren't what they said they were. How could we have known?"

"We should have guessed. Catcher and Nabb—that's not their names, of course it's not—he was making a joke on us. Fancy us being so dull! And when you mentioned Victor Pugh—remember?—they didn't know he was the policeman, not till you said. If they'd been real police, Granny, no matter even if they did come from London, they'd be bound to know that. I don't believe they've so much as spoken to Mr Pugh."

"But who are they, then?" said Mrs Bowen.

"I don't know. I couldn't make out the meaning of half of it, but I think they're just as bad as ever they can be."

And sitting up whispering in the candlelight, holding both her grandmother's hands tightly for comfort, Amy told her all she had heard; and anxiously at the end of it she asked her:

"What are we going to do?"

Mrs Bowen was silent for a while. Then she said:

"That poor man, Amy. It's not us they're after—it's him."

"And he's not a murderer—that was a lie they told us, like all the rest."

"It seems likely, indeed."

"Granny—if he went back to Tyler's Place they'll find him. The big one said he was somewhere close—he said he knew it. They'll find him. And when they find him, they'll kill him. They said he'd got to be *quite dead*. That's what they said, those very words. I heard them."

Again Mrs Bowen was silent.

"What are we going to *do*?" whispered Amy.

Many a night in the past Mrs Bowen had sat up in that same feather-bed and asked herself the same question, to which there had seemed to be no answer but the one she suggested now:

"We can say our prayers, Amy."

"I don't think that's going to be enough, Granny."

"Sometimes it has to be," said Mrs Bowen.

"But you've told me and told me—prayers aren't meant to be instead of doing something, they're as well as."

"Amy," said Mrs Bowen more firmly and louder, "there's one thing you're going to promise me here and now—you're not going down to Tyler's Place, nor anywhere near."

Amy was mute.

"Amy," said Mrs Bowen, very earnestly, "those are bad men, you said it yourself. You've got to promise me."

"All right then," said Amy, staring in front of her and seeing, not the brass knobs at the foot of the bed or the flickering outline of the chest-of-drawers, but the dark and ruined walls of Tyler's Place. "We don't know for sure he's there, anyway. But supposing he is, then it must be because he thinks he's got more of a chance, hiding, than out in the snow on a hill where they'd see him plain and catch him easy with those ski things of theirs. They wouldn't have to catch up with him, even. That little one—he's got a gun. I saw it, night before last, when they were searching. They've both of them got guns, I daresay. You needn't worry about me, Granny—I don't want to show them the way down to Tyler's Place, and I might if I went, so I shan't go—I promise. But if only there was something we could do—there must be *something*."

14. Amy Decides

The day was a burden almost too heavy for Amy to bear. Each minute pressed upon her like a separate and agonizing weight. What could she do? Which way could she turn? There was no relief. She was afraid to speak for fear she might say something that would tell them what she knew; afraid to say nothing for fear her silence might appear suspicious; afraid to look up for fear they should read her thoughts in her eyes; afraid to look down for fear it might seem she was avoiding their gaze; she was afraid to go out and afraid to stay in and whatever she did or did not do, danger surrounded her, invisible, unavoidable as the air she breathed. She could eat no breakfast.

"I'm not hungry, Granny."

"Leave it, then—or give it to Mick. It's being cooped up and no exercise—no wonder you've lost your appetite. But you can't go out this morning, Amy—there's nobody could be out this morning," said Mrs Bowen, touching Amy's shoulder as she passed.

For the snow was driving across, an impenetrable blanket, and if it was impossible for anyone to start looking for the way to London in such weather, so was it also impossible for any person to set out to look for any other person. Mr Nabb—as Amy felt she would always think of him now, whatever his real name might be—prowled restlessly round the front-kitchen, opening, shutting, tapping, humming; and yet, when she pushed away her bacon and egg and glanced up, she found that in spite of all the fidgeting his eye was steadily on her. "I've been watching them"—she remembered his words.

"Shall I polish the brasses, Granny?"

"Well, yes, Amy—why don't you?" said Mrs Bowen as heartily as though she had no recollection of Amy rubbing every bit of brass they had only the day before yesterday.

Inspector Catcher, whose name, like Mr Nabb's, was really something quite different, lay back in Mrs Bowen's basket-chair, his legs stretched out across the hearthrug like the long straight legs of a heron. The tips of his fingers rested together; he appeared to be thinking. Amy, her head well down, polishing, peeped at him through her hair. Mr Brilliant!—what a good name it was for him, better than Inspector Catcher, better than Vigers. Even lying as he was now, supine in front of the fire, there was a sort of a dangerous gleam about him.

"Mr Brilliant," she said softly, trying it out; and immediately, horrified, looked up to encounter again the gaze of Mr Nabb fastened upon her.

"They come up nicely, don't they?" she faltered, giving the candlesticks a push towards him. "Brilliant they are, with a bit of a polish."

Would that do? Perhaps he had not heard her first murmur after all. But he had said she was sharp; he was watching her. She must be careful, so very careful.

"Shall I turn the radio on, Granny?"

"Why, yes, Amy, let's have some music—that's a good idea."

But instead of music they heard the nine o'clock time-signal, and then the news and the weather forecast: snow everywhere, still coming.

"Is there to be no end to it?" said Mrs Bowen. "Funny they made no mention of that criminal you're after, specially as he's a murderer—they usually put it on the news, don't they, when there's a prisoner got out, so as to warn people not to open their doors."

Amy caught her breath: was this wise of her grandmother? She dropped her head lower still and polished harder. Mrs Bowen was stirring a pudding at the other end of the table. A stream of pop music poured out of the radio into their little front-kitchen.

"Turn that noise off," said Inspector Catcher.

"Oh, no—I like it!" declared Mrs Bowen, stirring away briskly.

"Harris—you heard what I said. Turn it off."

Abruptly the music ceased. Mrs Bowen said nothing for a while, only her lips folded together tightly and she beat a little faster. She paused, scattered in currants, beat again.

"Inspector, I'm sure you won't mind me asking—but I understood you to tell me yesterday this gentleman's name was Mr Nabb. Why was it you just called him Mr Harris, then?"

In her mind Amy begged her to say no more—to wipe out somehow what she had already said. She knew what her grandmother was doing: she was setting Amy an example of courage; she was telling these men that whoever they were she was not afraid of them. She was defying them. It might be brave, but was it wise? Through a protective screen of loose falling hair Amy, deeply apprehensive, watched Inspector Catcher, who was not really Inspector Catcher, and waited for his annihilating reply.

It seemed at first that he was going to ignore Mrs Bowen, or even that he had not heard her. He neither moved nor spoke for a whole long minute. Then very slowly he turned round and looked at her.

Blue, pale, his eyes, intently focused, reminded Amy of the eyes of the Post Office cat, that huge fluffy creature whose time was spent dozing in the sunshine apparently unconscious but coming, at the faintest rustle or squeak, instantly alert. The Inspector looked at Mrs Bowen as though all at once she was of

131

interest to him. One hand hung lax over the side of his chair, but Amy noticed that the tips of the fingers were crooked slightly inwards. Again she was reminded of the Post Office cat; and then, with a sense of shock, realized why she had felt that the soft voice and easy manner were a disguise, and what it was they disguised: he was cruel.

She had stopped polishing. She thought he was never going to speak. When he did it was a relief and a surprise: he sounded the same as usual—amused, careless, with the tinge of contempt that was always in everything he said.

"Mrs Bowen, I can assure you in our branch of the police force we frequently change our names. As you were so quick to remark, Mr Nabb is also called Harris, and at Scotland Yard he's known by half a dozen other titles too which he can assume or discard whenever necessary—isn't that the case, my dear Nabb?"

Mr Nabb at the window gave an angry-sounding grunt.

"The same goes for myself: today I'm Inspector Catcher—tomorrow I may be Colonel Bramble or the Prince of Darkness or the King of Siam. It's all part of our job as detectives, Mrs Bowen—we have to adapt our identities according to the circumstances—blend with the landscape."

"Oh, blending is it?" said Mrs Bowen. "Well, I've never had much to do with the police, I'm thankful to say, so I'll have to take your word for it, won't I? But if that Victor Pugh ever comes to me with this tale of having another name to the one he was born with, I'll blend him."

The strain was too great. The room was too hot.

"Where are you going, Amy?"

"Just out."

In the shed she hugged Mick against her chest. He had been shut into the side-kitchen since half past seven that morning because, unlike Mrs Bowen and Amy, he made no attempt to conceal his real feelings.

"Oh, Mick—what are we going to do?"

She was desperate.

Her grandmother, provoked, would say too much, and what would happen then? Amy thought of how Mick had been kicked out of the way for no other reason than that he had barked, as it was his duty to do. She remembered the Inspector's curved finger-tips and the blue blaze of his eyes when he turned his head and looked across the room at Mrs Bowen. It was not just Bartolomeo who was in danger; they all were.

"If only someone could help us, Mick. If only Mr Protheroe knew—if he was to come up here, somehow, after his ewes—"

If only! But the snow imprisoned them. It whirled about the cottage as close, as thick, as though the air itself had clotted. How could anyone breathe in that for five minutes, much less force a way through it? Even within the shelter of the shed the five ewes were discouraged by the proximity of a storm so dire and huddled together, motionless, against the wall. Amy had flung handfuls of grain for the chickens before breakfast but they too, after pecking about for a bit, had lost heart and returned to the comfort of their stuffy little house. It was not a day for any living creature to choose to be out; not, at any rate, for as long as this blizzard lasted.

But of course it would not last. Presently it would ease off. The flakes would get smaller and the space between them greater, and the wind would drop and the light increase, and then there would be a huge still pause, like peace after a fight, and all the snow that had been in such a commotion would lie tranquil on the ground. And during this pause the Inspector and Mr Nabb would come out into a calm immaculate waiting white world, and put on their skis, and glide away to hunt for what they were so certain, sooner or later, of finding: in her imagination Amy saw them. And should she not then, while they were gone—before it began to snow again, before they came back—get on to her tin toboggan and shoot away down the hill in search of help?

Supposing she did?

It would be easy enough to reach the stream, but the track on the other side that skirted round the foot of the great hill towering above it would almost have disappeared by now under its three days' and three nights' accumulation of driving and drifting snow; almost perhaps, but not quite. If this had been her worst problem Amy could still have found her way, but there were other problems, more conclusive. At two separate points the track was cut through by deep wide rocky channels where every spring and autumn the rain-water was borne in torrents down from the hill above to swell the stream below. It was these channels, full to the brim, not with water but with snow, that would defeat her. If she tried to cross that seemingly solid floor of snow on foot she would sink like a stone in a bog.

Then she would not cross on foot: she would use her toboggan instead. All that was needed for her toboggan to skim safely over the danger zones was enough momentum. Would there be enough momentum? Amy wrinkled her brow. For the first of the channels the answer, she decided, was yes. It had a long steep approach where she would be able to get up the speed necessary to carry her in a rush to the top of the further side. But for the second channel the situation was reversed and it was the approaching pitch that was short and slight and the far pitch that was long and steep. Amy considered earnestly and had to acknowledge that with the slope against her and the snow profound she dared not attempt such a crossing, neither on foot nor yet with the aid of her little tin toboggan. It would need skis, she reflected grimly.

But in any case, even supposing there had been no snow-filled channels to stop her, the route she took each day to school would still have been impossible, for the road on from Casswell's Gate to the village would be thoroughly blocked, and once it was blocked it stayed blocked until the thaw set in; Ted Jones, who drove the snow-plough, had orders each winter not to waste the Council's valuable time clearing a stretch of undulating narrow lane that, officially speaking, led to nowhere.

Well then, supposing she were to use the frozen stream itself as a path? Might this be her answer? But the stream ran a devious course, twisting and turning, and there were deep black pools beneath its icy surface; waterfalls interrupted it, rocks overhung it. Branches and brambles would get in her way. Even on a sunny happy-go-lucky idle summer afternoon it was slow hard work to follow the stream down; she had tried more than once and always given up long before she reached the village. How much slower, harder now? They would catch her at some dark and narrow bend where there would be no one to hear her cry of terror.

And Bartolomeo—where was he? Suppose, when the snow stopped, his great clumsy figure should come shambling down the hill with no notion of what awaited him? He might; after all, he had taken such a risk before.

It was then—only then—that Amy remembered the letter.

He had taken the risk before for the sake of writing that letter; and he had given the letter to her, pressing it into her hands and her hands over it. And she, in haste and fear, had posted it under the newspaper of the shelf in the back-kitchen, stood a jar of pickles on top, and forgotten it.

The letter was real. It was lying under the jar of pickles at this very moment. She had no idea who it was to, or what was in it, but the more she thought about it the more she felt that it must be immensely important, that it contained the solution to the whole of this dreadful tangle, and that if she could only get it into a post-box, somehow, they would all be saved. But how in the world was she to reach a post-box?—*how?* And in her head once again, chance by chance, she began to go over the possibilities of escape.

Both the track on the other side of the stream and the stream itself were, for different reasons, out of the question; also the road from Casswell's Gate to the village would be blocked. As for Tyler's Place, it was worse than useless to think of fleeing there—no path existed beyond the ruined farmhouse, and her action might well betray Bartolomeo; besides, she had promised her grandmother not to go. There remained a single alternative, one so awful that until now she had managed to avert her mind from even admitting it was an alternative: the high wild short way over the top of the hills to Dintirion.

As she allowed herself to realize what that journey would mean, Amy's eyes widened and her breath came faster. It would mean for two miles or more tracing the course of a path, at the best uncertain and for much of the distance totally invisible, knowing that on either side were deep drifts like continuous white graves, waiting to bury her; it would mean wind and snow biting her to the bone for every step she took, and it would mean that if she missed her footing at the cliff's edge her rash venture would come to an end far from the bustle and glow of the great Dintirion kitchen, at the bottom, instead, of Billy Dodd's Dingle.

It was impossible—she could never do it, never! No, never! Or could she?

How many times had she been along that same path, alone or with the Protheroe boys? Times without number; she knew every inch of the way. Well then! Oh, but that was different! That was in spring or summer when there were harebells growing in the short dry grass and wild scabious and the wind blew warm and there was no hurry—that was different! It would be like another country under snow. She would feel lost before she started.

"I couldn't do it," she whispered in horror to Mick, holding him close.

But she knew all the same that she must; and from that moment she began to think of how it could be done.

15. Mr Nabb Shows His Feelings

Amy lingered on in the shed. Her head was teeming with plans. She was oblivious to the cold. One thing was clear to her: she was going to have to be extremely clever. Inspector Catcher thought her stupid, and she felt that this was to her advantage; she could hide from him behind a mask of stupidity. And yet she must not be so obviously stupid as to make Mr Nabb suspect she was up to something, for he, on the contrary, believed her to be smart.

It was another, even greater advantage that they neither of them knew of the short way over the hills to Dintirion. And then she wondered whether she might not be able to manage it so that they would never discover she was missing at all. Could they be made to think she was ill in her room, perhaps? But for this she would need her grandmother's co-operation, and Amy knew there was no hope of that. If she could mislead them, though, into thinking she had gone by a different way from the way she had gone by she would gain time, and it was time that was more precious than anything else to her because of the terrible swiftness of those pursuing skis.

When should she go? By night? But she had no torch, and a hurricane lamp would show for miles; besides, by night she would undoubtedly get off the path—be lost either in a drift or over the cliff-edge of the Dingle. On the other hand in daylight the risk of being seen was much more. And then there was the obstacle presented by her grandmother who would never agree, under any circumstances whatever, to Amy setting off on such a trip. Consequently she too would have to be deceived, and this was indeed a problem for her grandmother was a person not easily deceived. In addition Amy was worried by the risk of Bartolomeo reappearing. How could she warn him to stay away without the warning being understood equally well by Inspector Catcher and Mr Nabb-Harris?

Her difficulties were many, and for each and all of them she had to find an answer. So preoccupied was she in searching her head for the necessary solutions that Amy forgot how long she must have been standing outside until Mick, still hugged in her arms, began to growl and she heard the door open behind her.

"So that's where you are," said the harshly grating voice of Mr Nabb. "I was beginning to wonder where you'd got to."

"Amy!" called Mrs Bowen. "I've made you a cup of cocoa—come on in and drink it. You'll catch your death of cold out there."

Amy ducked her head and slipped obediently into the cottage past Mr Nabb.

"Granny," she began presently, armed with her cup of cocoa, "I'm worried about Mr Protheroe's ewes."

"Why—what of them?"

"I don't think the hay's enough—they ought to be having cubes as well. And they're going to lamb soon, Granny. Any moment now they might start lambing—I've been having a look at them, out in the shed. Mr Protheroe doesn't even know we've got them up at our place. He ought to know, shouldn't he? He ought to be told. I've been thinking, Granny—couldn't I get down to the village and tell him?"

"Get down to the village?" exclaimed Mrs Bowen, and in her astonishment she stopped kneading dough and rested her floury hands on the sides of the bowl while she gazed at Amy as though she thought she must have gone out of her mind. "Whatever possesses you, child? In this weather? You might as well think of flying!"

Amy dipped her nose into her cup of cocoa. She was aware in the silence of a sharpening of attention. They were all listening to her. She said, carefully looking at no one:

"It's just I can't help but worry for those ewes, Granny. I'd like for Mr Protheroe to know we had them."

"Why, Amy—" Mrs Bowen started to say, and then stopped. Amy could tell she was wondering what was the purpose of these remarks. She would have realized that they could only be a cover for some other deeper meaning; both of them knew perfectly well that the ewes were not due to start lambing for another two weeks at the earliest and that they would come to no harm if for a few days they were fed on a diet of hay alone. But why should Amy deliberately talk of getting down to the village when she knew it was impossible? Mrs Bowen started to knead the dough again with a thoughtful air.

"Well, maybe the Inspector here and his friend could take a message," she suggested tentatively. "It wouldn't be much trouble for you, would it?" she said, speaking to him directly. "With those slidey things on your feet you could be down to the village in no time, I daresay, once it stops snowing."

"We're not here to run errands for sheep, Mrs Bowen," he replied in his slow contemptuous drawl.

Amy kept her back turned on him; she was afraid that otherwise he might read secrets in her face. Loudly, with a show of eagerness, she cried out:

"But I could get down, Granny, I'm sure I could—I was thinking just now, the stream's bound to be frozen over. I could go on the ice, like it was a pathway."

"And how about the pools?" said Mrs Bowen sternly. "Deep they are—dangerous! And waterfalls—they'll not be frozen. How do you think to get by them, with ice on the rocks, and

139

steep too, slippery? Oh, Amy, no!—you never could and I'd never consent to such a folly, so you can put it right out of your head this minute."

She was puzzled, Amy could see, as well as stern; for if Amy had really intended to make her way down the stream, why speak of it in front of these men? And if it were not her intention, why speak of it at all?

"I'm sure I could do it, Granny."

"I've said no, Amy. That's enough."

Amy bowed her head meekly and finished her cocoa. She hoped it *was* enough and that when the time came this conversation would be remembered.

Towards midday the snow stopped. The sky lifted away from the earth and the air cleared. Amy had been so immersed in her calculations she had scarcely noticed the morning go by. She sat at the table polishing brasses, already as bright as brass could be, and working out detail by detail her complicated plan of campaign, aware only vaguely of her grandmother opening or shutting the oven door, filling the kettle, making up the fire, rattling the poker; more aware of the presence of the two men, the stillness of the one and the restless movements of the other providing a background to all of her thoughts.

Now, with the feeling of having at last made her arrangements and being ready to begin to put them into practice, she looked up and there was the Inspector pulling his cap over his ears, zipping his jacket. Mr Nabb, however, continued to sit hunched on their oak chest, tying intricate knots in a piece of string. For some reason it had never occurred to Amy that one of them might set off as hunter and one stay behind. This being so, it was just as well she had changed her mind about going today. But her confidence was disturbed. She saw how easily a plan that counted on other people behaving in such and such a way could go wrong: they might behave differently. It was worrying.

"Don't you mean to go with him?" she said to Mr Nabb.

He pulled the string at both ends and the knot in the middle magically disappeared.

"I'm staying here," was all he said.

"Oh, I see."

She wanted to ask him why he was staying. Was it so as to keep that eye of his on them, or because he had had enough of being out in the snow, or what? But the question was too difficult for Amy to phrase.

Instead she put on her Wellingtons and coat and scarf and gloves and went outside to watch the Inspector fasten his skis. In spite of all doubts and fears it was still a wonderful sight to see him glide away, gathering speed. He was gone, disappearing into the trees at the bottom. She waited and presently there he was on the far side, smaller now, heading west up the valley that they had come skimming down as lightly as birds the day before yesterday. So that was all right—he was welcome to find whatever he might in that direction.

"What about the Inspector, Granny—isn't he coming back for his dinner?"

"Wherever are your eyes, child? He took some food with him in his pocket—bread and cheese. I declare, Amy," said Mrs Bowen kindly, "sometimes you seem to live in a world apart. You've no more idea of what's going on round you than a bat in a barn. Though I'm not saying it's such a bad thing, now and again—it's one way of taking a holiday."

Amy was alarmed to learn that her absent-mindedness had been so apparent, and she strove to make up for it, chattering on with unflagging vivacity throughout the meal.

"You're clever with that string, aren't you?" she said to Mr Nabb. "That was a conjuring trick you did, with the knot in the middle. Where did it go to? Will you show me how you did it? Will you do more tricks for me, after?"

But the others were unresponsive. Mr Nabb merely sucked in his soup more noisily, his expression of gloomy disapproval

141

unchanged, while Mrs Bowen eyed her granddaughter with a growing uneasiness.

"I'm going outside to play, Granny, soon as I've done the dishes. I'm going to take a shovel up and make a snowman."

"Don't you go far then, Amy," said Mrs Bowen, remindingly.

"Only just to the top of the hill—that's all."

"Well, you mind and see it's no further."

"I shan't go far, Granny, I promise. You don't have to worry yourself. Will you come up with me, Mr Nabb? Will you help me to make a snowman?"

But he shot her a glance so savage she was silenced.

It was not play at all, this part of her scheme, it was very exhausting work, for she had to make two snowmen—two men of snow, standing right on the summit, in the middle of the track that went between cottage and haystack, barring the way. This was her plan, the method by which she hoped to tell Bartolomeo—supposing he still was somewhere close at hand and supposing he did venture on another visit—that he must come no nearer. But would these two snowmen Amy wondered, stepping back to consider the results of all her hard labour, would they be unusual enough to stop him, to make him think: why *two*? Would they have for Bartolomeo the meaning she meant them to have? And at the same time for Mr Nabb, toiling up the hill towards her now, would they be just snowmen with no meaning other than the amusement of a little girl playing by herself on a wintry afternoon?

"Hullo!" she called down to him, very friendly, and waited anxiously for what he would say. First he got his breath. Then he looked at her handiwork, then at her flushed cheeks, then back again.

"And what are those supposed to be?"

"Why, snowmen of course," she said, surprised, ready to be suspicious. Was he trying to trap her into saying more than she meant to say?

"I'm glad you told me—I'd never have known it, else."

Amy's vision faded. She looked where he looked and saw what he saw: not the warning figures of Mr Nabb and Inspector Catcher sculpted in snow—almost too dangerously obvious, it had seemed to her—but instead two dingy lumpy piles of nothing in particular. Bartolomeo might stumble against them in the starlight and knock them over—that was all. She had worked with such desperation of purpose and for all the use it was going to be she might have saved herself the trouble. Was every plan of hers going to turn out so poorly?

"What did you want to go and make two for, anyway?" he asked her.

"I'd finished the other one, that's why," she answered lamely.

Her woollen gloves were soaking wet and the fingers inside them ached with cold. She felt the tears rise up, hot, into her eyes, tears of discouragement and vexation; tears of doubt. Had she set herself, in fact, a task that was impossible? Had she?

"You certainly get the view from here," said Mr Nabb with grudging appreciation. He had lost interest in Amy's snowmen and was scanning the huge deserted landscape that stretched below and around them. "I reckon you could just about see a fly move, and a couple of miles off at that."

Again Amy felt the old sick squeeze of fear inside her. What he said was true. From the top of this, or any other hill, he would be able to see the movement of a fly a great distance away trying to escape; only the fly would really be a man, or perhaps a little girl.

With an effort she blotted the picture from her mind and caught at his sleeve.

"You can get a better view than this," she said. "Further up, by that rock, see? Come on—I'll show you."

And she capered off to the right along the boney ridge like somebody giving way to a fit of high spirits, kicking the snow up in showers ahead of her, while Mick, affected by her exuberance, pranced alongside, tripping over, recovering himself, barking, shaking the white fluff from his muzzle. Mr Nabb trudged morosely in the rear.

"Look at us, Mr Nabb!" she called out, shrilly insistent. "Look at us!"

He looked and looked away again, annoyed by a display of such silliness. But Amy was satisfied: he had been made to notice so that if, in due course, the snow should be found to be trampled here along the ridge he would remember that it had been messed up during that afternoon—not later—by the girl and her dog playing the fool. It was probable even, Amy had reasoned, that remembering this neither he nor the Inspector would bother themselves to go again as far as the rock, but if they did they would still find no tell-tale footprints beyond it. This rock marked the point at which, invisibly, the path that led to Dintirion crossed over the summit. On its downward slope any faint indentations left by the corrugated tin of her toboggan would surely not show enough to catch the attention of pursuers.

Snow, Amy knew, could give away so much, and most of the morning's concentrated thought had been devoted to the particular problem of footprints. They were the great betrayers. Often and often she had studied the marks of a fox or a pheasant or a blackbird or a hare when the creature itself had been gone for hours yet left its movements recorded as clearly as writing on the page of an exercise-book.

Mr Nabb was not inclined to linger. It was higher by the rock and therefore a slightly better point of vantage, but correspondingly more exposed. The air was like ice. He made sure in one glance that there was nothing new to be seen from here and immediately, ignoring Amy, turned back along the ridge. With his hunched and hurried walk, hands in pockets, elbows askew, he looked, thought Amy following behind, like a small black disappointed spider.

They reached the snowmen and as they passed by he let loose an idle swipe at one of them which knocked its head off, and a kick at the other, toppling it. Amy, indignant, cried out in protest but he took no notice; he paid her no attention at all until down in the shed, stamping his feet to get rid of the chunks of snow, he said:

"You're a rum one, you are."

"Me?" she said, startled.

"You—yes! I've had my eye on you and I'll tell you what I think—you're a funny sort of a child and that's a fact."

"Funny?"

"Very funny, I think. Only I don't mean the sort of funny that makes me want to laugh. More like the sort of funny that makes me wonder what's going on."

Amy leant against one of the posts that supported the shed because she felt in need of support herself, suddenly dizzy, as though the root of her breath had been cut away and she was left with only a puff of it in her mouth and no more to come. She feared and hated him: hated because she feared. In that moment of terrible weakness she longed to kill him and longed at the same moment to run away, anywhere, or to burst into tears, or best of all simply to vanish; and longing for all these things did none of them, only said, looking round at him with huge frightened eyes:

"I don't know what you mean, Mr Nabb."

"Oh, you don't, don't you! What about this morning, eh? Not a word to say for yourself—not one word this morning. You couldn't hardly lift your head up, could you? I was watching. And then all of a sudden, what have we got?—talk, talk, talk! Mr Nabb this and Mr Nabb that—why, you even had your old granny guessing—I saw! One minute you're moping around as good as deaf and dumb, and the moment after, what have we got?—all this talk, talk, talk stuff. And making out we was best of friends, and smiles and waves, and jumping up and

K   145

down in the snow like a flea in a fit. Well now, that doesn't make sense to me. That strikes me as very funny, that does. You're a rum one, you are, like I said, and I don't understand what's behind it—but I shall! I'll find out—you wait and see!"

Amy heard herself say, as though the words were spoken by somebody else in a dream:

"I don't understand you either, Mr Nabb. It wasn't very nice of you to go and spoil my snowmen back there. Why did you have to do it?"

"Why did you have to make them?" said he, roughly.

Amy's arms tightened round the post.

"I was playing, that's all."

"Well, all right then, that's what I was doing—playing, same as you."

"Oh, no, you weren't," said Amy. She was trembling all over. "You did it so as to spoil my snowmen, that's why you did it. I think you just like to spoil things."

He took a step towards her. Mick began to growl.

"Never mind what I like," he said in a voice choked by the bitterness of some old resentment. "I'll tell you what I *don't* like and that's children, so you can cut it out, your pretty little angel-on-top-of-the-Christmas-tree act, because it's not going to get you anywhere with me. I know about children, I've had experience. They're crafty, they're cunning. They're always scheming, trying to make a monkey out of you—little devils, they are. I don't like children, or their ways, or anything to do with them."

16. The Inspector
Talks of Roman Geese

Amy found herself alone in the shed. She sank down on the chopping-block and took Mick in her arms.

"Mick!" she said, almost sobbing. "Mick, oh Mick!"—over and over for no reason except simply the comfort of saying the name of something dear to her, something affectionate, while she held him warm and close.

The light was beginning to fade, the whiteness beyond the shed turned bluish, and in the air once again was the vague drifting movement of flakes coming down. So the lull had ended and soon it would be dark, with snow falling, and nothing certain, nothing safe.

"Oh, Mick—if only they'd go away. If only they'd never come."

She got up wearily and pulled a bale of hay to pieces and scattered it at the far end of the shed; whatever happened the sheep had still to be fed and watered. Amy filled two buckets at the tap by the side-kitchen door and poured the water into an old zinc bath they were using as a drinking-trough, for she had decided it was less trouble for her to do this for the ewes than it was trouble for them to have to lick snow.

"Make haste before it freezes," she urged them.

For freezing it was. The icicles hanging down like silver meat skewers from the roof of the shed were glitteringly dry, whereas this morning there had been occasional drips plip-plopping off them. So far their outside tap, heavily lagged with straw and sacking, had not frozen but if it did freeze there was another tap above the sink in the side-kitchen. And as for their actual water-supply, it came from a spring deep underground a little further up the hill and was unfailing, no matter how low the temperature or how dry the season. Winter or summer, they had never wanted for water—never wanted for food either. In all of her short life Amy had never wanted for anything until now. There had been—not perhaps plenty—but always enough; until now. And now for the first time it was not enough to have food and water and clothes and a bed and a good warm fire, and Mick and her grandmother, and sticks to chop and chickens to feed. She was afraid; and fear destroyed the security of her little world, destroyed the sufficiency of it. Because all that she had was no longer safe, it counted for nothing.

She opened the side-kitchen door and Mick, glad to be home, rushed inside.

"Is that you, Amy?" called Mrs Bowen.

"Yes, Granny."

"I'll make the tea then."

But Amy had still another task to do before she took off her Wellingtons and her coat. The door through to the front-kitchen was shut. Mr Nabb was certainly on the other side of it, but where? Close to it?—just about to open it? Or over by the fire? She had to know. She looked in and there he was, humped up again on the chest at the far side of the room, tying knots in his piece of string. He never even looked at her. Mrs Bowen was lighting the lamp.

"I shan't be long, Granny. I've done the ewes but I haven't shut the chickens in yet. Have you got enough sticks for morning?"

"You might as well fetch in a few more when you come."

Amy closed the door quickly and a second later was lifting the heavy jar of pickles off the shelf and standing it on the floor. It was essential to hide the letter in another place, for once she had gone to bed the side-kitchen was going to be inaccessible to her.

When she raised the sheet of newspaper and found the letter lying where she had hidden it the day before, she felt a curious thrill of discovery, even though she had known it must still be there. She pushed it into the front of her coat. The question that had occupied her thoughts a good deal that morning was in what new place to conceal the letter until she was ready to start out on her journey. It had to be somewhere from which she could retrieve it easily, yet somewhere absolutely safe. Even for those few hours she dared not keep it in her bedroom, not with Mr Nabb forever on the prowl, nosing into everything. Then she had had what had seemed at the time to be a flash of inspiration: she would hide the letter in a nesting-box in the hen-house. No one would think of looking there!

But she had reckoned without the dislike of all hens for being disturbed. They were accustomed to Amy's regular visit at nightfall to push across the slide of their own small entry and turn the catch on it; but they were not accustomed, once they had roosted, to having the main door of the hen-house swing wide open, and when it happened now it had a most unsettling effect upon them.

They began to cluck and ruffle their feathers in the dim light. One hen fluttered down from the left-hand perch and stepped jerkily out on to the gang-plank. Amy shooed her back. The hen tried to dodge her way out again and when Amy again prevented her the general agitation and clucking increased. Feeling about a little desperately for the nearest nesting-box Amy put her hand directly on to a sitting hen. There was a loud squawk and then pandemonium as the rest of the hens began to flap and squawk as well, and to topple each other off the perches. With deep dismay Amy realized that hiding the letter in the hen-house was another one of her bad ideas. It would never do. If they made only half as much noise as this when she came to fetch the letter she would be utterly betrayed.

"Oh, you are such stupid creatures," she muttered. "Why can't you have some sense?"

"I hope they've provided plenty of eggs for my breakfast," said a voice behind her pleasantly.

Amy let go of the letter, dropping it on to a bunch of indignant feathers, and whirled round. There he was—Vigers, the tigerman, Inspector Catcher, Mr Brilliant—leaning his skis up against the wall beside the side-kitchen door, smiling at her. She caught the gleam of his teeth in the dusk.

"I never heard you come," she stammered.

"I'm not surprised, with all that hullabaloo going on. What happened?—why are they so upset?"

She shook her head, dumbly.

"Perhaps there's a fox about," he suggested. "One should never under-estimate the instinct for danger that birds and animals have. The Romans put it to good use—they guarded their citadel with flocks of geese. If anyone came creeping up to the walls at night the geese would start cackling, and then of course the alarm was raised. I've always thought that was a very ingenious idea. What—weren't there any eggs at all?" he added, seeing her empty hands.

"Oh, yes—I fetched them in before. It was just this one old hen—she was still sitting—I thought she might have laid by now. She hasn't though," said Amy, shutting the door with such a thump the hens protested again. "Did you—did you find—anything?"

"Not today," said Inspector Catcher, and he held open the side-kitchen door for Amy to precede him.

"I've some sticks to get yet," she mumbled. "You go on in—Granny made the tea a while back. I shan't be many minutes, tell her."

150

The very moment he was out of sight she snatched open the hen-house door and her hand was actually on the letter when she heard an appalling rumpus break out in the side-kitchen—Mick's frantic barking, some kind of a crash, and angry shouting.

Mick! She had forgotten that Mick was in the side-kitchen!

With the speed of despair Amy slammed the hen-house door shut and, stooping, managed to tilt the great chopping-block just enough off the ground to be able to push the letter underneath. In such a hurry it was the best she could think of doing. Then she sprang for the side-kitchen door, and as she wrenched it open the surprised and questioning faces of Mrs Bowen and Mr Nabb appeared in the doorway opposite.

Inspector Catcher held Mick suspended at arm's length. Mick had stopped barking. He had almost stopped breathing as well, so tight were the fingers that gripped him by the scruff of the neck. His jaws were gaping stiffly, his eyes bulged, his hind-quarters wriggled spasmodically.

"Mick!" screamed Amy.

Inspector Catcher tossed the dog towards her like a rag. Mick tried to double back at once, but Amy grabbed and held him.

"However did those pickles come to be on the floor?" cried Mrs Bowen, her eyes on the broken jar and spreading mess.

"I put them there," said Amy, and the tears began to roll down her cheeks. "For tea, Granny—I thought we could have them for tea. I forgot to bring them in, though—it was my fault —I forgot."

Mrs Bowen knelt down on the stone flags and embraced both dog and child together.

"There now, Amy—it's all right. Mick's fine—see! He's not been harmed."

"If that dog ever comes near me again," said Inspector Catcher, wiping his hands fastidiously on a silk handkerchief, "I shall kill him. So if you want to preserve your pet you'd better make sure he keeps away from me."

Some hours later Amy sat on her grandmother's bed, the ironing-blanket round her shoulders, and watched while the old woman combed and plaited her grey hair. Mrs Bowen's candlestick stood on the chest-of-drawers and was reflected in the small square swing mirror. Her face was reflected mistily beside it. Amy, wriggling her toes to keep off the cold, regarded this familiar and peaceful picture with a yearning she was not able to express to her grandmother. They had been discussing the day's events, Amy with some evasion here and there.

"It can't go on for ever, Amy—that's the way I look at it," said Mrs Bowen. She reached for a piece of white tape, twisted it deftly round the end of a pigtail and tied it in a bow. "There's bound to come a thaw, sooner or later—or they'll tire of being here—or we'll run out of food, even. I wouldn't mind to go hungry if it only got rid of them."

"There may not come a thaw for days and days—it's freezing tonight as hard as ever, and look what the forecast said—getting worse."

The flurry of snow at tea-time had turned out to be no more than a passing shower. When Amy had let Mick out for his last run the stars were glitteringly bright in a vast unclouded black sky, and the air was so icy it hurt her to breathe it and she had had to cover her mouth and nose with a gloved hand. But at that rigorous moment all the doubts that had nagged at her courage since early afternoon suddenly vanished. She was staring at the Inspector's skis, propped up against the wall. Here was Bartolomeo's warning! Better than snowmen; better indeed, more explicit, than anything she could have planned, and provided by the Inspector himself. Her spirits had lifted then on the wings of a wild conviction: luck must be on her side, and no matter what mistakes she made, what miscalculations, luck would see her through.

Would it, she wondered now, do more than see just her

through? How about those she left behind? Were they going to need luck as well, or would care be enough?

"Granny—you'll watch out for Mick, won't you? He meant what he said, that man, I'm sure he did. He'd *like* to kill him."

Mrs Bowen, holding her second pigtail in both hands, leant forward to peer in the glass at Amy and not getting a clear enough sight of her there, turned round to stare across the shadowy candlelit room.

"What do you mean by that, Amy—*me* watch out for Mick? Of course I do, when he's by me—but he's mostly with you, not me."

"I know he is—only sometimes perhaps—well, I might be outside, mightn't I?—and Mick might be inside. What I mean is—you won't forget to watch out for him, will you? I think he'd better stop in my bedroom."

"Why, yes—maybe that might be best," said Mrs Bowen uncertainly. She turned back to the chest-of-drawers, rapidly tied the remaining pigtail, and then came and sat down on the bed beside Amy. "You've had something on your mind all day—I've known it well enough. That nonsense you were talking of—going downstream to the village—you can't surely be thinking of that still? You must know as well as I do, Amy, it would be madness for you to try, even."

"I don't mean to try, Granny—don't worry. I only said it for —for something to say." Amy's voice faltered a little and she crossed her fingers under the ironing-blanket. She wanted to get her grandmother away from this unsafe subject and so she hurried on: "Do you know what I've been thinking, Granny? I think they're both of them cruel. One of them's clever and cruel, and the other one's stupid and cruel, and I don't know which sort of cruel is the worst, do you?"

"Ah! It's a poor job either way," said Mrs Bowen. "What should make people want to hurt others, let alone to kill them— that's a mystery I've never been able to fathom. But it's my belief it's catching, Amy, same as the measles. It could be they had those who were cruel to them once and they merely took the infection. If the truth were known, we might even find it in our hearts to feel sorry for them."

Amy considered this.

"Maybe a bit for Mr Nabb," she said at last, remembering the rage in his voice when he had declared that children were devils, always trying to make a monkey out of you. Supposing it were true that years and years ago, in school perhaps, he had been made miserable, tormented, jeered at—why then she might find it in her heart to understand, at least a little, why hate had lodged in his, and to pity him for it.

"But I'd never feel sorry for that other one," she said. "I couldn't, no matter how hard I tried. Did you see his face when he had Mick by the neck? He was smiling, Granny. He's terrible!"

17. The Small West Window

Amy had intended to stay awake. She waited until she judged that her grandmother would have fallen asleep and then she dressed herself again and sat on the floor with an arm round Mick and her back against the iron framework at the foot of the bed.

Her legs were encased in the sleeves of her spare brown jersey which she had put on upside-down and fastened tight round her waist with a safety-pin; her usual leggings, being scarlet, were out of the question. She had thought at first that her legs would have to do without any extra covering—it was better to be cold than to be seen; but then she thought that if her legs got too cold they might not be able to move as fast, so she improvised trousers out of the brown jersey. Her scarlet scarf had been traded earlier on for her grandmother's scarf, the colouring of which was more subdued. Amy had considered every detail in advance; or so she hoped and believed. And every eventuality that it was possible to prepare for, she had prepared for. All she could do now was to get her escape-line ready, and then wait until the right time came for her to go. Three o'clock in the morning was the right time, she had decided. People were always asleep then, and yet it was not so very much before dawn; the worst of the night would be over.

It was seven days past full moon, a piece of information supplied by the calendar in the front-kitchen which she had discreetly consulted. Amy felt this to be propitious: a waning moon, rising late, would suit her very well. Although even starlight without a moon would really be bright enough, she told herself optimistically; the only real essentials were that the snow should hold off and the sky remain clear, and for these conditions Amy had no guarantee.

There were other uncertainties too. For instance, she was not positive how much time it would take her to lay a false trail. She planned to go right down to the frozen stream and back again, treading in her own footsteps on the return journey and trusting her pursuers would be in enough of a hurry to skim past the single set of prints without inspecting them very closely. A proper false trail would have necessitated walking backwards on the return journey, and the distance was too great for this, and time was too short. The whole manoeuvre, allowing for limited visibility, was going to take about three-quarters of an hour, she had reckoned. Secretly Amy was worried by a lurking suspicion that it might take her much longer, and might also exhaust her before she had even started on the real journey over the top.

Her most serious handicap was to have no easy means of knowing the time. She had racked her brains to think of a plausible excuse for borrowing her grandmother's bedside clock, but without success. Mrs Bowen would have stared at Amy, her eyes as sharp as needles: "Borrow my clock?" Regretfully Amy had come to the conclusion that she might just as well tell her grandmother everything as ask to borrow her clock. Her only alternative was the grandfather-clock in the front-kitchen whose soft but resonant strike she could hear when she was lying flat on the floor with her ear against the boards and concentrating. But it was too soon for listening yet. They were still talking down below.

She had brought a bunch of hairy binder-twine upstairs with her when she came to bed, having failed in an attempt to make off with the new clothes-line. Mrs Bowen had seen her.

"Whatever are you doing with that clothes-line, Amy?"

Mr Nabb was watching too.

"Well, I've got to have something for tying Mick up with. I used my stockings last night," she added truthfully, "and I couldn't hardly get the knots undone this morning."

"But you don't need a whole clothes-line for tying Mick, and I certainly don't intend for you to cut a piece off—not off that good line. Why don't you take a few bits of the binder-twine that was round the bales? There's plenty lying about in the shed."

So Amy had to be content with binder-twine, although it was not as strong as a clothes-line or nearly as comfortable for the hands. Sitting cross-legged on her bedroom floor and yawning, she began to unravel the bundle and to knot the pieces together so as to make a single length. When she had finished she tied one end of it to the bar at the foot of her bed.

It was much too short.

Amy regarded with dismay the line that was meant to dangle down over the roof of the shed. It reached as far as the window and not an inch further. If only her bed had been close to the wall instead of clear out in the middle of the room then the line would have been long enough, but it was too late to think of trundling her bed about now—the whole household would be aroused.

Holding her candle high Amy looked round the small bare room in search of inspiration. Her eye fell on the pair of stockings that tied Mick to the bed-post. She could lengthen the twine with her stockings, and she could tie Mick up with her patent-leather belt instead. But when this change-over had been made, and Mick attached by Amy's belt to the leg of the bed, and Amy's stockings added to the twine, still her home-made line was not as long as it needed to be, and what more could she use? She did have a third pair of stockings, but they were airing on the string above the range in the front-kitchen. There was nothing else that she could think of. And then, miraculously, her exploring fingers came upon last year's outgrown skipping-rope, lying dusty and forgotten underneath the chest-of-drawers. It was so exactly what she wanted that her confidence returned with a rush, and she felt as she had felt in the shed earlier that evening when she saw Inspector Catcher's explanatory skis leaning up against the cottage wall: luck must be on her side!

With the skipping-rope knotted to the toe of the second stocking the line was fully long enough and Amy, satisfied, coiled the strange conglomeration that composed it on her bed and sat down again by Mick to wait.

How much time had passed since she came upstairs? It seemed like hours. She stretched herself on the rag-rug with her ear to the boards, and listened. It must be late: the sound of talking had ceased. Then she heard the grandfather-clock strike a single blurred note. One! Could it really be one o'clock? If it were, she had only to stay awake for two more hours. On the other hand it might have been striking half past anything. She must make quite sure not to miss how many times it struck after another half-hour.

But suppose when it struck again it was only once? That would mean that the last time had been half past twelve, or one o'clock—either. Which? Three ones in a row. Three ones were three—three o'clock? She struggled to sit up but realized then that she had been making a muddle in her head. One strike—it had struck once. How cold it was! She reached up a hand vaguely and pulled the unfinished patchwork quilt down on top of the ironing-blanket, forgetting her home-made line, which came with it. What was the thing that hit her head? A skipping-rope handle? How funny! And how hard her bed had become! No, of course, it was not her bed—she was on the floor. She was there so as to listen. It was very important for her to listen and count. She must listen and count. Listen. And count. But when the grandfather-clock struck eleven times Amy heard nothing at all.

She awoke feeling cramped and uncomfortable and with an overpowering sensation of having done something wrong. Wrong ? What had she done ? And then she knew: she had fallen asleep, and now she had no idea of the time. Her candle had gone out. It must have been burning for hours. Amy crawled across the floor on hands and knees to the chest-of-drawers, raised herself, groped for the candlestick, found the box of matches, struck a match and examined what was left of her candle. The wick had burnt down almost to its root and then drowned in hot melted wax which had set again, hard and white, over it. With her finger-nail she prised the little blackened fragment of wick upright out of the wax and lit it, using another match. If it stayed alight for only a few minutes more it would be enough.

She had to hurry and yet, hurrying, she had to make no noise at all. Amy lifted the wooden chair beside her bed, taking great care not to scrape it, carried it across the room on tiptoe and set it down beneath the west window.

There were two windows in her bedroom. The bigger one faced east. It came so low and the wall was so thick that the ledge formed a natural seat and here Amy used sometimes in warmer weather to station herself when day was over and her jobs all done, like someone on the look-out, gazing at the empty land-scape beyond with a faint indefinable ache of longing for she never quite knew what.

The window in the west wall was only a quarter the size, not much more than a peephole, but big enough to let in a shaft of golden evening light at sunset and to let out now—so Amy hoped—a smallish girl. It was situated directly over the shed-roof, and because of the slope of the hillside, roof and ground were closer together at this end of the cottage than at the other end, which would lessen the final drop.

Amy stood on the chair and cautiously pushed the little

window open. Immediately a rush of air seemed to smite her face like a blow. She was shocked. Was it really so dreadfully cold outside? Then Mick whined. She turned and looked down at him. There he sat, stiffly expectant, ears cocked, waiting for the reassurance that she was not going to leave him behind. He had been watching all of her movements intently, treading his front paws up and down whenever anxiety became too much for him. Now he whined. Amy climbed off the chair and hugged him. She said in his ear:

"You've got to stay, Mick—you've got to look after Granny. Lie down, then—wait, boy!"

Poor Mick—it was hard for him. But he lay down when Amy told him to, and rested his head on his paws: he would wait.

She took the ironing-blanket and climbing on the chair again pushed it through the window. With age, and countless scorchings and scrubbings, this blanket had become a deep creamy-yellowy colour, the colour of fleece, and the thought had occurred to Amy that if she were to wrap it round her shoulders she might from a distance be mistaken for a harmless old sheep. It would help to keep her warm as well. The ironing-blanket, Amy considered, was one of her best ideas.

Now all that remained was to fetch her home-made line, fling it out of the window after the blanket and follow both herself. But as she got off the chair her regenerated candle gave a final guttering flicker and expired. She had to move forward in what seemed by contrast to be total darkness. Reaching the bed she felt about with blind patting movements for her line. She had coiled it all ready on the bed; she could remember doing it. Then her toe kicked against one of the skipping-rope handles and it rolled, bumpety-bump, across the floorboards.

Amy stood perfectly still.

Several moments passed. When there was no indication of anyone, either below or in the bedroom next door, having been disturbed, she forced herself to take courage. Stooping down she got hold of both skipping-rope handles and grasping them tightly stepped back towards the window. At her third step she collided with the chair.

This time they must have heard! Sick with fear, she waited. But again there was silence; only silence.

Amy counted fifteen thumps of her heart and then she mounted the chair for the last time and threw her line out of the window. The room, when she turned for a farewell glimpse of Mick, was a pool of shadows and he was lost to her. What she did notice, now that the candle had gone out, was the big pale square in the wall opposite. It was the window that looked east. Was it starlight or moonrise that made it so pale, so luminous? Or was it the dawn?

The dawn? Could it be as late as that? Amy stared unbelievingly at the bland grey patch facing her. If it was the dawn she had already left it too late. Too late! But she *had* to go! It *had* to be not the dawn, not too late!

She turned and gripped the window-ledge, took a breath and sprang. The chair-legs grated as she sprang but she was in no position now to pause and listen for what might be the consequences. She was scrabbling against the wall, heaving and wriggling to scrape herself on to the window-ledge. And because the window-ledge when she got there was too narrow for her to be able to twist herself round, Amy emerged from the little west window in the only way she could: diving out, head-first; and at once the old ironing-blanket, receiving her weight, began to move off like a magic carpet. She grabbed for her line, but the roof was too slippery. The stockings slid uselessly through her fingers, and the knob of the skipping-rope handle broke her grasp. Borne swiftly down on the ironing-blanket she reached the edge of the roof where, unable to stop herself, still head-first, over she went.

It was the bale of hay she had earlier put for a step that cushioned her fall and although she was scratched and shaken, she was not hurt. The sheep were startled. She could hear them shifting about on the other side of their enclosure. Amy picked herself up. It was snowing. Soft flakes blew against her face and hands and the dim light, she perceived, was indeed the light of early morning. There was no time to lose. Certainly there was no time for her to trudge all the way down to the stream and back again, laying a false trail.

She knelt and pulled her coat from underneath the hen-house where she had stowed it last night when she let Mick out. Wrapped inside were her gloves and her Wellingtons and Mrs Bowen's scarf. She crammed the clothes on, buttons shoved through the wrong button-holes, gloves on the wrong hands. In the fright of her fall she had scarcely noticed the cold but her teeth were chattering and when she retrieved the letter from beneath the chopping-block, cold and haste and fright and wrong-way-round gloves all combined to make her clumsy so that she allowed the great chunk of wood to fall back on her toes. The pain was excruciating. Somehow she managed not to cry out, only gave a muffled groan. But there was no time to spare for nursing injuries. Amy pushed the letter down inside the neck of her jersey, thinking to herself that it was less likely to get wet there than in a pocket, and so, ready at last, hobbled out on to the hillside.

Dawn was coming and yet when she looked up she could see nothing. Instead of a lightening sky above her head there was a darkness, a void, and the snowflakes that she felt on her cheeks came from nowhere, touched her, vanished. But when she looked at the ground she saw it glimmering faintly all about her, and across this glimmering unmarked snow she stamped a trail of deep clearly defined footprints that curved away downhill until they merged with the tracks made by the coming and going of the Inspector and Mr Nabb. Further than this she dared not go: time was too short. She could only hope that if her footsteps indicated plainly enough at the start which way she had gone, it would simply be assumed that from there on down to the stream her trail was indistinguishably mingled with the general disorder.

Then quite suddenly she was in a fever, a frenzy of impatience to get away from the cottage, right away from doors and windows. The snow and the light were increasing together. She should have been far from here by now, out of sight, out of reach. Panicking, she floundered back uphill in the tracks that had been made last night by Inspector Catcher returning from his hunt, and round the corner of the cottage as he had come when he had so dreadfully startled her, and into the shed.

Her corrugated tin toboggan was propped ready. She seized hold of it, snatched up the old ironing-blanket, and without wasting another moment set off as fast as she could go on the much-trodden north-westerly track to the top of the hill. And when she reached the top, quite breathless, already beginning to sweat, she swerved instantly to the right, not pausing, and kept on along the ridge, bent low, straining to see, stumbling as she went. Twice she called out words of encouragement to Mick before remembering that she was alone.

The rock was her goal and when she arrived there she did allow herself to stop for a moment and then her heart lifted in triumph: she had done everything wrong—overslept, fallen headlong—but in spite of all her mistakes here she was standing on the Dintirion path, and down in the cottage below still nobody stirred, nobody knew she had gone.

Amy dropped the blanket in a heap on the corrugated tin, settled herself on top of it, dug in her heels once, and was off.

18. Quite Alone

It was a gentle slope at first. She glided rather than flew and there was no need to use her heels either to accelerate or to slow herself. The snow that had thickened so ominously when she was toiling up the hill had suddenly ceased. Probably it had been the fringe of a storm passing further north. Whatever the reason, Amy was thankful—visibility was bad enough without snow to make it worse. She leaned forward, trying to distinguish landmarks ahead, prepared to change direction at any moment. But it seemed almost as though her care was unnecessary, as though the tin toboggan knew its own way. It moved down the invisible track like an engine running on lines, quite slowly, slow enough at one point to come sedately to a halt, whereupon Amy dug in her heels and they were off again.

She was surprised at how easy it was after all, much easier than she had expected, and dreamily slithering past one familiar rock after another she failed to notice her toboggan gathering speed. But the whizzing noise of metal on snow and the coldness blowing sharper in her face alerted her: she was going too fast. Fully awake, she jammed her heels down and the toboggan stopped. Amy sat and considered what came next.

Until now the path had traversed the broad open flank of the hill, so broad and flat and high and open that almost as much snow as fell was swept up again by the wind and taken on. But from here the ground fell more and more steeply, and the

164

path fell steeply with it, dropping down towards the verge of Billy Dodd's Dingle, the deep cleft or gorge—so gently named, so savage in fact—that every year claimed its toll of unwary sheep. At the bottom of the gorge, sunk between nearly vertical cliffs of scree, there trickled in sunnier weather a thread of bright spring water, the same small stream that lower down passed close to Tyler's Place and accounted for its real name, Cilnant.

The head of the Dingle was formed by a ridge, high and narrow, that ran between two great neighbouring hills and joined them together in a sort of everlasting partnership. This natural causeway carried the path over from one hill to the next, and on the further slopes of the further hill, Cader Ddu, lay Dintirion, the Protheroes' farm which had once belonged to Amy's father and before him to her grandfather, and to Bowens before him for as long as and longer than anyone could remember.

Sitting there astride her toboggan Amy was not really considering what lay ahead of her. She knew well enough what lay ahead of her; she was trying to nerve herself to face it. If she could only get to Cader Ddu then endurance, she believed, would take her the rest of the way—just simply endurance—but what she needed now was courage. From where she sat to where it crossed the head of the Dingle the path became increasingly dangerous, drawing ever closer and closer to the cliff's edge until, for the last twenty-five yards, it skirted along the extreme brink, a distance Amy had already resolved she would cover on foot. Now she decided that it would be prudent to negotiate the few yards immediately in front of her on foot as well. Here the path fell away with the abrupt steepness of a ladder to a lower level where it made another right-angled turn and then resumed its more gradual descent.

Step by step, down she went, letting the toboggan slither in front and holding on to its string. With every passing minute the sky grew lighter. She looked over her shoulder: nobody there. But with every passing minute the likelihood of someone appearing increased, and step by step was a terribly slow way to escape in daylight in broad view. Trying to hasten she slipped and nearly let go of the string. She must be more careful. It was awkward just here, with no landmarks to show her the way; she had to rely on her memory and blamed herself for not having thought of bringing a stick—with a stick she could have probed the snow and found out where the ground was stony and safe and where bilberry-bushes and heather lay hidden beneath the smooth surface.

All at once her Wellington boot went in too deeply. She lost her balance and fell sprawling, snow in her mouth, inside the neck of her coat, up her sleeves, everywhere. In a panic she strove to recover her footing. How easy it was after all to go wrong, for the path itself was her only guide and her only guide was one she could not see.

Suddenly Amy was very frightened. She wanted to cry. She wanted someone to be with her, to take her hand and tell her what to do, someone to help her. There was no one. The great stillness surrounding her seemed to say: you are quite alone. And even as she stood up, swaying to keep her foothold, per-plexed and afraid, her teeth chattering, her breath coming in sobs, day drew on. The sky had paled to grey and now, raising her head, she saw the grey was laced with pink. She should have been on the other side of the further mountain when the sun rose and instead she was here, not even half-way to the end of her journey, with the worst still to come. Desperation brought calmness. As a flurry of wind subsides, her fear fell. She must get on—that was all there was to it: *must*!

The path had gone down short and sharp, like a ladder, and then turned away at right angles. Amy, having reached the bottom of the ladder, had descended one step further: this was her mistake. She realized it now and flung herself forward, attempting to scramble back to the higher ground. But it was slippery and there was no branch or root for her to catch hold of. Try as she might she could not haul herself up until she had the idea of turning her toboggan over and thumping it down hard enough for the curved end of the tin to sink into the snow like an anchor. With something to grip she managed then to wriggle herself, inch by inch, on to the level above.

At once, not pausing for so much as a sigh of relief, she stood the toboggan on end and banged it all over with the flat of her hand to make the snow fall off. Then she wrapped the ironing-blanket round her shoulders; the light was strengthening every moment and she felt the need of some kind of protective colouring. Also she was shivering. The snow that had got down inside the neck of her coat had melted, and so had the snow up her sleeves and in her boots. Still, it was no use minding about being wet. Amy glanced ahead once briefly to note the course she must take and then resolutely sat herself down on the corrugated tin, stuck both her heels well out ready for braking or steering, and again set off.

The path which now veered along the side of the hill was normally about six or eight feet wide but the angle had been so filled in by snow that only a narrow strip of it was left, a just visible ledge in an otherwise smooth white surface. The outside edge of the strip was uncertain. Amy went very carefully, riding whenever she could and occasionally walking when she had to, so absorbed in her task of navigation that she presently forgot her wet and cold condition and almost, but never quite, the dangers of pursuit. The further she went the more care was needed for as she drew nearer to the head of the Dingle so was she also drawing nearer to the cliff-edge that marked the side of it. Soon she meant to get off the toboggan altogether and depend on her legs. Not yet, though: the path rounded a bluff and swooped ahead of her, gently down and gently up again, in a switchback that was irresistible. Amy pulled in her heels and let the toboggan go.

Almost at the bottom of the downward swoop it hit a bump, a concealed rock, which, like a spirited pony meeting with the challenge of an unexpected fence, it leapt clean over. It leapt the rock successfully, but the sudden jolt had wrenched it round. Still at the same hectic speed it shot off the path, and the spirited pony had become a runaway, out of control, plunging straight down the side of the hill towards the Dingle.

Amy had only a few seconds in which to brake, or to turn the toboggan, or to throw herself off it: something—anything! But she had been taken completely by surprise. She tried to put out her heels and they were tangled in the tow-rope. The ironing-blanket swaddled her limbs, encumbered her. And then it was too late. At the very edge of the gully, as it might be at the edge of life, she screamed, or cried out, some sound of anguished terror escaping her before there was another more violent concussion, followed by an extraordinary bodiless sensation of tumbling, sliding, falling, down and down.

Everything stopped. Everything was still. Amy thought that if she were to stay quite still as well and keep her eyes closed nothing else would happen. All she wanted was for nothing to happen, ever again. And so she remained, unmoving; and nothing did happen.

It was the persistence of a sweet thin chirping that eventually made her open her eyes. There in a bush close by a small brown bird was busily hopping to and fro amongst the maze of brown twigs. Amy, seeing it, felt a pang of intense pleasure: so she did have company after all. The little creature seemed to be quite at home in its bush. It sprang about, cocking its head and darting its beak and behaving as unconcernedly as though she were not there. Amy lay passive and watched it. Then almost reluctantly she allowed her gaze to go past the bird and to travel up, up, following a trail of broken snow that led from herself to the lip of the gorge above. And there she saw, sil-houetted on the skyline, a shape that puzzled her, a sort of

triangle. No—it was a rectangle, only it was leaning over sideways with one sharp corner at the top. All at once she realized
that it was her toboggan, and that it must have struck an even
larger boulder at the very edge of the Dingle and she been
catapulted forward with the toboggan remaining erect like a
flag for all to see.

Amy wondered hazily how long she had been here. It might
have been hours, or not more than a few minutes. She knew she
could never climb up the way she had come down. Besides being
almost as steep as a wall there was no foothold underneath the
snow, nothing to grasp, only a loose sliding shale, impossible to
ascend even in summer. And yet she ought to try. She ought to
move; some voice inside her told her so. And another voice
answered it drowsily: later on—soon—not just yet. And so she
lay there and might have continued to lie, like a sheep that had
fallen into a drift or a cranny, never to be recovered, only that
presently she heard the sounds of someone approaching.

Someone was approaching in haste down the Dingle, sliding,
boots scraping on rock. Amy was not afraid: she knew who it
was. And when Bartolomeo came round a corner and found her
lying in the snow propped on an elbow, just as she had found
him propped in the murky shades of Tyler's Place, she smiled at
him gladly but quite without surprise, still so dazed that she had
an impression their meeting had been arranged—only she had
forgotten; but here he was!

Bartolomeo was panting when he reached her. He wasted no
time on any attempt at a greeting, but instantly lifted Amy up
and set her on her feet as though she had been a doll that had
toppled over. Then he took hold of each of her legs in turn and
bent them at the knee and ankle; he bent her arms at the
elbow; he took off her gloves and rubbed her shoulders; he put
his huge hand on top of her head and turned it like a knob from
side to side, all the while muttering to himself in his own strange
language. Finally, having made sure that she was in full working

order he spread his hand in the small of her back and pushed her ahead of him up the Dingle.

Amy had been numbed, mind and body. With the return of her senses came also the return of fear. Every hasty movement Bartolomeo made, every gasping breath of his, told her they were in danger, they must hurry—faster! And desperately she did her best to obey him. But attempting to cover this ground fast when to cover it at all would have been hard enough, was a kind of a nightmare. Not much snow had penetrated to the bottom of the gully but the bed of the stream was narrow and strewn with rocks and every rock had a coating of what was worse than snow, more slippery: ice. Everything was frozen. Whatever they touched with hand or foot seemed to refuse them help. Each boulder Amy succeeded in scrambling round or over was an enemy conquered, but always there was another in her way, and after that another. She felt Bartolomeo's hand behind her, steadying her, pressing her on, and sometimes with one sweep of his arm he lifted her clear over an obstacle. Twice she looked round at him wanting to rest for a moment or so, but when she saw with what savage expectancy his gaze was directed upwards at the cold empty skyline above them she did not dare to stop.

Presently she found that the ground was again covered in snow, not ice, and had tilted so that she was mounting on hands and knees. Then she did pause and raising her head saw they had reached the end of the Dingle and were climbing towards the top of the causeway that joined the two hills. A set of footmarks zig-zagged up from bush to boulder, and these they appeared to be following; but Amy also noticed that at a little distance apart from the footmarks the snow had been churned violently in a straight line from top to bottom as though some heavy object had come hurtling down at full speed. She was still confused and the significance of it eluded her then. It was only later she realized that the heavy object had been

Bartolomeo and that he must indeed have descended with no consideration whatever for the safest, only for the quickest route.

Surprisingly enough it was less difficult getting out of the Dingle than making their way along the bottom of it. At this end, in contrast to the cliffs of shale on either side, there were roots and stems to cling to and the rocks were kinder now and gave them footholds and handholds. Sometimes Bartolomeo helped her on with a mighty shove from below; sometimes he climbed ahead and yanked her up to him. But he would not let her stop, not for even half a minute. She was winded, sweating, her breath came in sobs, her legs ached, her arms had no strength in them, but still he urged her on, and forced her on, and thrust and dragged her on; and she knew that every yard or so he turned his head to look back at the vacant rim of Billy Dodd's Dingle with which they were gradually drawing level. And if all of a sudden the edge of the cliff should not be vacant but have on it a figure, she knew what that figure, looking the other way, would see: two flies, a big and a little one, crawling slowly in full view up a white-washed wall.

She stumbled forward: they had reached the top and stood on the rocky ridge that joined the two hills. Here there was no depth of snow, for the wind picked it off as a bird of prey picks flesh from a carcase leaving only bones. With his arm supporting her, almost carrying her, Bartolomeo made her run.

Then they were climbing again. Amy by now was so exhausted she followed Bartolomeo mechanically, plodding in and out of his footsteps while he, with a grip on her wrist, tugged her unremittingly along behind him. They were on the path, that was certain: the ground underfoot was firm as a road, and the snow reached no higher than half-way up her boots. Bartolomeo had found it. Bartolomeo would make sure they kept to it. There was nothing for her to bother about. All she had to do was to follow Bartolomeo; and somehow, head down, doggedly, on and on, Amy followed him.

When at last they stopped she saw it was where the foot-prints, that had all the while been going ahead and guiding them, stopped as well. Two long poles cut from saplings lay askew on the ground as though tossed there in haste. Amy turned. Below and away to the left, made small by distance, was that mute signal of disaster, her upstanding toboggan—and a whole sequence of events flashed suddenly clear into her mind: Bartolomeo cutting himself these ash-poles and setting off along Billy Dodd's Dingle in the precarious safety of near-darkness; Bartolomeo scaling the end escarpment, prodding and probing the snow with his two poles to find a pathway up the side of the hill until at this point he must have halted and turned, as she had just done, no doubt meaning to scan the landscape for followers and instead seeing as he turned an extraordinary object shoot into view—for whatever could she have looked like so far off, huddled low and wrapped in the ironing-blanket? Perhaps it was only when her toboggan struck a boulder and she was thrown forward to disappear over the edge of the cliff that he had understood what and who it was. Perhaps her cry of terror had reached him faintly. And he had instantly flung down his poles, flinging away his own desperate advantage with them, so as to come to her aid. She saw it all and was overcome by horror of what she had done to him.

"A-mee! A-mee!"

He was calling to her urgently to follow. For while she stood lost in retrospect, he had already picked up his poles and was forging ahead, jabbing the snow as he went to make sure of planting his foot at each step on solid ground. Amy had to struggle after him as best she could, unaided; but it was not for long. A few yards more and they had passed beyond an out-cropping of rock and were screened at last from the view of any possible pursuers. At last! Amy saw Bartolomeo lean forward over the poles with bowed head like someone achieving the winning-post in a race almost too hard.

On they went. They were not climbing now and so it was easier. The track curled round horizontally below the summit of Cader Ddu until, arriving on the further side of the hill, it began to descend the more graduated slope in leisurely bends, its route defined by thorn-bushes and sloe-bushes and by intermittent trees, mountain-ash and oak, which altogether gave the impression of a ragged sort of hedge offering, as well as guidance, a certain amount of protection. On this side the ground as it fell spread out in huge natural terraces, presently portioned into fields, and on one of these terraces about three-quarters of the way down was a big cluster of trees, dark against the snow, with a jumble of grey stone buildings set in amongst them. From somewhere out of the centre of trees and buildings there rose a column of smoke.

"That's Dintirion!" cried Amy, breaking into a stumbling run to overtake Bartolomeo. She seized hold of his arm. "That's the Protheroes' place, Bartolomeo—see!" She had forgotten he spoke a different language, but her triumphantly outflung pointing hand and the gladness in her voice needed no translation.

Dintirion looked wonderfully close. It seemed to be only a step away although, with the windings of the path, there was still a considerable distance to go. Their breath accumulated in a steamy cloud around their heads as they stood staring towards it with the eagerness of pilgrims sighting Mecca, the holy city.

Then Bartolomeo turned his back on their goal and gripped Amy tight by the shoulders. He was speaking to her earnestly, but she was too tired to understand. Like a match struck in a wind her last spark of energy had flared up in the joy of seeing Dintirion, and gone out. If he would only let her sit down she felt she might be able to listen better. But Bartolomeo held her upright on her crumbling legs and shook her gently, insistently, to *make* her listen, *make* her understand. His face was close to hers, the face that had once so terrified her. Now she scarcely noticed the black and filthy bristle covering it, seeing instead how deeply his eyes were sunk in under the overhanging brows, how bloodshot they were and how the skin surrounding them had a discoloured bruised appearance. He was ill, hungry, exhausted. Amy, for his sake, made a great effort.

"Gra-nee?" That was what he was saying. He was questioning her, wanting to know where her grandmother was. "Granee? Gra-nee?"

Why, she was at home of course. Where else would she be? And Amy waved her arm vaguely back in the direction from which they had come. But still Bartolomeo claimed her attention. He held up two of his fingers; he aimed an imaginary gun; he skated his feet on imaginary skis. Amy answered him with the same gesture as before. They were back there too, those men with guns and skis, at home in the cottage with her grandmother. Yes, yes, she nodded, gesticulating: back there. And still it was not enough. There was something else, something more she had to tell him. What was he doing now? She focused her eyes. He was writing on air. Writing what? Of course! *Writing!* Amy pulled off a glove with her teeth and got open the top button of her coat, and delving inside her jersey showed him the letter he had left in her care.

"Ah!"

Then he was satisfied to let her go.

"A-mee!" he said, patting her shoulder. "A-mee!"

He bent himself down to her height, and pointed onwards towards Dintirion, and gave her a little push, so that she tottered forward a dozen or so involuntary steps before halting to wait for Bartolomeo to catch up with her. But where was he? What kept him? She shuffled round in the snow. He was going away from her, back up the path, leaving her. Amy could hardly believe her eyes, or bear what she saw. Leaving her?

"Bartolomeo!"

It was a cry of agony and he turned; but only to wave and

motion her on and sign for her to hurry. And when she still
stood, stricken, he called out a sentence that ended in the one
word she could understand: "Gra-nee!" From the depths of
his duffle coat he pulled out their hacker and held it up, laughing. Amy shuddered—not because he was a monstrous figure
standing there in the snow, brandishing an axe: she shuddered
at the thought of the terrible journey he was about to retrace,
and at the danger he must believe her grandmother to be in to
undertake it; and she shuddered at her memory of the two
men, against whom his only weapon was the little hacker they
used for chopping sticks.

She must get help for him. All she had to do was to reach
Dintirion and tell Mr Protheroe, and he would tell Mr Pugh,
and they would save Bartolomeo, and save her grandmother,
and Mick as well. All she had to do was to reach Dintirion.
She could see it there, below her, waiting. Only now the trees,
the cluster of roofs, the plume of smoke, seemed to Amy not
close at all but impossibly far away like a cloud in the sky, or a
rainbow that would never get any nearer. And it was so tiring
to have to lift one leg and put it in front of the other, and then to
lift the leg behind and put it in front again—like this—and like
this—and like this. She looked round over her shoulder.
Bartolomeo had gone.

If only she were not so dreadfully cold—tired and cold, cold
and tired. If only, if only she could sit down for a little while,
for five minutes. Where was the sun? She glanced up. The rosy
flush of dawn had been false and the sky was dark above her, the
colour of lead. How long was it since she had struggled out of
her bedroom window? Not merely hours ago—in a different
life, surely. Ah! but she was so cold, so cold, and her legs were
so tired they would scarcely obey her even though every
fumbling step she took was downhill. But she must not stop,
she told herself. She must keep going, like a clock ticking, on
and on, on and on, towards Dintirion.

Dintirion! Perhaps there at this very moment they were having their breakfast. She could almost smell the porridge. How hungry she was! How cold! She could almost see the fire leaping up in the big kitchen. Dintirion!

It was strange to be able to picture them so clearly—Mrs Protheroe, the boys, their father—while they had no notion that she, Amy Bowen, was out here on the snowy hillside trying to reach them. They would think, if they thought of her at all, that she was far away, sitting comfortably with her grandmother in front of their own fire in their own snug cottage. And in the bitterness of her sudden recollection Amy actually halted and clasped her hands together and raised her face towards the sky and closed her eyes: for had they not themselves assured and persuaded Mr Protheroe that no harm could possibly come to them?

Something lightly touched her cheek, as it might have been the fingers of a friend, to comfort her. She opened her eyes. It was snowing. At the same time she heard the curious groaning sound of wind rising fast, and hearing it she floundered forward, trying with agonizing weakness to make herself run. This was no time to be standing still, for when wind and snow came together in a rush, and the sky was low and very dark, Amy knew what it meant.

It meant a blizzard.

19. An Empty Room

It was Mrs Bowen's habit to wind her alarm clock and set the alarm every night as soon as she had finished plaiting her hair and before she climbed into bed. But last night she had been worrying about Amy. She was sure the child had something on her mind and was keeping it from her. Distracted by anxiety she forgot to wind the clock and in the morning when she awoke it had stopped. She lay on her back for some minutes wondering what the time could be, and listening. Not a sound came from Amy's room, nor from below; everyone else, it seemed, was still asleep.

Her room was dark. She had left the curtains drawn across the night before, but even so there would surely be bright chinks of light showing round the edges of the window if it were late; and since there were no chinks of light to be seen, Mrs Bowen came to the conclusion that she must have woken earlier than usual. The day ahead was one that filled her with apprehension and to hurry it on by getting up before she had need to get up was sheer foolishness. Unaware that she had already overslept by more than an hour, Mrs Bowen allowed herself to drop off to sleep again.

She awoke for the second time with a definite sensation of something being wrong. It was too quiet. Then she heard Mick whimpering and snuffling on the other side of the closed door. She expected to hear Amy speak to him, hushing him, but the seconds passed without the murmur of a voice rebuking Mick. Was the child sleeping so soundly then? In the sudden access of a fear she could not have named Mrs Bowen scrambled out of bed and at once was struck by the extreme coldness of a draught, as though a window had been left open somewhere. She put her hand on the latch of the door and hesitated.

"Amy?"

Mick whined. She opened the door. The east window was uncurtained and one thing was clear instantly: Amy was gone.

How could she have gone? Gone where? Gone how?

The little west window gaped wide and a stream of icy air poured through it like water through a sluice. In a state of wonder and fear Mrs Bowen pulled in Amy's home-made line, marvelling at its composition, and shut the window. She picked up the chair and put it back beside the bed, so bewildered she hardly knew what she was doing.

How long had the room been empty? Where had Amy gone? Where was she now? Mrs Bowen took two wavering steps in one direction, two in another, turning as her mind turned in search of an answer. Only last night Amy had told her plainly that she had no intention of trying to reach the road by way of the stream; she would never have said that unless she meant it. And she had promised her grandmother not to go down to Tyler's Place again. Might she have broken this promise? It was unlikely, even in the present circumstances. Well then, suppose she had gone only a part of the distance? As far, say, as the site of the haystack, to leave a message—some kind of warning to Bartolomeo to keep away. Yes—that would be it—of course! Eagerly Mrs Bowen's mind fastened on this explanation because there was a third alternative so appalling she could not bear to consider it. Amy must have gone up to the haystack—she *must* have done; and probably not very long ago either.

Her movements had aroused the men in the front-kitchen. There was the sound of a cough from below, and then the scrape of a chair. Whatever was she to say to them? Should she tell them of Amy's disappearance? Or not? Suppose Amy were in danger? Which was the worse danger? How could she know? Mrs Bowen stood in the middle of Amy's deserted bedroom, one hand to her head and one to her heart, quite unable to decide on how she ought to act.

She would dress herself. That at least had to be done, no matter what else. And while she was putting on her clothes she would get it all straightened out in her mind. But when she had dressed, and combed her hair, and wound it into its usual knob, and pushed in the pins with trembling fingers, she was no nearer to knowing what she ought to do than before, except that she must go downstairs; if she delayed any longer they would start to wonder what it was that delayed her. Also, Mick had to be put outside. Mrs Bowen tucked him tightly under one arm and descended into the front-kitchen, which smelt disagreeably of tobacco and whisky fumes.

"I'm afraid you've let us oversleep, Mrs Bowen," said the man they still thought of as Inspector Catcher. He was stretched comfortably out in her basket-chair. His legs reached right across the hearthrug.

"Yes, indeed," she answered, scuttling past him with her head down. "I missed to wind my clock last night and what with a dark morning on top I'd no idea it had gone so late."

Mr Nabb, hunched up on the oak chest in the window, was blowing his nose on a dirty handkerchief. She avoided looking at him altogether and hurried into the side-kitchen where she drew the bolts back awkwardly, holding Mick tight against her. His body, she could feel, was braced to get free at the first opportunity and once outside, before she had a chance to set him down, he had wriggled clean out of her grasp and was nosing about to and fro like a creature demented. A sniff here and a sniff there and then he had shot off up the much-trampled left-hand fork. There were no footprints leading off to the right—she strained her eyes: no, there were none. Mrs Bowen told herself this surely did mean Amy had made for the haystack, or at the very worst for Tyler's Place, and in either case whatever her reason for going she would come to no great harm. As she called Mick back Mrs Bowen repeated this over and over to herself.

"Mick! Mick!" He was slow returning. "Mick!"

She called and called and at last, reluctantly, he came; but only, she could see, in order to fetch her before setting out again.

"No, Mick," she said, catching him by the collar. "We must stay here. She won't be long, boy—she's not gone far."

It was true, she told herself. Amy was somewhere quite close, would appear at any moment. Why then could she not rid her mind of the dreadful picture haunting it?

"She never would be so mad as that—not in this weather, not with snow on the ground, Mick—never!" whispered Mrs Bowen. And yet however much she stroked and patted Mick she saw it still—that high and winding track over the top to Dintirion and the sharp-edged unfenced cliff of Billy Dodd's Dingle.

Presently it occurred to her to find out if Amy's toboggan was gone as well. First she tied Mick to one of the posts with a piece of twine and then she made a thorough search. The toboggan was not in the shed. Well, that was hardly surprising. If Amy had gone down to Tyler's Place was it likely she would have set off on foot when she had a toboggan to take her? She had promised to keep away from Tyler's Place. It was wrong of her to break her given word and Mrs Bowen meant to scold her for it later—not too severely, though: right and wrong were sometimes hard to tell apart. If only she knew when Amy had started out she could judge when to expect her home. But there!—it was foolish to fret. She had always said that fretting never did anyone a speck of good. Amy would soon be back; and in the meanwhile the best she could do was to carry on with her accustomed tasks as though there were nothing amiss.

Resolved on staying calm and showing no trace of alarm, she went inside and set about lighting the fire in the front-kitchen, noting to herself as she did so that they must have kept a blaze going half the night through, for the logs were still smouldering and the ashes red-hot.

"Where's that granddaughter of yours, Mrs Bowen?" said Inspector Catcher affably, pausing on his way into the side-kitchen. Round his neck hung the towel he had asked for and been grudgingly given the night before, and from the ends of his long fingers dangled a neat little bag of washing and shaving equipment. "She should have been the first up, not the last— she ought to be cooking our breakfast by now. Isn't that what girls are for—looking after their elders and betters? I'm afraid you must spoil her, Mrs Bowen. Children ought to be disciplined, not indulged—aren't I right, Nabb?"

Mr Nabb, scratching himself by the window, merely grunted.

"There's no call to rouse Amy yet awhile," said Mrs Bowen evenly. She was down on her knees, her back turned, sweeping up the hearth. "I was only just then thinking—it'll do her good to lie on a bit. Not quite herself she wasn't, yesterday, it seemed to me—"

"No, she wasn't," said Mr Nabb, interrupting sharply. "I had my eye on that girl and I noticed the way she was carrying on. And I'll tell you this much—it was very peculiar. As a matter of fact I mentioned it to her."

"You did?"

Still on her knees Mrs Bowen slewed round towards him, brush and shovel raised in either hand. What had he said to Amy, what warning or threat uttered, that might have made her decide any risk, however fearful, was worth taking?

"Yes, I did," he replied in a surly voice.

"It could be she's sickening," said Mrs Bowen breathlessly. "They've got the measles at school. Have you two gentlemen had the measles? Better to part her from you, I daresay, just in case."

Oh, Amy! she wanted to cry—where are you? If only it were the measles! If only Amy were tucked up safe in bed, how thankful she would be—never mind the spots!

Abandoning all pretence of keeping an easy conversation going, Mrs Bowen cooked them their breakfast in silence; and three times while they were eating it she went outside to gaze up the hill in a state of growing agitation. She did not know what to do for the best, for the greater safety of her child. If she could only be certain of where Amy was she would at least then be able to weigh one peril against another. Surely it was true that she had gone down to Tyler's Place? And if she had, and if she were even now toiling homewards, Mrs Bowen had no wish, for the sake of easing her own distress, to give her away to those bad men. But just supposing—? Mrs Bowen was afraid to suppose it. She would wait another five minutes; another five. And perhaps she might have continued in this way to postpone her worst fears, interval by interval, were it not that when for the third time she went out into the shed it was snowing.

The low dark sky had begun to loosen its load in hurried flurries. The wind was rising. Something strange in the sound of it frightened her. She listened and heard it again—a sort of whistling, except that it was too low-pitched for whistling, and yet too shrill to be the usual moaning noise of wind. Wonderingly, Mrs Bowen stepped out from beneath the cover of the sloping roof into a ferment of conflicting currents of air. Her apron was torn almost off her. She fought her way to the corner of the cottage and there she crouched, not daring to set foot or even, for a few moments, to look beyond, one hand pressed to the stones of the solid wall for support, the other attempting to hold clear of her eyes the strands of grey hair whipping wildly across her face. But when she did peer round the side of the cottage all she could see was a huge shapeless moving mass filling the valley, travelling fast, an inky cloud blotting out the world, and at the sight of it her heart seemed to burst wide open with terror. Such a blizzard was not just a storm of wind and snow—it was more. It was a destroyer, out of whose path any frail or living thing must flee or perish.

The Inspector and Mr Nabb heard her in the side-kitchen calling aloud like a madwoman:

"I'm coming, my darling! I'm coming—I'm coming!"

When they reached her she was scarcely recognizable. Shaken by terrible sobs, her face screwed up, her mouth open, tears pouring down her cheeks, she was trying blindly to cram on boots and coat at the same time. They took hold of her arms but she fought to get free.

"Gone clean off her rocker," said Mr Nabb. "What happened? Do you think that dog went and bit her?"

And still she pushed at them feebly, striving to reach the door.

"Stand away from me—don't hinder me! I'm bound to go after her! Let me get by!"

"*After her?*" From the frantic babble of words Inspector Catcher plucked these two as a hawk plucks a mouse from the heather, and repeated them. "Was that what you said—*after her?* Harris—take a look upstairs."

Mr Nabb was up the stairs and down again in a matter of seconds.

"Nobody there—she's gone."

For one instant Inspector Catcher's face flamed at the other man a glance of total rage, as though it were Nabb himself who had conjured Amy away like a knot from a piece of string, and then it closed again over all betrayal of expression.

"Mrs Bowen," he said clearly, "where's that girl of yours? Where's Amy? Where's she gone?"

Passive in the grip of his fingers, Mrs Bowen stood looking down blankly at the floor. She had stopped crying. She had stopped struggling to get away. Her outburst over, she had become very quiet; only when she pulled a handkerchief from the pocket of her cardigan, the handkerchief shook in her hand. She blew her nose and wiped her eyes.

"I don't know," she said.

"How long has she been gone? When did she go?"

"I don't know," she said once more, in the same low flat voice. "I don't know where she is. I don't know when she went. But she's out there somewhere and I'm bound to go after her. She's been in my keeping ever since the night she was born. I can't leave her now, my Amy. I'm bound to go after her."

Inspector Catcher opened the side-kitchen door. Sheets of snow drove past up the hillside with a hissing noise. Mick, shivering at the end of his string, yelped.

"Why, you couldn't even stand up in that, Mrs Bowen, much less set off to look for someone. You'd better come inside and tell me whatever it is you haven't told me yet—everything."

"Didn't I say it?" declared Mr Nabb in a tone of spiteful triumph. "Didn't I say right from the start they knew a lot more than they were letting on to know? You didn't believe me, did you?"

"Be quiet, Harris! I haven't the slightest interest in what you may have said. Mrs Bowen, you can surely understand what you see with your own eyes? The weather's against you. So come away from that door—I want to talk to you."

But Mrs Bowen stared out at the fury of the storm, unheedingly. There was nothing she could do for Amy—nothing. Nothing! And the only prayer her dry mind managed to form was an agonized command: find her, Lord, as I would if I could; and shelter her as I would—as I would!

"Mrs Bowen—"

"Wait now," she answered dully. "I must bring the dog inside. I'll put him in the child's room. She told me to take good care of him."

"She told you that? So you knew she was going?"

Before replying Mrs Bowen took Mick upstairs and shut him

into Amy's bedroom. Then she came and sat by the fire obediently. She sat quite still except for the continuous fidgeting of her hands clasped together in her lap.

"I didn't understand her meaning. I said it was for her to look after him—Mick being her pet, like."

"You didn't know she was planning to run off—she hadn't discussed it with you?"

"Of course she had," said Mr Nabb.

Mrs Bowen shook her head.

"Then why were you lying to us? Why did you pretend she was still in bed when you must have known perfectly well she wasn't? What was your reason for pretending, Mrs Bowen?"

"I thought she'd maybe only gone to the top of the hill—I thought she'd be back any minute."

"But she'd been up and down to the top of the hill all day yesterday. Why was it suddenly such a secret? Come along, Mrs Bowen—I want an answer. I want to know what it is you're hiding from me!"

Mrs Bowen was silent. His voice went on and on. She wished it would stop, if only just for long enough to let her listen to her own unhappy mind and hear what counsel it gave her; but all she could hear was this insidious voice of his asking her on and on, question after question, and it seemed to Mrs Bowen like the silver thread a spider weaves, imprisoning its victim, binding it helpless.

"You're wasting your time," broke in Mr Nabb, roughly. "That's not the way. You leave her to me. I can soon get her to tell us what they've been up to."

Mrs Bowen looked at the scowling face on one side of her and then at the fair smooth smiling face on the other and she remembered Amy's whisper: "They're both of them cruel." Her hands ceased their restless fiddling and locked together tightly on her knees.

"Amy was afraid of you," she burst out in a passionate

undertone. "That's why she went—you frightened the very wits out of her almost."

"But why should Amy be afraid of the police, Mrs Bowen?" Inspector Catcher asked her softly. "Unless of course she'd done something wrong herself—had she?"

The confusion of truth and falsehood, of real danger and danger that might after all be imaginary, was too much for Mrs Bowen and she sat like someone stupefied, unable to answer. Yet an answer she was bound to give: he was waiting for it. After a long pause she said bleakly:

"You're not our sort."

"I see. And so because we're *not your sort* Amy was frightened and ran off without telling you in the middle of the night?"

Mrs Bowen nodded. She had fixed her attention on the fire; if she could only manage to keep her gaze steadily on a certain flame the right answers would come to her.

"And where do you suppose she has run to?"

Again there was a long pause.

"Most likely she'd go for Mr Protheroe, Dintirion."

"Protheroe—that's who she was on about yesterday," said Mr Nabb. "I remember the name. They were his sheep, she said, and he ought to be told—and she was saying how the stream was as good as a path, frozen—"

"Thank you, Harris—I heard as well, you know," said Inspector Catcher, standing up. "I too have ears, it may surprise you to learn. You'd better stay here. It shouldn't need both of us to deal with this."

Mrs Bowen raised her head. "You're meaning to go after her, then? But didn't you tell me just now no one could so much as stand up in such weather?"

"I said that *you* couldn't stand up in it," he corrected her calmly.

"And that's true enough," she muttered. "I don't have the strength. But it's different for a man. And then with those things on your feet, you can go fast, can't you? And no one could harm a child, not on purpose—I don't believe it. Not a *child*—"

Half to herself and half to him, she rambled on. Inspector Catcher watched her and listened as he did up his jacket. He was smiling. She seemed to amuse him very much.

"Why should I want to harm your granddaughter, Mrs Bowen? What a curious idea. I'm going to bring her back here, so that we can all be together again. Harris," he said, "I may be some time—that river winds about like the devil."

"Amy's not gone down the stream," said Mrs Bowen.

In an instant the smile had vanished from his face. He turned on her.

"How do you know?"

"She told me herself she'd no intention of trying the stream—better a lot if she had. Better a lot the stream than over the top."

"Over the top?" he asked her, bending down. "What's this—over the top?"

"Over the hills, up behind. The short way over—that's what we call it, and that's what it is, in fine weather—over the top to the Protheroe place, Dintirion."

"It's the first I've heard of a short way over the top to anywhere," said he savagely. "Why didn't you tell us about it before?"

"Why? Because there's no such way, that's why—not now, not once the snow's come—no way fit for a sheep to venture on, let alone a child. Madness indeed it would be for her to try to find that path today," said Mrs Bowen, beginning to rock herself to and fro. "And supposing it was dark still—worse than madness. Worse! And yet I can't get it out of my head it's where she's gone."

"You really think that girl's got so little sense she'd have taken a path that wasn't even fit for a sheep?"

"I might be wrong. There's a chance yet she could be down at Tyler's Place. But I know how it is with children—if they've set their hearts on never mind what, they believe they can do what

187

can't *be* done, not by human endeavour. They don't understand there's some things are plain *impossible*. And Amy had her heart set on Dintirion. I know she had. I knew it all the time, deep down inside of me. She was wanting to get there bad enough to believe she'd manage to find her way over the top to it somehow—find her way home, you might say—she was born at Dintirion all those years ago. Only I know better—terrible that path is at night, in winter, with cliffs to go by and the side of Cader Ddu steep as a mountain. I know she can't ever reach Dintirion, not in the snow—never! My poor child," said Mrs Bowen, her eyes stretched wide as though she were actually seeing the horrors of which she spoke.

"Well, that's all right then—what are we worrying about?" said Mr Nabb, harshly.

But Inspector Catcher had caught hold of Mrs Bowen's wrist. "Where's this Tyler's Place?" he said.

She was startled. "Tyler's Place?"

"You mentioned it just now. You said that Amy might be down at Tyler's Place. Where is it?"

Still for a moment she hesitated and in the pause heard, louder than the tick of the clock and the whirr of the flames in the grate, the ravening noise of the storm outside battering doors and windows as it swept over the cottage and on. She said:

"It's down the other side of the hill, below the haystack, down right at the bottom. Nobody's lived there for years—it's nothing more than just an old ruin. But she'd be back here by now if that's where she'd gone. No, indeed—it's not to Tyler's Place she went. I know in my heart it was over the top."

He let go of her wrist then, and when he looked at Mr Nabb his bright pale eyes were half shut and the corners of his lips curled up.

"So I wasn't mistaken, Harris. He was close—I knew it. I could feel it. In that case I don't suppose I shall be very long after all."

"No need to hurry yourself on my account," said Mr Nabb, carelessly. "Take your time—enjoy yourself."

20. The Enormous Snowman

The sound of the side-kitchen door closing roused Mrs Bowen from her own despairing reflections and she started up.

"Stop him—tell him to wait! I must go up the hill with him—I must put him on the path. He won't ever find the short way over by himself. Let me by!"

For Mr Nabb had thrust an arm in front of her, barring her passage. She was trying to dodge round it.

"You might as well save your breath," said Mr Nabb. "He doesn't want to know about your short cut. That's not where he's going. Where he's going is to this old ruin you just happened to mention—this old ruin you've been keeping so specially quiet about. Tyler's Place you called it, didn't you? That's where he's going—straight on down past the haystack, you said. I don't reckon he'll need your help to find it."

"But Amy's not there. Indeed, I don't think so! It's Dintirion she's trying for—I'm sure of it—over the hills. I told him so."

"Well, if you're right and she went that way we shan't have to trouble ourselves, shall we? She's never going to reach the other end alive and talking—that's what you told us. She hasn't got a chance, you said. She'll be done for. You said it yourself."

Mrs Bowen backed away from him. Her eyes were shocked. "Done for?" she repeated, painfully. "I don't understand what you mean."

"Oh, you don't, don't you?" Mr Nabb had dropped his arm.

189

Now he got out his piece of string and began to practise knots. "You're a crafty old woman, Mrs Bowen, that's what I mean. You and that Amy of yours—you're both of you crafty. I've been watching you and I'm willing to bet you know a lot more than you've ever let on to know. You can't fool me that easy."

"But he said he'd find her," stammered Mrs Bowen. "He said he'd bring her back."

Mr Nabb looked at her stricken face and a gleam of satisfaction crossed his own.

"He won't have to now, will he? Why should he? It's not Amy he's after. You've been a bit too cunning for your own good, Mrs Bowen. There's somebody else down at Tyler's Place, that's what I think, and I think you've known it all along. We've got a little business to settle with this somebody else and when that's done we'll be off."

"Business?" she said.

"Ah! You'd like me to tell you what it's all about I daresay, but you know a lot too much already, Mrs Nosey-Parker. Which is why, just as soon as ever Vigers gets back, you're going to be sent out to look for the missing girl. Well, that's what you wanted before, wasn't it? You were all set to go and we stopped you, didn't we? This time we'll make sure you go—and that ought to round things off nice and natural, I'd say." He twirled his piece of string, eyeing her derisively. "Comes in very handy, this blizzard does. There'll be no talking, no questions asked, nothing awkward—just a couple of headlines in the local paper: Victims of the Storm. He'll like that, Vigers will. He's fond of a joke—a bit too fond in my opinion. One of these days it's going to get him into trouble, as I'm forever telling him. Now I don't care for jokes myself. What I like is for everything to be neat"— he tied a knot—"and tight"—he tied another—"and no loose ends left lying about." He held up the string and it had turned into a wheel with three spokes. He gave a pull, and it fell into a single length again.

"I don't understand what you're saying," whispered Mrs Bowen. "I don't know why you're talking so much. You never used to speak a word, hardly."

"Now that's very sharp of you, Mrs B.," said he, nodding at her approvingly. "Very noticing you are—like me in that respect. And you're right, too—I'm not a talker by nature, not one of the chatty ones, I'm not. And I'll tell you why—I've always had to be on the look-out, that's why. But I can talk if I want to, same as anyone else. I can have a good time—I can let myself go."

"A good time—is that what you're having now?" she asked him in dread.

He was perched on the oak chest, winding the piece of string between his fingers to form an intricate web.

"I'm celebrating, Mrs Bowen," he said. "The job's over, and as I'm not partial to snow, nor yet to Vigers, I'm glad of it. Though I must say, it's turned out very satisfactory, which I didn't expect."

"Over?" she said.

He held up his cat's cradle and squinted at her through the mesh of it. He was as near to laughing as she had ever seen him.

"People shouldn't go poking their noses into other people's affairs, Mrs Bowen," he said. "It doesn't do them any good. Now take that sailor for instance, him you've been keeping such a secret from us—if only he hadn't gone and picked up private information about a certain matter that wasn't anything to do with him, you'd all be pulling crackers next Christmas and carrying on the same as usual—him and you and that Amy of yours. Instead of which,"—he jerked his hands and the tangle disappeared from between them—"all gone! See what I mean? That's a valuable lesson—pity some people learn it too late. Your kettle's boiling. I could do with a cup of tea. Make it strong, and I want plenty of sugar in mine."

"You'll get no cup of tea from me," said Mrs Bowen.

He was surprised. He looked across at her disbelievingly. Then his old scowl reappeared.

"If I tell you to make a cup of tea, you'll make it," he said.

But Mrs Bowen was no longer the befuddled creature of a few minutes before. It was as though she had all at once emerged from a fog of doubt into daylight where the view was terrible but clear.

"I can't stop you from taking whatever you choose to take, and I can't stop you from doing whatever you choose to do—I know that," she said, "but I will not offer you hospitality again under my roof, not by so much as one bite or one sip. It would be as great a sin to entertain such wickedness as the wickedness itself, and I'll not do it."

Her face was colourless and her voice quavered a little but she stood up in front of the fire as stiff as her own brass poker and her fists were clenched. Mr Nabb had nothing to say. He made no movement to prevent her from going into the side-kitchen. When she returned she was wearing her boots and her overcoat and her hat was tied on to her head with Amy's scarlet woollen scarf. She crossed the room and opened the door at the foot of the stairs. Then at last he did speak, with a lowering uncertain glance at her from under his brows:

"And what do you think you're up to now, I'd like to know?"

"I'm going to Amy," she said. "And I'm taking Mick with me. I couldn't leave him here."

But by the time, carrying Mick, she got downstairs again he had recovered his equilibrium and was standing in her way.

"You can't just clear off whenever you happen to fancy— don't you understand that? You'll go when you're told to go, and not before."

The room was as dark as though evening were closing in. What light there was came more from the fire than through the snow-choked windows. In the flickering glimmer of the flames Mrs Bowen saw that he held a gun. Mick was snarling.

"Let me by," she said.

"Oh, no, you don't! Who do you think you are, ordering me around, telling me what to do? You're not clearing off now. You're going to stop on here till Vigers gets back—haven't I just told you so? And you'd better watch that dog of yours too, unless you want him to have a bullet in him—I'd about as soon shoot him as look at him."

Before she could utter a word in reply they heard the side-kitchen door bang shut.

"Here, Vigers!" called out Mr Nabb. "Come on in here—I want you. He's been quick," he added in an undertone.

There was no reply from the side-kitchen. Mick had stopped snarling. His ears were pricked and although Mrs Bowen had him clamped tight beneath her arm she could feel the slight welcoming movement of his tail. Hardly knowing what she said, or even why, but impelled by an instinct to protect whatever might need protecting, she spoke in a rush:

"I didn't fasten that door properly, I don't believe."

"Is that so?" said Mr Nabb. His eyes were on Mick. "Is that so?" he repeated. "You'd better see to it then, hadn't you? Go on—fasten it!"

There was absolute silence from the side-kitchen.

"Go on," said Mr Nabb softly, and he motioned at Mrs Bowen with his gun, waving it towards the side-kitchen. She went past him slowly and slowly opened the door between the two rooms. Then she screamed, for there propped up against the door opposite to her was an enormous snowman.

It was Bartolomeo.

His eyes were closed. His one good arm hung limp at his side. He was covered thickly in snow, every inch of him, from head to foot. Neither he nor they moved until Mr Nabb exclaimed in loud exultant tones:

"Would you believe it? All we had to do was to sit here and wait for him. And what happens? He walks in at that door—just walks in!"

As though two lumps of coal had been put into the face of the snowman, Bartolomeo opened his eyes. He opened his eyes and looked at them, but still he made no movement of any kind. Mr Nabb thrust his way past Mrs Bowen. His voice was peculiarly gloating.

"They said he was big—he's big all right. And what's the use of being so big after all? Size won't help him now. He's finished! Why, look at him there—with all that size he can't lift a finger to save himself, not a finger! Not this time, he can't!"

The great black burning eyes spoke to Mrs Bowen as they had spoken once before. She stepped towards him in horrified compassion:

"Bartolomeo!"

Without bothering to glance at her even, Mr Nabb reached forward and grasping the old woman by her shoulder pushed her hard out of his way. She staggered, loosening her hold on Mick, who, like a launched arrow, sprang straight across the intervening space at Mr Nabb's throat. But he missed his mark and fell to the floor. Kicking at him, cursing him, Mr Nabb swivelled and backed away from Mick's hysterical attacks.

"Mick!" cried Mrs Bowen. "Mick!—Mick!" For although the light in the side-kitchen was poor and the skirmish confused she saw the gun being raised and aimed. "Mick!" she shrieked.

What she failed to see was the one and only gesture made by Bartolomeo. He lifted his hanging right arm quite slowly and brought the back of their hacker down on the top of Mr Nabb's head. Mick went on barking. There was Mr Nabb full length on the side-kitchen floor and still Bartolomeo leant up against the door as though he had not enough strength to take even a single step away from it. The hacker had fallen from his hand.

"A-mee," he said.

"Yes?" asked Mrs Bowen, sick at heart. "Where is she? Where's Amy? Tell me."

"A-mee," said Bartolomeo, just nodding at her. He turned his eyes as though if he could have done he would have pointed somewhere over the hills, and he held his fist out towards Mrs Bowen, its thumb stuck up to tell her that wherever Amy might be she was quite all right.

21. Ivor Makes His Own Plans

At seven o'clock in the morning the Protheroes' big kitchen had a dishevelled appearance as though pots of tea had been endlessly brewing and people coming and going there all night long. The electric light, which was on, somehow gave Ivor the impression of having never been switched off. There were jars of pickle on the table and crumbs and the loaf of bread had been left out. Ivor began to cut himself a thick slice.

Upstairs a door banged and he heard his brother Colin shouting. The dogs were barking in the front yard. Then there was the sound of the landrover's engine, a renewed slamming of doors and more shouting. His father was about to start off for the village. It had been well past midnight when Mr Victor Pugh the policeman had gone from their place having agreed with Ivor's father to ring police headquarters first thing in the morning, provided his friend Mr Protheroe stood by him and gave him the support he felt he would need in asking for the immediate return of the snow-plough which had only completed its official task of opening up the road as far as the village yesterday evening just as darkness fell.

If they were successful in winning back the snow-plough and the remaining couple of miles of road beyond the village was cleared, the rescue-party—consisting of Mr Protheroe, his two elder boys, Colin and Ray, and Mr Pugh the policeman—intended to force its way on from Casswell's Gate up the valley and across the stream to the Gwyntfa. Whether it would be better to go on foot or mounted was still undecided. Ivor had lost interest in the argument as soon as he heard, with indignant amazement, that he was not going to be one of the rescuers.

"This isn't a bit of fun, Ivor," Mr Protheroe had said in reply to his youngest son's beseeching look. "By all accounts we might get into something real nasty before we're through. I wouldn't want to have you mixed up in it. And in any case, nasty or not, it's going to be hard enough work to fetch out Mrs Bowen and Amy without having you to think about on top."

"You wouldn't have to think about me—I can think about myself," protested Ivor, his feelings, usually deeply hidden, showing for once in the desperation of his entreaty.

"I've said no, Ivor. You're not coming. That's all there is to it."

Ivor relapsed into silence. It was a waste of energy, he knew, arguing with his father and so he held his tongue and concentrated instead on making plans of his own. At least he could do what nobody else had thought of doing: he could climb to the other side of Cader Ddu and survey the territory that lay between the Gwyntfa's back entrance and Dintirion, the route of the short way over. It was true there would be nothing for him to see except acres of snow, but the idea of appointing himself as solitary look-out appealed to Ivor, and by giving him the dignity of a purpose helped a little to relieve the smart of having been excluded from the rescue team. He would go on his pony Ginger, and without telling anyone, and without even stopping for porridge first. A slice of bread and butter and jam would do him for food, he reflected, sawing away at the loaf—or perhaps two slices to make sure. At this moment his brother Ray burst into the kitchen in stockinged feet, carrying a coil of rope.

"Hey, Ivor! What have you done with my pocket-knife?"

"Nothing," said Ivor. It was a vulnerable position, being youngest of the family, and Ivor's defence, built up over the years, was imperturbability. He buttered his slice of bread calmly and heaped it with spoonfuls of gooseberry jam.

"Your knife's in the drawer, Ray—I put it there," said Mrs Protheroe, appearing in the doorway. She was dressed and neat but her eyes were tired, as though she had slept little, or badly. "Oh, Ray—just look at those heels! In all my life I never knew anyone to make such holes in their socks as you do. You'll have to take another pair from the basket—you can't go off in those. Ivor, will you fetch me in some sticks from the back porch—I must get the fire going, no matter what else. And I only hope there'll be a better end to this day than there's been a beginning."

"Fire's not out, Mum," said Ivor, inspecting the jam on his slice to make sure it had enough actual gooseberries in it. "All it wants is just a bit of blowing up, that's all. Suppose they say we can't have the snow-plough back—what then?"

"Oh, Ivor, they're bound to, when your Dad puts it to them—all that about kidnappings and political prisoners and plots and escapings and I don't know what else—you heard what Mr Everest was telling us. We can't leave poor old Mrs Bowen and Amy all alone up at the Gwyntfa if there's a chance even of such people about in the neighbourhood."

"That's not his name, Mum," said Ivor.

"Well, no, not quite I daresay—but near enough. And don't you put on airs with me, Ivor Protheroe, for if I didn't get hold of his name exactly right, you didn't either, nor anyone else, and where's the difference? He won't mind, I'm sure."

Ivor took a large bite and then chewed rapidly so as to clear it out of the way before speaking. "He won't mind if we can't get hold of his name, Mum. But he'll mind if Dad and Mr Pugh go saying on the 'phone why it is they want the snow-plough back in such a big hurry. They promised they wouldn't."

"Then they won't say it, not if they promised."

"Then perhaps we won't get the snow-plough back."

"Oh, Ivor!" exclaimed Mrs Protheroe. "How is it you were born so provoking! Wait and see. We'll know soon enough."

But Ivor was right. Down in Melin-y-Groes police station Mr Victor Pugh and Mr Protheroe were finding it by no means an easy task to convince the sergeant on duty at police headquarters eight miles away of their urgent need for a snow-plough which had only left them a few hours before, without giving away to him over the telephone more than they had sworn not to give away.

The sergeant thought their request a surprising one and particularly unreasonable for being made so early in the morning. In any case it would be a matter for the County Council to deal with, he said, and suggested they should wait until nine o'clock and then ring the Highways and Byways office, although in his opinion they were bound to be refused. After all they had had their turn and there were plenty of other roads as badly blocked or worse, and not enough ploughs to go round as it was. They were lucky, he added, to be on the telephone still— many of the villages had their lines down, no means of communication at all. And the two miles they wanted cleared beyond their village never had been cleared, not any previous winter; it was a dead end, it served no other village, no hamlet, not even a farm for that matter. Victor Pugh, getting his word in at last, said that it served old Mrs Bowen who lived up the valley alone with her little granddaughter, and he had reason to believe that she was in difficulties. When the sergeant asked him what reason and what difficulties he looked helplessly at Mr Protheroe, who whispered in his ear:

"Measles!"

"It could be the measles, Sergeant," said Victor Pugh aloud into the telephone. Mr Protheroe nodded at him encouragingly.

"Who's got the measles then?" asked the police sergeant, eight miles away in Llwynffynnon. "Is it the old lady you're speaking of or the little girl?"

"Well, now, it could be either," said Victor Pugh cautiously. "Mind, all I'm saying is, it *might* be the measles—I'm not saying for certain it is."

"Just a minute then—hold on."

Fragments of conversation reached the two anxiously waiting men.

". . . measles in Colva school right enough . . ."

". . . can be nasty . . ."

". . . shouldn't like to think that . . ."

The telephone receiver began to speak again:

"I tell you what we'll do for you then—we can count it an emergency, and if we were to get on to Ted Jones right away— he's a good lad, he won't mind making an early start when he hears it's special circumstances. And he can have it done and still be back for the Brynmawr road on time, or near enough. I don't suppose it'll take him many minutes to clear that bit on from you, not once he's up there."

Victor Pugh thanked the sergeant and put the receiver down.

"I didn't like to have to give him that part about the measles," he said. "Good as a lie, it was."

"No, it wasn't," said Mr Protheroe. "They've got the measles at Colva school—that's no lie. And we don't know but Amy might be covered in spots by now—she could be. And didn't that chap say for us to keep this tale to ourselves, not to go spreading it around?"

"He wasn't having us on, you don't think?" said Victor Pugh. "Suppose it is no more than a tale? Some fellow killed down Cardiff way and another fellow on the run with information like dynamite, dangerous enough to blow a whole country up. Well, I ask you, Tom—does it sound likely? And both off a foreign ship, foreigners—same as this chap himself is, come to that. Mind, I'm not saying a word against foreigners, Tom— but there's no denying it, they're different. You can't be sure exactly where you are with them, and that's a fact."

"I don't know are you right or not, Victor," said Mr Protheroe. "All I know is, I liked him."

"Maybe you did, but there's no proof in liking a chap. He

turns up here on Ted Jones's snow-plough with fur on his coat and a name we can't any of us pronounce, and says he's an Ambassador. Does he look like an Ambassador to you?"

"Well, I don't know, Vic," said Mr Protheroe again. "I've never seen one before, have I?"

"There you are then—that's what I mean! Suppose he's one of these practical jokers you read about? Or raving mad, he could be. We'd look pretty silly, Tom, if it turned out he was a lunatic."

"We didn't any of us think he was a lunatic last night, Vic. We believed his tale last night—you did just as much as me."

"So we did, but what you believe at night you don't always believe in the morning. I'm not saying it is a tall story, mind— I'm just saying it might be."

"Now you look here, Victor Pugh—if this was a question of you and me maybe having our legs pulled and no more than that, I'd be inclined to agree with you and say—leave it alone, boy! Keep out of it! But you stop a bit and take it the other way round. Suppose he's telling us the truth—just you think of the fright old Mrs Bowen's going to get, and Amy too, if any of that lot he was talking about should happen to come knocking at their door. Why, it could put her in her grave! And even suppose it is a tall story like you say, Vic, I'd rather risk being made a fool of than fretting myself sick the way I'm doing, and that's another fact."

"Right then," said Victor Pugh, and the two men climbed back into Mr Protheroe's landrover and drove through the still dark and dozing village to Dintirion to collect shovels and ropes and whatever else might be necessary in the long and difficult trudge up from the road to Mrs Bowen's cottage; and also to collect the two Protheroe boys, Colin and Ray, and to tell Mrs Protheroe what arrangements had been made, and to have a quick bite of breakfast before setting out again to meet Ted Jones and the snow-plough.

Ivor had blown up the kitchen fire for his mother and brought her in a supply of wood, enough to keep it going for some time. Without a word he had watched his brothers adding to the pile of equipment they were getting ready for their expedition and listened to them disputing each other's choice of essentials. He finished his first chunk of bread and butter and jam and cut and spread himself another. Then, with this in his hand he wandered out of the kitchen into the stone-flagged scullery where all the coats and oilskins, caps and hats and scarves belonging to all members of the Protheroe family hung from a long row of wooden pegs. Wellington boots littered the floor.

Having parked his slice of bread and jam on a shelf, Ivor proceeded to dress himself in a random selection of outdoor garments. This done, he went and stood in the back-yard and wondered as he munched what the darkncss indicated. Some mornings arrived, it was true, more slowly than others and of course it was early yet. But it seemed to Ivor that this darkness was not the remains of night lingering on: it was a new darkness brought by the day, a warning of worse to come.

On the other side of the house their landrover was returning home from the village. Ivor could hear how his father swept it in a circle round the front-yard so as to leave it facing in the right direction, ready for starting off again. The doors slammed, and then he heard Mr Pugh's voice, and his father's answering laugh. They had gone into the house together. Now they must be in the kitchen.

He had finished his second slice of bread and jam. Unless he meant to get himself a third slice he might as well go. Ivor glanced about, consideringly. Yesterday he and Ray had cleared the snow from the whole back-yard, shovelling it into a huge blotched mound in the centre. But on the sloping roofs and beyond the yard the snow lay still untouched and smooth. It looked in the gloom not white but a pale dull grey. The buildings were black and brown. There was no colour or brightness in anything. There was no wind either, no movement except for the vaguely tossing heads of the ponies as they jostled against the railings of the enclosure where they were always penned in exceptionally bad weather.

Ivor crossed the yard to the big barn to fetch a bridle. He trod warily. The ground was rough and slippery with lumps of frozen dung and frozen slush. Inside the barn he was given an ecstatic welcome by the smallest and youngest of their three sheepdogs, named Kettle for having been the only one of his litter without a white hair on him; Ket for short.

"Why, hullo, Ket! Didn't you go down the village with Dad, then? Seems like he means to leave you behind, boy, same as me."

It was almost pitch dark in the barn but he could find what he wanted by touch. Beyond the further partition the cattle were shuffling and heavily sighing. Ivor lifted the bridle off its nail and picked up a sack.

Supposing his father changed his mind at the last moment and shouted out that he could go with them after all? It was unlikely, but there was just a chance he might. Ivor stood, biting his lip. Then he sat down on an empty oil-drum to wait.

Presently he heard the front door slam, and voices calling; not for him. He sat quite still in the darkness, holding the bridle across his knees, listening. Ket nudged at his legs, but Ivor took no notice. He heard the doors of the landrover bang shut, and the engine cough into life. "Colin!" his father was yelling. Colin always kept everyone waiting. There was a grinding of gears—"*Colin!*"—a final slamming of doors, and they were driving away. Ivor stood up.

"Come on then, Ket."

As he approached the ponies' enclosure he could see them crowding together to meet him, restless, fretful at being confined in such a small space, all eager for him to set them free. But Ivor leaned across the railings and winding his hand in the coarse mane of his own pony, Ginger, tugged him along to the gate, opened it narrowly, urged him through, and shut it again quickly before the others could follow. In the yard he bridled Ginger and flung the sack on his back instead of a saddle. Then he led him out on to the hillside and there mounted.

"If you want to come with me, Ket, you'll have to ride. That snow's too deep for you to run in. Up boy—up! Quiet, Ginger! Come on, Ket, then—up! Up, boy!"

Ket ran to and fro as though trying to decide whether or not to take the risk. Suddenly he gathered himself and sprang. With one arm Ivor caught him and held him, while keeping the reins close in his other hand in order to steady Ginger. But the pony, unconcerned by Ket's flying leap, only backed a step or two: he was used to carrying a dog as well as a boy. Then Ivor tapped with his heels and they were off.

Ginger knew the way better even than Ivor. He had been born and bred on this hill and was as tough as one of the native thorn-trees marking their path, and as well adapted to all exigencies of weather. He plodded on at an energetic walk, not too close to the bank on their right where the snow had drifted deep, nor far enough to the left to get off the track, and when his hooves slipped, as they sometimes did, he recovered himself nimbly.

Every so often Ivor pivoted so as to look back towards Dintirion. The light, though reluctantly, was increasing and the blurred group of trees and buildings showed further and further below him. All at once he was seized with exhilaration. He hugged Ket and bent forward to pat Ginger's rough neck, although really it was himself he wanted to pat and hug for having had such a good idea. Whatever his brothers did it would be what they were told to do by their father and Mr Pugh, and here was he, out on his own, quite independently. Nobody knew where he was, even; and no one but he had thought of climbing Cader Ddu for a view of the short way over.

But the higher he went the colder it grew, and the colder it grew the more Ivor hunched himself up and dug his chin into the collar of his coat to save his face. And after a while his mind began to dwell on the numbness of his fingers and toes instead of the triumph of reaching the far side of Cader Ddu. Also, he found himself wishing very much indeed that he had had that third slice of bread and butter and jam. Then, with a terrible pang of longing, he remembered the bowl of porridge he had gone without, and he began to imagine what he would do if it were steaming in front of him now—how he would scatter on the sugar, cover it with cream, scoop up a dripping spoonful... Tormented beyond bearing by this vision he raised his head sharply so as to get rid of it, and found with surprise that during his absence of mind it had started to snow.

Ivor forgot at once about numb fingers and empty stomach. He tightened the reins and the little pony halted. He listened: there was wind on the way—he could hear it. And even as he sat there the first few puffs of it reached him like ripples, every ripple stronger than the one before.

"We'll get on a bit yet, Ginger boy," said Ivor, signalling with his heels, and on they went.

But the wind grew more violent with each step they took, and buffeted them more harshly, and transformed the gentle snow-flakes into whips which lashed them with such cruelty that soon Ginger shook his head and dropped it down between his legs and refused to go further. Then Ivor realized that he could only raise his own head if he shielded it with his arm, and, having raised it, that he could see no more than a yard ahead. He was surrounded by snow rushing by him, over him, an avalanche borne on the wind, and it was so sudden and so fierce that he was shocked and even for a moment, in spite of all the storms he had ever known, afraid. A moment later and he was turning Ginger round, at the same time trying to quieten Ket who was behaving like a dog gone insane.

"It's all right, Ket—we're going home. Keep still or I can't hold you."

But Ket wriggled and twisted and uttered short high-pitched barks and then, with a final contortion, jumped clear out from the grasp of Ivor's encircling arm.

"Ket! You fool!"

Frantically shouting at him, Ivor slithered to the ground. He was too late. Ket dodged and doubled round and vanished uphill straight into the driving snow. So his father was right: he had declared that Ket would never make a good working dog because he was unreliable. What a time to prove his unreliability! Ivor's perplexity at what to do was so great that he actually laid his head against Ginger's shaggy flank and groaned aloud. The next moment he was ashamed of himself, for Ket reappeared, bursting out of the storm like a bullet and wild with the delight of a good sheepdog who comes to tell his master that he has found a lost sheep.

"Never, Ket! You don't mean it—you can't!"

But Ket continued to insist unmistakably that he did mean it, that he did have something to show Ivor, and that Ivor must follow him. Whatever old ewe could it possibly be? There were none missing that Ivor knew of, except for those few over at the Gwyntfa and it was hard to believe one of them could have strayed this far in such conditions.

"Come on, Ginger—we'll have to see what it is. Wait, Ket! Good boy! Come on *round*, Ginger—come *on!*"

But not all the tugging in the world would induce Ginger to turn again. He was adamant. His nose was pointing now towards home and he meant to keep it there. The best that Ivor could finally do was to shove him far enough into the snow at the side to be able to tie his reins to the very tip of a branch. It was more of a hint to Ginger to stay where he was than an anchorage to hold him.

"Right then, Ket—show me, boy!"

Bent almost to the ground, one arm flung up to protect his face, one hand holding on to Ket's collar, groping, slipping, struggling, Ivor allowed himself to be guided forward into the fury of the storm. It was only for a few yards. Then Ket turned aside and scrambled through the deep snow and up the bank and crept, whining with excitement, under the low branches of a thorn-tree. Here it was that Ivor found Amy. Not one single word did either of them say. They could only stare in amazement. Amy was crouching against the stem of the thorn-tree, as close as she could get to it, shivering. Ivor was on hands and knees. For each it was such a marvel to see the other that speech was unnecessary and neither noticed the lack of it. Then Ivor grabbed her by the hand and backed out from under the prickly branches, and Amy crawled after him.

The moment they stood up the wind hurled itself on them from behind like a savage attacker determined to tear them apart and beat them to the ground, but Amy clutched the pocket of Ivor's coat and he had hold of the belt of hers, and hooked together in this way they stumbled downhill. Through sheets of snow a tail materialized. It might have been the only part of Ginger to have survived, for his brown hind-quarters were already invisible beneath a coat of clinging white like the fur of a Polar bear. But he was there all right: he had waited, and Ivor loved him for it.

To get Amy on to the pony's back was unexpectedly difficult. She had spent her last effort to reach the shelter of the thorn-tree and was stiff with cold and fatigue. Somehow between them, using the bank as a mounting-block, they managed it, and Ket jumped up in front of Amy, and Ivor took hold of the bridle and went ahead, meaning to steady Ginger on the downward slope, but at the second step he slipped and almost brought disaster to all of them by hanging instinctively on to the bridle to save himself. It might be better, he decided then, to let a hill-pony find its own way down off a hill. And so, relinquishing the bridle, Ivor clambered up behind Amy, and Ginger bore all three of them, boy, girl and dog, home to Dintirion.

22. A Way of Telling

"Wherever has that boy got to, I wonder," said Mrs Protheroe, worriedly. The table was covered with dirty cups and saucers and plates and she was leaning across it, stacking them together. "It's a real blizzard come on—you can't hardly see out of the window."

But no sooner had she spoken than the clatter of hooves sounded in the back yard, and barking and the whinny of one pony answered by others.

"That'll be Ivor now," she exclaimed, a note of relief in her voice. So far as any answer went, she might as well have been alone and talking aloud to herself in the big dark shadowy-cornered kitchen. But Mrs Protheroe chattered on, undeterred. She was not someone who required the encouragement of a reply; a listener was enough, and she had a listener. "Off on that pony of his, and never a word to me, of course! Though I might have guessed he was bound to follow the snow-plough—he never could bear to be left out of anything. Oh, well, I don't blame him, not altogether. He's a boy, after all. I suppose his father let him keep on as far as Casswell's Gate and turned him back there—he certainly didn't intend Ivor to set one foot beyond, and a good job too. After what we've been hearing I shan't feel easy till they're all of them safe home again, Mrs Bowen and Amy included. Though mind you, I don't believe there's a soul could have got across the forest this weather—indeed, I don't!—not unless'they had wings, and from the stories you were telling us last night it sounds more as though they'd have forked tails than wings. Ivor! Is that you?" she called.

There was a bursting open of doors, a rush of cold air. Ket came bounding into the kitchen, scattering snow.

"Out of this house, you bad dog! Look at the mess! Ivor—what are you thinking of to let him in?"

"Ket's the best dog we've ever had, Mum," replied Ivor exultantly. "Don't you scold him—he found Amy."

Mrs Protheroe whirled round. There in the scullery doorway stood, not one, but two figures.

"Amy?" she whispered, incredulous.

With a proprietary arm across her shoulders, Ivor brought Amy shambling further into the room.

"She was up the hill, Mum, under an old thorn-tree. She must have come the short way over—just fancy that!—all on her own, and got caught in the snow. Lucky me and Ginger and Ket happened to have gone up there on the look-out."

"And me so sure you were with your father! Lucky indeed!" said Mrs Protheroe, attempting to draw Amy nearer the fire. But Amy resisted her. As though there were something of which she had to make quite sure before she could move another inch, she stood transfixed, struggling with powerless fingers to undo the buttons of her coat. Full of solicitude and wonder, Mrs Protheroe went to her aid.

"Oh, Amy—is it true what Ivor says? Have you really come over the top?—just now? I wouldn't have thought it was possible, not for a grown man, even. It's a marvel how you ever got by the Dingle, let alone up Cader Ddu! Whatever made you do it, Amy? It's not your granny, is it? Did she go and slip on the ice, maybe? We've been in such a fret for the two of you. Dad and Mr Pugh and the boys are on their way up to the Gwyntfa this very moment, so they'll see your granny's all right, whatever the trouble. Did she slip or was it something else?"

But Amy seemed unable to respond to Mrs Protheroe's anxious questioning. She had allowed her coat to be unbuttoned but dumbly and obstinately refused to have it taken off her afterwards. And still she fumbled awkwardly with her clothes, plucking at her jersey.

"Leave her alone, Mum—don't keep on at her so. It's food she wants—she's just about famished, and so am I. And half-starved as well. Cold! You've no idea what it's like out there," said Ivor, a little boastful after what he had been through.

Amy by now had achieved her object and was holding a crumpled envelope in both hands flat against her chest.

"I've got to post this," she said to Mrs Protheroe. She pronounced the words, which were the first she had spoken, with some difficulty, as though her tongue had been frozen to the roof of her mouth and was not yet properly thawed.

"What is it, then—a letter? Why, you don't have to bother your head about that now, Amy. You give it to Ivor—he'll take it down the village for you later—won't you, Ivor? But there's no hurry for it—they don't clear the box till close on five, if they clear it at all today, which I doubt, the way things look at the moment. Never you mind about that now. You just let me have your coat and come by the fire. A good bowlful of porridge inside you, that's what you need, like Ivor says—you're famished, the two of you."

"I've got to post it myself," said Amy.

"Then so you shall, my darling. We'll have to put a stamp on it first, though. Where's it going to—Australia? Is it a letter for your father?"

Amy shook her head. "I must post it *now*," she said. "I must—I promised I would. I promised Bartolomeo."

Mrs Protheroe's attention was arrested as suddenly as though she had collided with a stone wall. All at once she became aware

210

of the obsessive nature of Amy's concern. "Promised?" she echoed. "*Who* was that you said you promised?"

Amy licked her lips. She had to explain and it was hard to explain when her lips were dry and her head was buzzing. "It's Bartolomeo's letter," she said. "He wrote it. He gave it to me to post. It's very important. I've got to do it."

"But *Amy*," said Mrs Protheroe, increasingly apprehensive, "who's Bartolomeo?"

"I don't know who," said Amy. "He came—and they're after him—and he wrote this letter." She held it up in front of her to study, for the first time, the address on the envelope. "London, he's put—or at least I think it's London, meant to be. And then there's something above with a capital P, but I can't read the rest of it. He's not very good at writing—and it's foreign, of course. I can't make out what the name at the top is— it looks like Senior, and then there's a word that starts with an A and ends with a Z. Suppose the postman can't read it either— how's it ever going to get there?"

Amy looked towards Mrs Protheroe for an answer; and she may have answered, but if she did Amy heard nothing of it. Her ears seemed to go dead with the shock of what her eyes saw over Mrs Protheroe's shoulder: a movement which, unbeliev- ably, became a man. Believably after all, for it was a man, some- one she had never seen before, rising up from the settle where he must have been sitting the whole time concealed by its high wooden back. And her ears were not dead, for when he spoke she heard what he said, although each word sounded like a separate and horrifying piece of nonsense.

"We shall have no need to trouble the postman," he said to Amy. She thought he was smiling. His eyes, though dark, were very bright. "If you give it to me you can feel quite confident that your letter has reached its destination."

Amy's breath came in short gasps. His sudden appearance filled her with terror. He was a total stranger and strangers were terrifying; they were dangerous. Those other two had been total strangers. If she could have run away from him she would have done, only she was incapable of any kind of movement.

"It's all right, Amy," said Mrs Protheroe, putting her arm round Amy's waist so as to reassure her. "He won't hurt you. He spent the night here," she whispered. "He's from London."

"He's an Ambassador," added Ivor loudly, not feeling it necessary, as his mother did, to lower his voice when giving information about their visitor.

But still Amy drew her breath in painful gasps and she had begun to shiver again. She tried to control herself, tried to see him better, to understand what he meant. She felt as though her life depended on seeing and understanding this man completely but it was hard to do either and getting harder every moment. She made a supreme effort: from the way he spoke he was not a Welshman, nor was he an Englishman. Perhaps he came from wherever it was that Bartolomeo came from—but if so did that mean he would be a friend to Bartolomeo or an enemy? He was saying something, speaking. She actually saw his mouth opening and shutting before she heard what he said, as though he were standing a great distance off and the sound took time to reach her.

"Yesterday," he said, "when I was brought here on a—on a—what do you call it?—a snow-plough, as one might somewhere else have arrived in a taxi, I was naturally hoping for news of some kind but I never dreamed there would actually come a messenger with a letter! Shall I tell you what you are for me? A miracle!" He nodded his head at her, repeating with lingering emphasis, "A miracle!"

Amy was steadier now. The black mist of her panic had receded; she could see him and she could hear him. But how was it possible to be sure by listening to a voice if the words it uttered were true or false? Or to know by staring at a face if the thoughts it concealed were good thoughts or bad ones? She had been frightened at first of Bartolomeo and thrilled at first by Inspector Catcher. This man standing in front of her was middle-aged or perhaps older, with thick grey hair and a leathery skin, brown and lined as though much weather-beaten in years past. His face was long, and his nose was long, and his eyebrows were bushy, and his mouth, when he had finished speaking, shut together in a firm line. One by one she noted each of his features: but although they would enable her to recognize him should she ever happen to see him again, they were of no help to her now in deciding what he was like. And even though he gave an impression of friendliness, that was no guarantee: it was easy enough, Amy knew, for anyone to pretend to be pleasant. With hands behind his back and head tilted to one side he was watching her watching him. Mr Nabb had watched her too.

"Don't be alarmed," he said, observing how tightly she still pressed the letter to her chest. "I am not going to compel you to give me your letter—I am merely suggesting it. You are quite right to hold it so tightly. That's very good—I like to see it! What you have there in your hands is information more precious than diamonds. It concerns not only the life of the man who gave it to you, but the life of a whole nation. Now listen to me very carefully, for I am going to tell you my name and also my address, and if you pay attention I think you will be able to see for yourself that what is written on that envelope is the same name and the same address."

When Amy continued to stare at him fixedly with no change of expression, he added:

"I am trying to tell you that I believe that the letter you are holding is addressed to me."

Then slowly and clearly he told her his name and his address, spelling them out for her while Amy, with painstaking obedience, traced the counterpart with the tip of her finger.

"Yes," she said. "That's what he's written here."

213

But still she kept hold of the envelope, merely going a step or two nearer without relaxing her grip on it, to gaze up searchingly into the man's face.

"For what are you looking, my child?" he asked her, smiling a little.

"You can tell by the eyes," said Amy briefly; and then she gave him the letter.

He received it from her with a curiously formal bow, as though he were paying homage to more than either a letter or the person giving it: to a moment in history.

"Will you excuse me, please?" he said to Mrs Protheroe as he tore open the flap of the envelope.

"Why, certainly I will. You carry on and welcome," she said, going to the switch at the door. "You'll need a bit more light, though. It's as dark in here as the inside of a whale. There—that's better."

"Mum, if I don't have a spoonful of porridge soon I swear I'm going to die," said Ivor. He had cast off his outdoor clothes and was slumped in a chair, his elbows on the table, chewing at somebody else's discarded crust.

"Wait now, Ivor—I've not forgotten your porridge, don't think it! But I'll have to make you a new lot—those boys scraped the pan clean. It wouldn't have tasted so very special by this time, even supposing they *had* left any! Only I'm bound to get that coat off Amy first—sopping it is! You'll let me have your coat, Amy, won't you? Now you don't have to go out again there's no reason for you to keep it on, is there. Look at you, child—shivering! I'm going to fetch a blanket and wrap you up in it, top to toe, and put you to sit close in to the fire. That's what you need—a real warm right through."

"I lost our old ironing blanket," said Amy dreamily. "It must have come off me when I went over the edge of the Dingle."

"Oh, Amy—you never!" cried Mrs Protheroe, aghast. "I can't bear to think of that journey for you. How you ever came through it I don't know. But you're here now, and safe—that's all that matters. Come by the fire—come and sit down," she coaxed her.

But Amy instead went up to the man who stood on the hearth-rug. He had finished reading whatever it was Bartolomeo had scrawled on the two sheets of paper and was gazing intently over the top of them as though his mind were focused half a world away. Amy touched his arm respectfully to attract his notice.

"I just wanted to ask you something, if you don't mind. Bartolomeo isn't a murderer, is he? They said that he'd killed somebody—did he?"

The man Ivor had called an Ambassador put his hand on her shoulder.

"Bartolomeo Cordoba is not a murderer," he said. "He is a hero. And Luis Alvarez, who was killed three days ago in Cardiff—he too was a hero. He was an old man, and a very brave man. He was also my cousin. It was to prevent him from telling me this"—he held up the letter—"that Luis was killed. And yet," he added, more to himself than to Amy or the others, "because by chance there happened to be a certain sailor and a certain child, he has told me just the same. By chance! Is it chance that arranges such matters? I wonder! Life is very strange."

"I'm sorry about your cousin," said Amy, "but I'm glad about Bartolomeo. I knew it wasn't true, though, him being a mur-derer. When he saw me go over the cliff he was nearly up the top of Cader Ddu, safe, and he came all the way down to fetch me. If he'd been bad like those others he wouldn't have bothered, would he? And he wouldn't have gone back to the Gwyntfa after, on account of my granny. He was worried for her being left on her own there with *them*. But she's got Mick—I told Mick to watch out for her. And I told my granny to watch out for Mick. Because I *had* to go, didn't I? Somebody had to go. And we didn't know where Bartolomeo was, not then. He thought I'd be all right, soon as we got over Cader Ddu—he couldn't tell there was going to come a blizzard, could he? So that's what he did," said Amy in a slow sing-song voice. She had shut her eyes, as though to see more clearly the events she was describing. "He went off back to our place, and he's only got our hacker with him, and they've got guns. Or at any rate Mr Nabb's got a gun, and if he's got a gun I should think Inspector Catcher's got a gun as well, bound to have. That's not their proper names, Catcher and Nabb—he said it for a joke. He likes jokes, that's why; the tall one does. He's called Vigers. And it rhymes with tigers, and he can tell where people are—like a tiger can, he said. And the little one, Mr Nabb, he's called Harris. I listened when they were talking, that's how I know. That's how I found out first they weren't the police. And Bartolomeo's got a horrible great gash in his arm," said Amy, all the facts in her head becoming more and more confused. "It's horrible to look at—worse than any gash I ever saw before. My granny put a bandage on, but she said by rights he ought to have a doctor. I've come for help," finished Amy in a rush, thankful to have unwound the tangled skein of her account and reached the point of it at last.

The Ambassador took both her hands in his. She felt their strong grip, and noticed how cool they were, and for a moment fancied she was back in the snow and that these were the hands she had then so longed for, hands that would rescue her and take charge of her. But of course it had been all right because Bartolomeo had come. By another great effort of will she recollected where she was, and that this was not Bartolomeo. This was somebody else who was speaking to her now.

"Are you sure," he was saying, "that one of these men is called Vigers? Was that the name you heard—Vigers?"

She nodded.

"You are quite sure?"

She was surprised at the way her head nodded again for her; kept on nodding until she stopped it.

"Can you describe him?"

Instantly Amy seemed to see Inspector Catcher leaning against the mantelpiece in their front-kitchen.

"He's tall," she said, "and he likes to make jokes—and he's got long fingers—and he's the same colour all over like cream toffee—and his eyes—" She stopped. "It's his eyes are so awful," she whispered. "I can't look at them—but they look at me. They look right inside my head and they can see everything I'm thinking. Brilliant, that's what they are. Blue—same exactly as the eyes of that old fluffy cat they've got down the Post Office."

He let go of her hands. "I know who you mean. I know him well. His name is Vigers, as you said, and he is a very extraordinary man; or you could say, a devil. There are some men who play tennis for a sport. His sport is cruelty. That is the game he chooses to play for his amusement, as well as for his profit. I am astonished to learn that Vigers has actually come here himself. I should have thought the risk would have been too great—but no doubt for such a man it is the risk that gives flavour to the sport. And now—let us see if I have understood correctly what you tell me: this old lady, your grandmother, she is alone in her cottage with Vigers and with an associate of his, someone called Harris—yes? And Bartolomeo Cordoba, the sailor, who has been wounded, is now at this present moment returning to your cottage, having previously made his escape—something of that sort. Am I right?"

For the third time, Amy nodded.

He looked at her a full minute longer, seriously, compassionately. "It is always the same old story," he said. "Always it is the innocent who suffer in order that evil may be overcome."

With a sound like a sigh he turned away; but then immediately his manner changed, became decisive again.

"Mrs Protheroe, I shall have to use your telephone—at once."

"Oh, yes, of course, you must," she cried. "I'll show you where it is."

"Please—don't trouble yourself. I know where it is. This child is the one who has need of your attention. Her hands are very hot. I think she has a fever."

Mrs Protheroe's agitated energies were promptly diverted into caring for Amy. She hurried off to fetch a blanket, swathed in which, unresisting at last, Amy was deposited in Mr Protheroe's big baggy armchair. As an extra precaution her feet were propped on a footstool to be out of the way of draughts. Her flushed face was sponged. A cup of warm milk was held for her to sip. Only when she had done for Amy's comfort all that she could think of doing, did Mrs Protheroe set about making Ivor his long overdue porridge.

But no matter how busily she occupied herself, her mind managed to occupy itself quite separately, fitting together bits and pieces of the jigsaw to complete a dreadful picture. And however much she kept her thoughts inside her head and closed her lips tightly to keep back the questions which, partly for fear of upsetting Amy and partly for fear of what her answers might be, she dared not ask, still she could not prevent herself from seeing over and over, as though in miniature, the figures of her husband and her two sons and Victor Pugh the policeman toiling up the steep hillside towards the Gwyntfa, unaware that the danger they had never really believed in was already ahead of them, was waiting for them, even perhaps watching their progress through the little snow-bound cottage windows; or that it was worse, far worse, than anything any of them had ever suspected. Mrs Protheroe could restrain herself no longer. She paused in her stirring and turned towards Amy, whose cheeks, framed in the folds of blanket, were now scarlet.

"Amy," she said, hesitantly, "I'm sure it will all come out

all right for—for everyone, so there's no cause for us to fret ourselves, not unduly. But did I hear you say there's two men up at your granny's place? Or was it three? And all with guns, and likely to use them? Mind, I'm only asking. I don't mean for you to excite yourself, Amy. But who are they?"

"I don't know," answered Amy. "I can't say—they just came to our place. First of all there was Bartolomeo—"

"He was the one who gave you that letter?"

"Yes—and he took the leg of mutton you sent up for us, only it wasn't cooked then, so we took it back off him and we cooked it and Granny wrapped it in newspaper and put it inside his coat—to keep him warm, she said, same as if it was a hot brick."

"Ivor—do you think she's wandering?" asked Mrs Protheroe in a low voice.

"If you don't hurry up with that porridge, Mum, you'll have me wandering," said Ivor emphatically.

"That was when those others came," said Amy. "They came on skis—fast!—like they were flying. Beautiful, it was—a sight to see. I never did see skis before, except at the pictures. They told us they were policemen, but that was a lie. And it kept on snowing, and snowing. And he said to keep Mick away or else he'd kill him next time for sure. So then I got out of the window and—and then I took my toboggan. I made a toboggan, Ivor, just like you showed me, with a bit of old corrugated—not as good as yours, though. And we brought down the hay on it, bales and bales of hay. We've got your ewes over our place, Mrs Protheroe, all five of them. One was lost, but I found her—I found her down Tyler's Place. There's a lot more to tell, only I don't think I'll bother just now."

Mrs Protheroe felt her forehead and then looked significantly at Ivor.

"Don't you say another word, Amy. There's nothing for you to trouble yourself about now—it's all going to be all right," said Mrs Protheroe, still wretchedly seeing in her mind's eye four figures, unwarned, unguarded, plodding on through the snow towards the Bowens' cottage. "Ivor—just you hand me over two of those bowls, will you?"

"At *last!*" said Ivor.

He gave her the bowls and watched while she doled out the steaming porridge.

"Mum," he said, "did you tell the Ambassador about that man who was asking questions in the Post Office a day or two back?"

"Why no, Ivor, I don't believe your father did happen to mention him. But he had nothing to do with what's going on. He was a teacher, Mrs Ames said, in charge of a party of schoolboys back in Llwynffynnon, making enquiries—" She suspended her operations and stared across the kitchen at Ivor in sudden dismay. "He was asking Mrs Ames about suitable places for teaching boys to ski. Oh, Ivor!—was it just a story, do you think?"

"Sure to be," said Ivor, calmly. "But never you mind, Mum—it won't make any difference, not now."

He had managed to swallow only four scalding spoonfuls of porridge when their visitor came back into the kitchen wearing the fur cap and the black overcoat with the big collar that he had arrived in the night before.

"Can you direct me to some other telephone, Mrs Protheroe? I am sorry to have to tell you that yours is out of order."

"Oh, dear!" she exclaimed, deeply distressed. "It must be this blizzard just now that's done it. You'll have to go down the village—there's nothing nearer. Right at the far end of the street you'll see a kiosk. But if you were to ask Mrs Ames, she'll let you use the one in the Post Office, I know—that would be a lot more convenient for you. Only what if it's out of order too?"

"We must hope otherwise, Mrs Protheroe—I hope it very much. How can I get there? I must go quickly. Do you have a horse I can ride?"

"You can go on my pony, Ginger," said Ivor. "I tied him in the shed and he's still got his bridle on. I'll saddle him for you."

Mrs Protheroe followed them out to the scullery.

"I don't a bit like the feel of Amy, nor the sound of her, neither—she's as hot as fire and rambling in her talk. I was wondering, would you 'phone the doctor please, while you're down there. Or just mention it to Mrs Ames and she'll do it. And Ivor, before you come back in could you see to the animals for me? They need to be fed and watered, same as usual, the poor things."

"Well, so do I need to be fed," said Ivor. "I haven't hardly begun on my porridge yet."

"I'll keep it warm for you, Ivor. It won't take you many minutes—better to get it done. We have to carry on like it was any other day, that's what I mean."

He saw her haunted eyes. "All right then, Mum, I'll do it. But you don't have to get in such a fret about Dad—he knows how to take care of himself—he won't come to any harm. And he'll watch out for the others too, you see if he doesn't."

"Oh, Ivor—you're a good boy," she said, giving him a squeeze.

To Ivor's great relief the blizzard had passed. He had felt guilty at sending Ginger out to battle with it again. But his conscience was spared. Moving with the speed and the violence of a hurricane, the storm had blown over and on, leaving behind a residue of exhausted snowflakes floating down in a fine soft veil. There was a brightness irradiating the fine veil, and a gleam to the snow lying on the ground, like a promise of peace ahead.

Ivor saddled Ginger.

"Are you really an Ambassador?" he asked, as he tightened the girths.

"I am—yes. Really! Why do you ask?"

"Well, you're the first one I've ever seen, and last night you turned up here on Ted Jones's snow-plough, and now you're going to ride my pony. It's just I thought Ambassadors were different. I thought they went about in big cars and that."

"Sometimes I have to use a big car, and sometimes I have to use a snow-plough. It is a matter of circumstances. And for me to be an Ambassador—that is simply for me to be a man. There are good men, and there are bad men, and there are stupid men. This Vigers is a bad man, and I am beginning to believe that I must be a stupid one for otherwise I should have provided myself with skis, as he has done, and I should then have been in your village by now—instead of which I must beg of you to hurry with those buckles."

"Hadn't I better drop the stirrups a bit? Your legs are longer than mine are."

"Very well—if you think it necessary, do so. Only let us make haste."

Ivor led Ginger through the back-yard and round the side of the house to the front-yard. Here the Ambassador swung himself into the saddle with an ease that surprised Ivor.

"All you have to do is, just leave it to Ginger. He'll take you down the village all right. He won't slip—he's a marvel in snow."

Having said this, Ivor still held on to the bridle, for there was something more he had to ask:

"My dad—he won't come to any harm, will he, up at the Gwyntfa? Or Colin, or Ray?"

The dark foreign face looked down at him gravely.

"That is not a question I can answer, Ivor," said the Ambassador. "What I am able to do I am now going to do."

23. Ivor's Luck

Ivor let go of Ginger's bridle and stepped back. The last remnant of snow blew away and the sky was transfigured, blue, and the world lit up. He watched the solid black-coated figure being carried away from him by Ginger's quick neat agile walk. The sun shone and the pony's flanks were the colour of a conker and the long black tail hung down, swaying, almost to the ground. Everything about him sparkled, brilliant and clear: the storm was over. Slowly Ivor turned and walked past the side of the house and into the back-yard. He picked up two buckets. The animals had to be fed and watered, as on any other day; his mother was right.

But it was not a day like any other day all the same. The words his father had spoken earlier came back to Ivor: "We might get into something real nasty. I don't want you mixed up in it." He had said so from prudence, because it was his nature to be cautious, but he had not really believed it himself, Ivor knew. And after all it had been the truth. Somewhere out of sight, out of earshot, on the other side of those silent hills his father and his two brothers were involved in danger and he, Ivor, could do nothing to help them. And however speedily their visitor was transported to the Post Office by Ginger and however urgently he there summoned aid, and whatever the aid was, however fast and willingly it came, it would still be too late. There was nothing he or anyone else could do about it—nothing! A bucket dangling forgotten from either hand, Ivor leant against the yard gate to gaze with despair at the great empty snowy waste that stretched up and up to the summit of Cader Ddu.

But it was not empty!

A man was racing downhill towards him, fast, as though he were flying, as though he were a bird planing on the wind, swooping and swerving, lower and lower—a man on skis.

Ivor clenched his fists on the bucket handles and glanced quickly over his shoulder at the scullery door. Should he run and tell his mother? Tell her what? To bolt and bar the house? There was no time. He glanced uphill again and the man was nearer—nearer. The sun shone and the sky was blue and the snow spurted glittering from his long skis and his slender sticks as he turned and turned again. It was a beautiful sight: Amy had said so. And Amy was sitting now by their kitchen fire, wrapped in a blanket, feverish—with nothing to worry about, his mother had told her. What else had Amy said? He had to remember everything so as to prepare himself, to be ready—for what?—for whom? There had been two men on skis, she had said. Which one was this?

With a final graceful curve, a hiss of metal on frozen snow, a final sprouting of white feathers, the solitary skier drew up beside Ivor. Only the gate was between them. His pale brown clothes were sunny in the sunshine. His pale blue eyes blazed as bright as the blue sky blazing above; as blue, as bright, as pale as the eyes of the Post Office cat. Ivor knew who it was: it was Vigers.

"Hullo," said Vigers, with a careless friendly air. He was breathing hard, smiling at Ivor.

"Hullo," said Ivor.

All the things he had heard about this man crowded into Ivor's mind: he was a devil; his sport was cruelty. He could look right into your head and know what you were thinking—but that, of course, was just silly talk. Vigers could not possibly tell

224

that Amy was in their kitchen now; she was far more likely to be at the bottom of a snow-drift, she and her tidings of terror. Unless, Ivor reasoned with himself, Vigers were actually to see Amy he would most probably believe that no one here at Dintirion knew anything about him. Therefore, he had to be kept out of the kitchen; he had to be kept out of the house altogether. And he must not be allowed to guess that except for Ivor and Ivor's mother the farm was deserted. Whereupon Ivor's heart gave a sudden thump, for it had come to him, sickeningly, that there was indeed nobody else to deal with this situation but himself. His father and brothers were miles from home, their visitor half-way to the village by now—even the telephone was out of order. It all depended on him. He put the buckets down with a clank and rubbed his hands on his knees and slowly picked them up again so as to give himself time to get accustomed to this uncomfortable idea.

Vigers was scanning the yard, the buildings, the house beyond. "Is your father about?" he asked.

Ivor shifted the buckets uneasily.

"Well—that all depends. What was it you were wanting him for?"

There was a pause. Ivor stared at the ground. Using the toe of his boot he dislodged an icicle from the lowest bar of the gate. The silence went on for so long that at last he was compelled to raise his head. Vigers was still scrutinizing the yard. Ivor was much relieved—he had been afraid that Vigers might have been scrutinizing him; but it was plain that his interest lay elsewhere.

He was standing rather to one side of the gate so that a holly-bush partly screened him from the house, and with a flash of insight Ivor realized that he was not just looking to see whom he could see, but was looking to see if he had been seen. "I am astonished that he should have come himself," the Ambassador had said. "I should have thought the risk would have been too great." Vigers was hoping his approach had passed unnoticed except by Ivor, a stupid young boy, who would provide him with the information he needed and could no doubt be bribed not to give his presence away. These thoughts occurred to Ivor with the conviction of absolute certainties, and in the light of his new understanding he was emboldened to say, craftily:

"Do you want me to fetch my dad for you, then? He's busy, but I daresay he'll come if it was for something important—is it?"

"Oh, no—if he's busy there's no point in disturbing him," answered Vigers, just as Ivor had trusted he would. "I was only wondering—there's been a rumour of a child missing from home—some little girl. Have you heard anything about it?"

With his expression as dull as he could manage to make it, Ivor shook his head.

"That's what I thought," said Vigers. "Ah, well—there's no need to worry on that account then. But as a matter of fact I'm really trying to trace a man who's had a bit of an accident. He's damaged his arm and he doesn't speak English. I was thinking he might have turned up here—or he might have simply passed by without stopping. You haven't seen any strangers about by any chance, this morning? Or yesterday?"

Ivor dropped a bucket and opened his mouth. Up till now his main preoccupation had been to get rid of Vigers, simply to send him away from here, and with this as his object he was on the very point of declaring categorically that no stranger of any description had been seen near Dintirion, today or at any other time, and advising him to try down in the village which lay over in *that* direction; but even as he raised his arm ready to wave it obligingly towards Melin-y-Groes there came before his eyes like a warning, suddenly, a picture of the sturdy brown hind-quarters of his pony, black tail swaying and black-coated rider sitting solid as a rock on top, disappearing down the road at a quick walk: not quick enough. Skis, he had seen for himself, travel faster on snow than hooves. Vigers would be bound to catch up with Ginger. And then whatever news there had been in the letter Amy carried through a blizzard it would certainly cease to exist somewhere between their farmhouse and the village. With his mouth open, his arm half-raised, Ivor checked himself.

"Yes?" prompted Vigers; and now his attention was entirely fixed on Ivor, who felt, with a tightening sensation of his chest, that Amy might have been right after all when she had described those eyes as being able to look inside a person's head and know what they were thinking. Curiously enough, although Vigers was not touching him, Ivor had the impression of being gripped and held, so that he could not move.

"Yes?" said Vigers again, quite gently. "You were just going to tell me something, weren't you? What was it? And why did you suddenly decide not to tell me? Why was that?"

As though he had been gripped and held Ivor could not move his limbs, but his mind in contrast had never moved so fast. It surveyed the problem from every angle at lightning speed. Vigers must be kept from going into the house—that was certain. Equally certainly he must be kept away from the village. Somehow he had to be prevented—delayed. He had to be kept—kept how? Kept where? And then the solution dawned on Ivor like the sun rising on a dark world. Of course! There was only one thing that could be done. He had to do it.

"Answer me!" said Vigers, and his voice was different: low still, but passionate.

During those few long seconds Ivor's arm had remained upraised, arrested in the middle of his intended gesture. Now Vigers reached across the gate and took him by the wrist with fingers that bit like teeth. This physical contact had an unexpected effect on Ivor. While Vigers had not touched him he had felt captured; as soon as Vigers caught hold of his wrist, he felt freed—angry too, and reckless and confident, all at the same time.

"Are you looking for that murderer, too?" he blurted out, almost joyously because the moment of fear and indecision was past.

Across the surface of Vigers' face there passed a flicker—not more—of surprise. His eyes contracted. He let go of Ivor's wrist.

"Why ever did you have to grab hold of me like that?" Ivor grumbled. "That hurt, that did."

"What murderer?" said Vigers.

"The same one as you were talking about, I suppose. There wouldn't be two of them on the loose, would there? Both foreign, and sailors, and both got awful great gashes in their arms?"

"You seem to know a good deal about this man; what else do you know?" asked Vigers, speaking in the sort of pleasant conversational tone that Mr Williams used at school when it was a Current Affairs lesson.

"I know everything," replied Ivor boastfully. "He killed a man down Cardiff way, didn't he? We've had the police here all night, off and on—there's two of them in our kitchen this very minute, eating their breakfast," he added, on an extra burst of imagination; and was pleased to see Vigers cast a fleeting glance towards the scullery door and move a step further behind the holly-bush. He waited hopefully. Would Vigers believe him? Had he sounded convincing?

"So the police have been brought in, have they?" said Vigers, reflectively. "I suppose, sooner or later, it was inevitable. And do the police have any idea where this murderer might be?"

"Oh, they know all right."

Again there was that flicker of surprise.

"They *know* where he is?"

"Well, of course they do," said Ivor, with a show of impatience. "They caught him, didn't they? They've got him trussed up like an old hen. And now they've cleared off, the most of them, gone to fetch transport I heard. Only they've left these two chaps behind—to keep a watch on him, they said."

"I see!" It was a long-drawn-out considering exclamation. "So he's been caught, has he? By the police! And he's here now. In that case I'm just in the nick of time, it seems. Well, that's time enough," said he musingly—caressingly, almost. It sounded as though he were uttering his thoughts aloud and his thoughts pleased him. "The nick of time is time enough—a perfection of timing, in fact! If these two policemen are having breakfast in your kitchen," he went on to Ivor, "then presumably their prisoner must be in your kitchen too—is that right?"

"Oh, no! He's not in our kitchen," said Ivor, hurriedly. "They put him somewhere else, out of the way, but I can't tell you where. We had to promise to keep our mouths shut, not to go spreading the tale around. It's a secret—I shouldn't have told you as much as I have done, only you made me. I'd rather you didn't hurt my arm again," he added truthfully, retreating.

"Now listen to me," said Vigers. "I'm a detective—I come from Scotland Yard. You've heard of Scotland Yard, I suppose? It's the most important branch of the police force—can you follow what I'm saying? Very well, then—I've got to see the prisoner for a couple of minutes. That's what I've come for. But I don't want your local police to know I'm here because local police don't like Scotland Yard—do you understand me? If you don't, it really doesn't matter—you'll understand this, I'm sure. Here is a pound—"

He was holding it up as he spoke and Ivor enjoyed a split second of delighted self-congratulation at this proof that he had been right when he guessed Vigers to be a born briber, the sort of man who, in his contempt for people, believed enough money could buy anything from anyone.

"It's yours," he was saying. "You can have it if you tell me where he is. You're lucky, aren't you? A pound is very much nicer than a twisted arm."

"I promised I wouldn't tell," mumbled Ivor. "I don't want to get in any trouble."

"Why should you get into trouble? If you say nothing, no one will know. I have to see him for a few minutes, that's all, and then I'll be gone. Now come—if you want your pound, be quick. I'm in a hurry. Where is he?"

Ivor judged it best to allow himself another moment of hesitation before giving way.

"He's down in our cellar, over the far end behind some barrels—that's where they put him. He wouldn't ever get from there, they said."

"They were right," said Vigers, very softly. "He'll never get from there. And where is the entrance to this cellar of yours, boy? In the kitchen, I suppose."

"No, it's not," said Ivor. He was pointing. "It's over by the scullery window, see? Under the shed roof."

"*Outside!*" exclaimed Vigers. "Is *that* where it is?" His eyes shone with an extraordinary brilliance. "A cellar with its entrance outside! What luck! Luck? It's royal treatment by the gods of chance! Fate only grants such favours to the very few— did you know that, boy?—to the selected winners! To those who can do *as they like*," he breathed, "and never lose!"

"He's mad," thought Ivor. Aloud he said, "But supposing someone was to come to the door while you're down inside the cellar—what then?"

With all his heart he hoped his mother would not suddenly decide to help him to feed and water the stock. He and Vigers stood silent, both intently studying the house, both calculating the risks involved.

"What's on the other side of that window?" asked Vigers.

"Nothing much—it's where we hang the coats and that."

"And no one's come to the door for the last five minutes. Five more—that's all I need. Another five will do it," said Vigers, deciding. "Here, take your money."

He had already propped his ski-sticks in the holly-bush. Now he bent and freed his feet from the skis. Then he pushed up the latch of the gate and slipped through.

"Come along—show me," he said brusquely to Ivor.

They crossed the yard together. There lay the slab of stone with an iron ring let into the centre of it. And without doubt the slab had been recently lifted out and then set back again: the crack surrounding it was chipped clear of ice, and the iron ring lay loose. Ivor had been able to count with certainty on this corroborating evidence when he spun his story, having himself held the torch the previous night while his father raised the stone so as to fetch up a supply of best cider for their unexpected visitor, the Ambassador; moreover, his mother had only that morning sent Colin to the cellar for a bottle of her home-made cherry brandy to carry up to the Gwyntfa as a form of medicine in case of need. There was nothing, as Ivor had known, in the appearance of the flagstone to arouse Vigers' suspicions.

"I'll keep a look-out for you," he volunteered, as one conspirator to another, "and if I bang the bucket down loud it'll mean you're to wait a bit, see?"

Vigers nodded. He bent and caught hold of the iron ring and swung the flagstone to one side, partially uncovering a square black hole, the cellar entrance. A flight of stone steps led down into the darkness below. Used to his father's deliberate movements, Ivor was taken by surprise at the speed with which Vigers twisted around and lowered himself, sinuous as a snake, through the narrow gap.

"Hey—mister!"

"Yes? What is it?"

Vigers had paused. His head was already several inches lower than ground level. Ivor, kneeling at the brink of the hole, saw that he now held in one hand a torch and in his other a revolver— the gun that Amy had said he was bound to have. Somehow the actual sight of it was shocking to Ivor: a gun imagined was different from a gun seen.

"Don't you mean to put the top back on, then?"

"No," said Vigers, curtly.

Ivor had been certain that Vigers would replace the flagstone for the sake of his own safety.

"But supposing they come while you're down there—those policemen?" he whispered urgently. "I can't get the top back over myself, not fast enough. What am I going to say to them?"

There was no reply from Vigers. He had reached the bottom of the steps. The shaft of torchlight pierced the gloom below, darting left and right. Ivor felt sick with dismay: it was all happening too quickly. He was losing his opportunity. He needed more time. In a state of frenzy that was genuine, although the reason he gave for it was not, he called down:

"I've got to pull the top over—there's somebody coming— I'll tell you when they've gone."

Then with all his strength he dragged at the iron ring. The ground was slippery. More easily than he had expected the slab slid forward and bedded into its groove. For an extra warning, he clattered the bucket.

Would Vigers believe him? Or would he spring up the stairs and heave the flagstone out from underneath with as little effort as he had swung it off from above? Or would there be just sufficient doubt in his mind to make him wonder, and, wondering, wait? Wait for how long? How long before the beam of his torch had probed into every corner, behind every box and barrel, and found there was nobody tied up, nobody else in the cellar at all, that he had been deceived, betrayed into making a fool of himself, mocked? How much time was there? Ivor asked himself as he sprinted, or tried desperately to sprint, uphill across the frozen yard, his feet slithering as he ran. How much time, counted in seconds, did he have, and was it going to be enough?

On the further side of the yard, flanked by the big barn, sheltered by the hay-loft above it, stood their old red tractor. To Ivor there seemed to be an immeasurable distance stretching between him and that old red tractor. It was too far off; he would never reach it in a hundred years. And then he was there, clinging to it, panting, scrambling up into the seat, which was surely higher than it had ever been before. And now was the moment, now, when this terrifying gamble could be utterly lost: now, if the engine refused to start. Sometimes it fired at the first pull and sometimes Ivor had seen his father try and try, and curse the machine, and climb down again to tinker with screws and wires. But it had to start for him—*now*—it *had* to! Ivor shut his eyes and pulled, and the engine roared into life. He shoved the gear lever forward, let in the clutch, let go the brake. Like a bull unchained the tractor charged across the yard.

For one suspended beat of his heart Ivor thought he was going too fast, that the tractor was out of his control and he would never be able to prevent it from crashing full tilt into the wall of the house. As hard as he could he trod on the foot-brake, and so as to make doubly sure, hauled on the hand-brake as well. The wheels locked. The whole huge contraption slewed round at right angles to the scullery window, smashed into one of the posts that upheld the shed roof, splintering it like a matchstick and bringing down a noisy shower of slates; and stopped. The scullery door flew open. Mrs Protheroe stood there, white-faced. Ket, barking, bounded past her.

"Ivor! Whatever happened?"

"Get inside, Mum! Get away from the door!" shouted Ivor, almost falling down from the high seat, frantic to find out whereabouts this unpremeditated skid had landed him. It could be disastrous, absolutely.

He was still yelling at his mother when his feet struck the ground. Then he saw how it was, and his eyes widened in awe, and the warning died on his lips. His intention had indeed been accomplished, though not by himself. Accident had done for him what his own wild efforts had failed to do, and one of the giant rear-wheels of the tractor rested squarely and fully across the cellar flagstone, sealing it.

Ivor drew a deep breath.

"Oh, Ket—what luck!" said he, not realizing that he was quoting Vigers. "What beautiful luck!"

"Ivor, Ivor! Are you all right?"

"And to think he gave me a pound for it, too!"

24. Storms, and What Came of Them

Amy had measles, made worse by exposure and exhaustion. She lay in the Protheroes' big spare bedroom with her temperature rising and rising. She would do better, the doctor said, when the spots appeared. Meanwhile she panted and tossed, uttering, in her sleep, cries of fear and warning, and when she was awake calling for her grandmother over and over. Mrs Bowen hardly stirred from her side.

"It's all right, Amy—Granny's here. I shan't leave you. See— I'm here!"

But Amy, clutching her hand, stared at her with wide open eyes and called for her still, not knowing who she was.

For days people went softly up and down the stairs. Meals were eaten almost in silence and even the most interesting news was of no interest to them now. Everyone knew that everyone else was wondering if Amy were going to die.

But she did not die. In due course she became covered in spots. Mrs Bowen said there were so many it would have been hard work to put a sixpence in between them, glad of a joke, no matter how small, to have something to smile at after so long. But when she overheard Mr Pugh declaring that Amy's measles came as a relief to his conscience, since he had more or less promised the sergeant over at Llwynffynnon it was the measles she had, Mrs Bowen was very angry indeed.

"Victor Pugh, I'm ashamed to hear you say so," she blazed out at him. "You surely don't count your conscience more important than that child's life?"

"Why no, indeed, Mrs Bowen, I never meant any such thing," he stammered. "They tell me she's getting better—on the mend, I was told."

"So she is—no thanks to you and your conscience," retorted Mrs Bowen severely.

Amy was getting better. One afternoon, awakening from a long sleep, her forehead cool and her thoughts tranquil, she lay watching rain hitting against the window. There had been a change in the weather. She liked the sight and the sound of rain: it made her feel wonderfully snug and safe.

"No more snow," she said aloud.

Mrs Bowen, who had been sitting by the fire, put down her sewing and came across to the bedside.

"So you've woken up!"

"I've been awake for a long time."

"Well, I never! Why didn't you let me know before? I've got some soup for you downstairs, keeping hot."

"I'm not hungry, Granny."

"I don't suppose you are, but you must try to eat—you've gone so thin this last week or two. Now that the fever's over we've got to see if we can't feed you up, Amy. You're going to need your strength."

"Am I? What for, specially?"

"I didn't say specially for anything. It's just that I want to have you looking yourself again. With those big eyes and those white cheeks you're like a little ghost instead of my girl."

"I don't feel I want to eat now, though, Granny. I'd rather you stopped here and talked to me a while."

"I'll talk as much as you like, Amy, so long as it's not about anything that's going to send your temperature up. The doctor said it was very important for you to rest your mind, remember. You know how particular he was you weren't to get excited."

Mrs Bowen had already a day or so earlier given Amy a carefully sedated account of what had taken place at the Gwyntfa on the morning of the great blizzard, her aim being to tell only as much as would keep Amy from worrying about it. There would be time enough later on, she felt, to fill in the details and the drama. And Amy did not press her, possibly because she too felt there would be plenty of time later; or possibly because she was in any case not short of enthralling conversation, having managed to evade her grandmother's ban on exciting talk by the simple device of sending for the boys at frequent intervals, using one pretext or another.

"Can I have Queenie up for a bit?" she would say. "Can I have Mick? I'd like Colin and Ray to bring them. Ivor can fetch them away later."

These requests caused Mrs Bowen to purse her lips and hesitate:

"They mustn't stay for more than a few minutes, then."

But the three boys had no such hesitation. They responded with alacrity, and the more Amy summoned them the better they liked it. Amy wanted to know what had happened, and they thoroughly enjoyed telling her—and listening to each other telling her, and interrupting each other, and remembering bits they had forgotten before and telling it all over again. It was not just what they had done that had to be described but also their varying emotions, what they had felt and supposed and feared and expected, moment by moment. One way and another there was a great deal to recount, and as the visits were short there had to be as many visits as possible.

At first this continual coming and going benefited Queenie and Mick. The Dintirion cats and dogs had deeply resented the appearance of newcomers in their kitchen, and had shown their resentment by spitting and snarling, and scratching and

237

snapping, until, for their own protection, Mick and Queenie had been relegated to a distant outhouse. During the worst of Amy's illness their life had been very dismal; as she improved, their existence too took a turn for the better. And Amy was so pleased to see them again, and minded so much when they were taken away from her that soon Queenie was accepted as a resident in the bedroom and even Mick, who could never learn to be quite as discreetly silent in his behaviour, was carried out only when she dropped off to sleep. But by this time the visiting habit had been established and Amy was spared the need to invent new reasons.

So, little by little, she had assembled from Colin and Ray the history of how they and their father and Mr Pugh had set out for the Gwyntfa on that memorable morning and been overtaken by the blizzard; of how they had struggled on, shouting and calling as they drew near to the cottage, and in reply heard only Mick barking. As clearly as though she had been there herself, Amy could imagine them bursting into the front-kitchen, and imagine the glances they must have exchanged of misgiving and worse, when they found it empty and heard Mick still hysterically barking in the next room. And she could imagine, as though she had been there with them, the horror of the scene that met their eyes when they threw open the side-kitchen door. Only Mick, clutched tightly in Mrs Bowen's arms, had shown any signs of life. Mrs Bowen herself had seemed to be turned to stone. Opposite to her loomed a figure of gigantic proportions, while a second smaller figure lay stretched uncon-scious on the floor at her feet. Entirely misunderstanding the sit-uation they had hurled themselves like heroes on the wrong man.

"Well, of course we did," said Colin. "I've never seen anyone so ugly in all my life—and *big* ! We were bound to think it was him was the wrong 'un, a great monster like that."

"Bartolomeo isn't ugly," Amy had protested.

"Oh, no!—like a gorilla, that's all."

"He's coming to our place, to convalesce," said Ray, "once he's out of that hospital. Mum said he could. And you're to be his teacher, Amy—that's what the Ambassador told him. He told him you'd teach him to speak English."

Amy had laughed. "What, *me* teach him?—Granny's the one for that." But after considering a moment or so she had changed her mind. "I might have a try, though. I think I'd like to have a try. Yes, I'll teach him."

Ivor, when he had first been allowed to visit Amy alone, had wasted not a second. Kneeling up on the foot of her bed, with a glance every so often over his shoulder for fear of being stopped by Mrs Bowen and sent away before he had finished, he poured out as fast as he could talk the tale of his triumph in outwitting and out-manoeuvring the terrible Vigers.

"I thought he was a marvel, to start with," said Amy. It was true: she felt bound to confess it.

"Then all I can say is, you must have been barmy," retorted Ivor. "I could tell what he was like, straight off. He'd got it written all over him, plain as print—*wicked!*"

"Well, it was getting dark, the first time I saw him," said Amy, excusing herself. "And anyway, Ivor, that's not fair—you'd heard about him already. I hadn't. 'Tisn't easy to tell what a person's like just by looking at him. People can turn out to be a lot different from what you think they are to begin with," she declared.

Ivor had agreed there might be something in this theory, and then proceeded to relate how, on the morning that now seemed so long ago to both of them, Harris—but here Amy had once again interrupted him.

"I still think of him as Mr Nabb," she said.

"Well, you shouldn't—that's not his proper name. That was just their silly joke, wasn't it? And I've got to be quick—do you want to hear about it, or don't you?"

"Oh, yes, I do, Ivor. Please go on. I won't say another word."

So Ivor had gone on, and told her how *Harris*, as soon as ever he had recovered consciousness, was escorted back to Dintirion by Mr Pugh and Colin, it having been decided that Mr Protheroe and Ray should keep guard up at the Gwyntfa; for at that time they had no idea of what had happened to Vigers or when he might return. There had indeed been a moment of alarm and desperate resolution when a figure was seen climbing the hill with a pair of skis balanced across his shoulder, and Mr Protheroe, watching his approach from Mrs Bowen's bedroom window, had felt no doubt at all but that it was Vigers, nor doubted that if he was obliged to shoot, he would. He had shouted a warning to the others, down below in the front-kitchen. Mrs Bowen had promptly mounted the stairs and joined him at the window.

"But that's not *him!*" she had exclaimed aloud in consternation.

And then Mr Protheroe realized it was their friend and visitor, the Ambassador, on whom he had Harris's revolver unwaveringly trained. For, as it later transpired, the Ambassador had taken it into his head to borrow Vigers' skis so as to pay a visit to the Gwyntfa in person and observe for himself the scene of so much hazard and heroism.

"He told me afterwards he looked at everything," said Ivor to Amy. "The window you climbed out of, and the rope you made. And he went on down to Tyler's Place, too. He had to see it all with his own eyes, he said. And then he went along the top of the Dingle and fetched back your toboggan. That's what they used for getting your old granny down on. I think it's good, your toboggan," said Ivor generously. "I mean that—it's *good*. Specially considering you didn't have me to help you. I took mine up when I went along with Dad to fetch away your chickens and our ewes, but only because mine's bigger than yours, Amy. We put the chickens in boxes, and tied the boxes on to my toboggan—that's how we got them down."

For the rest of that uncertain and anxious day Vigers had

remained in the cellar like an invisible Jinn corked up in a bottle, and Harris had been kept locked into the larder at Dintirion; all that day and until some hours after nightfall, when cars came for them. They were taken away in a buzz of subdued activity and orderly confusion, an atmosphere of lowered voices, of strangers' faces half-seen, preoccupied, grave; an atmosphere that made Ivor feel as though the familiar kitchen had become suddenly unfamiliar and that it was he and his family, not these people occupying it, who were shadowy, unreal. But in twenty minutes or less everything had returned to normal again: the anonymous crowd of invaders had come and before Ivor managed to distinguish one from another, or even to be sure how many of them there were, they had gone. The Ambassador departed with them. Both of the prisoners wore handcuffs, Ivor told Amy.

"I watched them go off. Your granny didn't, though. She said she never wanted to set eyes on them again."

"That's how I should have felt," said Amy.

"We've got to keep our mouths shut about it still, it seems—they didn't tell us how long for. 'Tisn't finished yet, that's why. There's more of 'em to catch and easier to catch 'em if they don't know exactly what's been going on. It's up to us to hold our tongues so as it doesn't get in the papers."

"I don't know exactly what's been going on, either," Amy had remarked.

"Of course you don't, and I'm not allowed to explain it to you, not yet," said Ivor, remembering belatedly his undertaking to Mrs Bowen. "I promised your granny I wouldn't say too much. You have to be kept quiet, she says—not excited, or it might start your temperature off again."

There was really no danger of Amy becoming over-excited. Her illness had curiously separated her from the terrible events that had preceded it, and she could look back at them with a calm detachment, as at a range of distant hills, between her and which lay a wide flat plain. They interested her extremely, but she no longer felt threatened by them. Nor did she feel in any hurry to hear all those colourful extras, recollections, embellishments, that she knew lay stored in her grandmother's memory, ready to be brought out for their mutual entertainment on many a patchwork-making evening of the future.

So it was that when, on this particular rainy afternoon, Mrs Bowen declared herself willing to talk provided it was not about anything too agitating, Amy replied serenely:

"It's all right, Granny—it wasn't about *that* I was wanting you to talk."

Mrs Bowen came and stood near Amy's pillows, and folded her hands, and smiled at her.

"What was it you were wanting me to talk about, then?"

"Oh, I don't know. Anything—just anything. You know what I was thinking, lying here? How much I like this room. I like the way the ceiling bulges, and the beams are so low if I was to stand up on the bed I'd hit my head on them. It's so big and dark—friendly. I don't know why Mr and Mrs Protheroe don't have it for theirs—I would if I was them—instead of keeping it for the spare."

"Molly chose not to have it on purpose, just because of it being so big and dark. She's such a cheerful soul herself she likes to have everything round her the same."

"Oh, but I think it is cheerful," said Amy, "specially with a fire in it. It's the sort of room," she went on dreamily, "that makes you feel you're welcome."

"Well, Amy! It's funny to hear you say that, because this is the room you were born in."

Amy was so surprised she sat straight up in the huge bed. "No, Granny!—was I really?"

"Yes, indeed you were—in the middle of the night, in the middle of a storm. Lie down, child!—whatever do you think you're doing, sitting up like a Jack-in-the-Box when you perfectly well know you're meant to stay quiet."

"Tell me about the storm, Granny. Was it a snow-storm ?"

"No, not that time, it wasn't. That night it was thunder and rain and lightning. Your father sent Benjy Cadwallader over to the Gwyntfa to fetch me. They weren't expecting the baby—which was you, as it turned out, Amy—not for some while, but there'd been an accident—never mind what, now; like many an accident, it was everyone's grief but nobody's fault. Anyhow, be that as it may, poor Benjy was so much afraid of the thunder no power on this earth would induce him to stir again from my front-kitchen once he got there. So I had to set off on my own and I was in such a hurry I took the short way over the top, Amy, the same as you did, and I as near as an eyelash went over the very same cliff as you did, too. I'll never forget that night and that journey, not as long as I live. Drenched! The rain came down so hard it all but washed me clean off the rocks. And pitch dark except for the flashes of lightning—there were plenty of those and just as well—it was all I had to see by. And afraid to my heart every step of the way—not of the storm but of what I should find when I got here, for your father's message was that Catherine—your mother, that's to say—was going fast. He was wrong, as it happened. She stayed with us a few weeks more, long enough to name you and love you and give you to me to care for."

"You came the short way over in a thunderstorm the night I was born and you never told me about it before, Granny, all these years ?"

"No, I never did. Well, it was a long while back and a saddish time for all concerned and I've never been much inclined to dwell on the past. I take more of an interest in the present, I suppose," said Mrs Bowen.

"But I like to hear about the past as well," said Amy, "even if it is a bit saddish. I'm glad you told me."

"Your father was born in this room too, as a matter of fact," said Mrs Bowen, laughing. "I'd almost forgotten it myself—that's going back a while further. There now, I've been chatting on for long enough. I mean to fetch you up your soup, and if you like I'll tell Ivor he can keep you company the few minutes I'm gone—I know he's got something he wants to show you."

Amy lay back to wait for Ivor. She was touched and a little awed by the drama of that far-off night, but it was too remote for her to be saddened by it now. Instead, she felt warm and safe, lulled by the movement of the flames on the ceiling, lapped round by love, empty of all desire, contented. The door opened creakily.

"Hullo, Ivor. What have you got there? Oh, it's a lamb!"

"It's our first. It came from one of those ewes you kept over your place in the snow, and Dad says he's giving it to you—that's why I thought you'd like to see it."

Amy touched the tightly crinkled wool on the hard little body with the tips of her fingers.

"Born today—but not in this room! Did you know it's where I was born, Ivor, and my father too—in this room. Granny's just told me."

"I'm not surprised," said Ivor. "Bowens have been at Dintirion for generations. Protheroes are new. Do you ever stop to think it might have been your home instead of ours, and wish it was, and wish we weren't here?"

"Oh, no!" said Amy, much shocked. "I like it how it is—you and Ray and Colin and Mrs Protheroe and Mr Protheroe at Dintirion, and me and Granny over at the Gwyntfa. I don't want it different. Besides, I've never known exactly how it did come to change."

"I do," said Ivor. "I know all about it. I've heard it talked about, time and again. Your granny was the school-teacher, wasn't she?—and she married your grandfather and came to live here at Dintirion, because in those days Dintirion was your grandfather's place. My mother says it was hard on your granny, her having no folks of her own round these parts."

"She hasn't got any folks of her own round anywhere," said

Amy, placidly, "except for me and my father. She was an orphan, raised in an orphanage down in Cardiff. She doesn't mind, though. She doesn't feel the need of folks. Some people don't. Friends are as good, and not too many of those either—that's what she says."

"Does she?" said Ivor. "I don't agree with her. I like folks, and I like friends, plenty of both. Anyway, what I was telling you was about your granny, how she married your grandfather and came to live here, only he got killed, and your father was born—or maybe it was the other way round. So that made Mrs Bowen a widow, didn't it, and she couldn't manage the farm on her own so she rented it off to my grand-dad. He was the tenant at Dintirion till your father grew up, and when your father grew up he took it back, so as to farm it himself. And I can't say for sure if Mrs Bowen came back here to Dintirion with him, but I think she did, and kept house for him till he married your mother—that was Catherine Davies from down Denver way."

"You don't have to tell me who my mother was," said Amy. "I know all about her. And when I was born Granny was living over at the Gwyntfa, and they sent her a message and she came in the middle of the night, the short way over, just like I did. It was a terrible storm, thunder and lightning. She's just told me."

"I never heard about the storm before," said Ivor. "Well, so then your mother died and your father didn't want nothing more to do with Dintirion after that, so he sold it, and my grand-dad bought it, the very same farm he'd been tenant of earlier on, only of course he was old by now and he'd retired, so it was his son he got it for—that was my dad—and he gave it to him and he came to live with us here, my old grand-dad, and he died here too, later. I can remember him, just."

"Everyone's always getting born or dying, over and over, on and on," said Amy, gently rubbing the snout of the lamb, who bleated for milk, not rubbing.

"Well, of course they are—what do you expect?"

"What I mean is, it takes such a long time when it's happening, but afterwards when people talk about it, like you've been doing now, it all seems so quick, and it doesn't even seem to matter very much because there's always more things coming undone the whole time, like a streamer. I think that's what Granny was meaning when she said it doesn't do to dwell on the past. Though I think the past's interesting—specially if it's somebody else's past, because then it sounds the same as a story."

"You didn't let me finish. I got to the part where your mother died and your father sold Dintirion to my grand-dad. Well, so then he went off to Australia, your father, and bought a sheep farm out there and married a second wife and had a lot more children."

"Oh, Ivor, how can you be so silly!—as if I didn't know that part for myself without you telling me. And it wasn't a lot more children, it was only three. They're my brothers and my sister and I've never seen them."

Mrs Bowen came into the room with a tray.

"Ivor—you'd better take that little creature back to its mother now. It's been away from her long enough."

"Yes, it has—it wants its supper as well," said Amy. "It was trying to suck my fingers for milk. But you're to come back again directly after, Ivor, because there's still something I want to ask you."

"Oh, Amy—I think you've had enough company for today," said Mrs Bowen. "I don't want you to get overtired when you're only just beginning to be on the mend."

"I shan't get tired, Granny—I don't feel tired a bit. Just weak, that's all, same as that lamb is. It's good for me, talking to Ivor—I'm hungry now and I wasn't before. So can he come back?"

"Well, we'll see," said Mrs Bowen.

She put the tray on Amy's knees and went over to the window.

"The rain's stopped at last—that's a good job. It's going to be a fine clear night. We could do with a bit of sunshine tomorrow to dry the ground up, and it looks as though we might be getting it. I must say, there's been quite a touch of spring in the air, these last few days, and evenings are getting longer too. And yet, my goodness, how the snow does linger on—it'll stay by those hedges and there'll be patches of it up on the hills, white, for days yet, just to remind us, I suppose, of what's been."

"I don't think I shall need any reminding, Granny—will you?"

"Well no, maybe not. Though I can't say I mean to let it worry me any. What's done's over."

"Bartolomeo's coming here when he's out of hospital, Ray told me."

"Oh, he told you that, did he?"

"Yes—and I'm glad. I was hoping I'd see him again. And Ray says the Ambassador said that I'm to teach Bartolomeo to speak English."

"I see. He has been busy with his tongue, that boy."

"He just happened to mention it."

"And did they any of them happen to mention about how the Ambassador's been on the 'phone from London every day since you've been ill, asking after you?"

"No—has he?" said Amy, pleased.

"Every day," said Mrs Bowen. There was something constrained in her manner, as though she were debating with herself whether or not to say more. She left the window and came across to the bedside and stood looking down intently at Amy's face.

"What is it, Granny?"

"I was wondering whether maybe you were well enough now for a letter that came for you a few days back."

"A letter? For me? Oh, Granny!—who's it from?"

"Now Amy, you're to lie still and you're not to get flustered."

"Yes, I will—I'm not."

"Maybe I shouldn't have spoken so soon. But I was thinking if I didn't one of those boys would go and let it out, the way their tongues wag."

"Who wrote it?"

"Well, it's from that Ambassador, Amy. He's a nice man. I liked him," said Mrs Bowen. "We got along together fine, him and me. He's someone you know where you are with—not one of these people who say one thing and mean another."

"I liked him too," said Amy.

"He liked you. Though that's not really what it's all about. He says you did a service to his country, Amy. He wants you to know how grateful he is, and his country is. That's what he's written in that letter. Mind—I haven't opened it—of course I haven't. I haven't read it, but—but that's what it is," finished Mrs Bowen, lamely.

More and more Amy was puzzled by her grandmother's manner: it was as though she were going downhill on a bicycle with both brakes jammed hard on and finding the slope steeper than she had expected.

"Can I have my letter?" said Amy.

Almost reluctantly Mrs Bowen took it out of her apron pocket and handed it to Amy.

"Oh, look!—it's been done on the typewriter: *Miss Amy Bowen*. I've never seen my name like that before—typed. Doesn't it look nice? It makes me feel I'm someone else."

Glancing up she noticed that her grandmother was tense with a mysterious expectancy; her eyes were bright and she was smiling.

Amy opened the envelope and pulled out a sheet of paper covered in black type with a signature in ink, very flourishing and big, at the bottom. Fastened to the top of the page with paper-clips was what appeared to be a long narrow strip of pasteboard. Amy fumbled weakly with the clips but they were too tight to come off; only the pasteboard slipped a little sideways, and she saw that it was a thin sort of a book and that there was another one underneath. Amy stared at them, confused, suddenly defeated—were they something to do with lessons?

"What are they, Granny?" she said. "I don't understand. What does the letter say? You read it to me. My eyes aren't so good for reading yet."

"Well, I expect he says thank you very much for everything you did," said Mrs Bowen in a strained voice, not attempting to take the letter from Amy. "I expect that's what those things at the top are for—to say thank you very much."

"Is that what they are? What are they, Granny?"

Mrs Bowen picked up Amy's limp hand and held it closely. "They're tickets, Amy, for you to go on an aeroplane—for you to go to Australia. It's so as you can see your father at last, and he can see you."

"Australia? Me?"

Mrs Bowen nodded. There was a long silence. Then Amy said:

"But why are there two tickets?"

"Well, there's one for going and one for coming back, I suppose."

"Is that what it says on them? See what it says."

Obediently Mrs Bowen freed the tickets and bent her head and examined them.

"What does it say?" cried Amy, watching her face. "What is it, Granny? Read it out."

"It says here that one's for a child, and one's for—one's for an adult."

"That's you, Granny."

They looked at each other.

"Both of us!" said Amy.

249

25. Ivor and Amy Disagree

"I'm glad you got a prize as well," said Amy to Ivor who was lying stretched at ease across the foot of the bed. Mrs Bowen had been persuaded to allow them an extra twenty minutes of each other's company before Amy was tucked up for the night "After all, if you hadn't been so clever, Ivor, and trapped Inspector Catcher it wouldn't have mattered what anyone else had done."

"Why do you keep on calling him Inspector Catcher? And you still call Harris wrong as well."

"It's because that's the way I think of them—I always shall: Inspector Catcher and Mr Nabb. I knew them before you did, Ivor," said Amy, with a touch of dignity.

Ivor yawned. The discussion of good news had had a soporific effect on him. " 'Tisn't a prize, either," he said. "It's a reward."

"I don't see the difference."

"Well, they are different."

"I don't see it, and prize sounds nicer."

"That's because you're a girl," said Ivor. "As a matter of fact, my dad didn't want me to have it at first."

"Didn't he? Why not?"

"He didn't like the notion of me taking money. That's what he said. But then the Ambassador wrote him this long letter, all about how there were lots of farms in his land that might have been spoilt by war if it hadn't been for me, and one day I was going to want to buy a farm of my own, and the money could go towards getting it for me, and that was only fair. So then Dad said all right. But it's my money. I don't have to use it for buying a farm with if I don't want to."

"Why, Ivor—what else would you use it for?"

"Oh, I don't know. By the time I grow up I might have some other ideas, mightn't I? I might decide to go to Peru. The Ambassador said I could stay with his family any time I wanted. They've got farms out there too. I'd like to see how they manage. I don't suppose even their tractors look the same as ours."

"Ivor," said Amy, reminded of her reason earlier in asking for Ivor to be sent back, "what *was* it all about? You said you'd tell me sometime, and I want to know now. Why would the farms in Peru have got spoilt by war if you hadn't done what you did do? I don't understand."

" 'Tisn't very easy to explain," said Ivor. The mere thought of the effort involved in explanation caused him to yawn again.

"But try!" she urged him, and as an antidote to yawning she directed a sharp kick towards the foot of the bed.

Ivor sighed, and rolled over, and propped himself up on his elbows.

"Well, you see, there's this big organization," he began, cautiously, "and Vigers is the head of it—*was* the head of it, I mean. The Ambassador said that it was like a sort of a business Vigers ran—he took on jobs, and people who wanted to make money paid him money so they could make more money."

They both considered this statement critically for a while. Then Amy said:

"I don't see there's anything wrong with that. It's the same as your father does when he pays Neville Evans to come and spread lime on his fields with his spreader so as he can get a better crop of hay."

"It may sound like that," said Ivor, "but it's not like that. I was trying to put it so as you could understand it. I told you it was going to be hard."

"You had it explained to you, Ivor—just tell it to me however it was you heard it."

So Ivor took a breath and knotted his brow and tried again.

"Well, for one thing it isn't just small money, it's millions and billions of pounds they're after; and for another thing they make it out of making trouble for people. The way Vigers first came to start up in his business was years ago when he happened to know someone who manufactured guns, and this person wanted to sell his guns, but he couldn't. So he paid Vigers to put round stories that weren't true in some part of the world that was far enough off for the rest of the world not to give it too much attention."

"Go on," said Amy, encouragingly.

"I was trying to remember where the place was, but I can't, and it doesn't matter for what I'm saying at the moment. Vigers was so clever he got the tribes out there, wherever it was, to believe these lies about each other, and so they started fighting each other—which they wouldn't have done if they'd been left alone, and then it turned into a war, and a lot of people got killed who never should have got killed, and the man who made guns sold thousands and thousands of them, and of course he made a lot of money, and so did Vigers. That's not the same as my dad paying Neville Evans to spread lime."

"No, that's not the same," agreed Amy.

"And ever since then people who wanted trouble stirred up so as they could get money out of it for themselves, or so as they could get power out of it, or something like that, something bad—they got hold of Vigers and paid him and he stirred it up."

"I see," said Amy.

"Well, this job Vigers had taken on this time was arranging

for some President of another country to be killed—assassinated—while he was on a visit to Peru, and then to put the blame for it on the wrong people. Only as it happened old Luis Alvarez heard of what was being planned, and he wrote to his cousin in London and told him, because his cousin was the Ambassador there."

"I know," said Amy.

"I know you know. I'm only saying it because it's important, because if he'd been just any old cousin it wouldn't have been much use to tell him. But being an Ambassador he was the right person to tell anyway. The worst part of it was that at that time there wasn't enough to tell. It wasn't much above a rumour—no facts, and you have to have facts to be able to act against them. So Luis Alvarez said he'd stop on in Peru and find out the names of the people in the plot, and when it was meant to happen, and where, and all about it. And he did find out all about it too, but the pity of it was he got caught by some of Vigers' men only a few minutes before he was intending to get on an aeroplane to fly to London to tell his cousin this information he'd found out."

"Oh, that *was* a pity," said Amy. "If he'd only managed to get to the aeroplane just a little bit sooner he'd have been all right, probably."

"You can say *if only* about anything," replied Ivor, impatient at such a point of view. "*If only* means what didn't happen, that's all. But it's what did happen you have to go by."

"Yes, I suppose so," said Amy, regretfully. "But when things have very nearly happened differently—that's when I can't help thinking *if only*."

"Well anyway, they caught him," said Ivor, brushing aside Amy's interruption in his haste to continue; for by now his imagination had been seized by the tale he was telling and his yawns were forgotten. "They caught him, but somehow or other, I don't know how, he gave them the slip, and he got on

253

board a cargo boat that was sailing to Cardiff. Of course he was a stowaway, and so he was locked up, but quite comfortably in a cabin because of being old, and ill as well. It seems that this cargo-boat came from Finland—it was a tramp-steamer—and only one other person on board could speak the same language as Luis and that was Bartolomeo, and he'd signed on for the trip at the very last moment when one of the regular crew went sick. So the captain gave Bartolomeo the task of looking after the stowaway and taking him his food and that. So of course they came to be friends, as was bound to happen. And Luis told Bartolomeo everything he knew about the assassination plot, and who he was meaning to tell it to in England, and how he'd been caught, and how he'd escaped. Well, they got to Cardiff at last—I don't know how long the voyage took them. It was late at night by the time they'd tied up at the docks, and when the rest of the crew had gone ashore Bartolomeo let Luis off the boat very secretly, so as he could 'phone his cousin the Ambassador in London—Bartolomeo went with him. And he did 'phone, but he didn't want to say too much on the 'phone—he just said that he was alive, and where he was, and how he'd got there, and that Bartolomeo had been a good friend to him. Well, the Ambassador told his cousin Luis that he'd come at once, and that Luis was to go straight back on board the steamer to wait for him there—it was the safest place for him to be, locked up in that cabin. But on their way back to the boat they were set upon by three of Vigers' men and I'm sorry to say in the fight and the scuffle poor old Luis—well, I'm sorry to say, Amy, that was the end of him."

Ivor paused apologetically.

"I knew we were bound to be coming to that bit soon," said Amy. "I was expecting it."

"He wouldn't have lived for much longer anyway, the Ambassador said—he'd been ill for years and it was only will-power had kept him alive till then. So you see," said Ivor, trying to make the best of that dark episode out of consideration for Amy's feelings and for her frail health, "it wasn't as bad as it might have been."

"It must have been very bad for him for a few minutes," said Amy, refusing to dodge the reality. "I shall always mind for him, for those few bad minutes, all my life."

"Well, all right then," said Ivor. "If you do mind, that's all right—it's good if you mind. People ought to mind. That's how people pay tribute to heroes. Heroes deserve it."

Amy thought these words over and finding, surprisingly, that they were comforting, she accepted them with a sorrowful nod and a little sigh.

"Go on," she said. "So what did Bartolomeo do then?"

"They tried to finish him off as well, but he got away from them. Of course, if anyone didn't know what was going on it looked like Bartolomeo had killed old Luis and then made a bolt for it, and that's what the Cardiff police would have thought except the Ambassador told them differently, and told them to hush it up for the time being, and told them why. But that wasn't till next day. Bartolomeo says he doesn't remember much of the first night. His arm was bad and he'd been knocked about a good deal as well—but he had it stuck in his head that he'd got to keep clear of Vigers' lot somehow—that they were after him— and he'd got to get hold of Luis's cousin in London and tell him what he knew. He hid on the back of a lorry, underneath a tarpaulin—that's how he got clear of Cardiff and a fair distance up north. Only then the lorry was stopped. He didn't wait to find out why, or who stopped it—he just slipped down off the back of the lorry as quick as he could, and he hid in a building all that night, and the next morning he set off across country. Of course he didn't have a map or anything, just a rough idea of what was the right direction for London. I think he looked at the stars and the sun and worked it out. I don't think he'd got a compass. Anyway, there was lots of Vigers' people trailing after him, and some of them spotted Bartolomeo up on the hills, heading east. Bartolomeo knew he'd been spotted—or at least he thought so, he wasn't sure—but he just kept going. It's all he can remember, he says, telling himself he had to *keep going, keep going*. Well, what the Ambassador thinks is that those men who saw Bartolomeo must have rung up Vigers in London, and Vigers said to them—'you go on after him, and get him'—and that's what they started to do, only then the snow came. So when the snow came Vigers said—'Ah ha!—I know the way to catch him now, and I'll do it myself.' But that's where he was wrong," said Ivor, with tremendous satisfaction, "because he got caught instead—by me! I caught the Catcher!"

"So you did," said Amy.

They looked at each other and laughed.

"And if you hadn't caught him, Ivor, me and Granny wouldn't be flying off in an aeroplane in six weeks' time. Six weeks and three days exactly, it is. I can hardly believe it yet—but it's true. It's really going to happen."

"You'll never come back," said Ivor, gloomily.

"Shan't I? Why not?"

"It's too far."

"That's got nothing to do with it. We're paid for, both ways."

"Yes, but all the same—once you get out there—Australia—why, it's the other side of the world. You won't ever come back here again."

Amy continued to look at the ceiling. She ran her eye up and down the beam immediately over her head as she had done so many times in the last two weeks. She knew every inch of it; every crack and curve was familiar.

"I shall," she said, after a full minute of contemplation. "This'll always be home, Ivor. People don't stay away from home for ever. They always come back in the end."